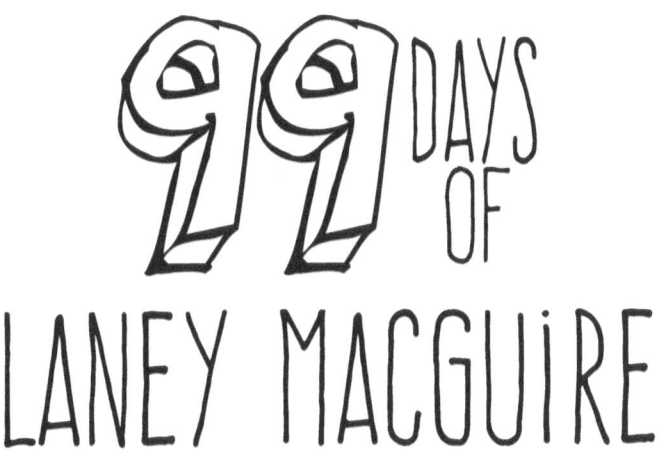

# LANEY MACGUIRE

# 99 DAYS OF LANEY MACGUIRE

## RACHEL BATEMAN

METAMORPHOSIS books

embrace the change

Metamorphosis Books
First Edition: November 2013
ISBN: 978-0-9899306-0-4

Cover Photo Manipulation by Stephanie Mooney
Cover Design by Rachel Bateman
Cover Photo © Lena Pantiukh / Shutterstock.com
Edited by Brenda Errichiello

Metamorphosis Books
www.metamorphosisbooks.com

Published in the United States of America

*For Kelvin,*
*for giving me everything*

*&*

*Connor Weston,*
*for being my all*

# 99 DAYS OF LANEY MACGUIRE

# DAY ONE

THERE ARE ONLY THREE THINGS you need to know about my dad's lake resort: 1) It's a place where nothing ever changes, 2) It isn't nearly as luxurious as it's made to seem in the brochure, and 3) It's twenty-five hundred miles away from my mother and her newest husband. Fiancé. Sex slave. Or whatever the hell *he* is to her.

It's a place where I can breathe.

Three days ago, I packed up Burt, my 1968 Ford Ranchero, and hit the road, not even sparing a look in the rearview mirror. The drive was a long one, filled with hotter than hot days, bug-filled nights, and sketchy hotel rooms.

Every drop of sweat, every disgusting hotel duvet, every bug smashed on Burt's grill, became completely worth it the second I turned off the highway and into the resort, cranking my window up to avoid the dust-bowl parking lot.

I dodged the giant pothole—definitely bigger than last year; Burt wouldn't fit on either side, so I straddled it, hoping I hadn't miscalculated and would be swallowed whole. After a few more evasive maneuvers, I pulled to a stop outside my cabin. Sunlight glinted off the metal roof of the rec lodge—was the left corner sagging more than last year?—and drew my attention to the rest of the grounds. A larger-than-normal expanse of lawn stretched to the beach. It took me a few minutes of staring to realize why: several of the tall pines that used to dot the lawn had been removed, leaving an open, sunny area rather than the shaded, pinecone-infested grounds I was used to. Winter must have been harsh this year.

Finally, I allowed my gaze to settle on the beach. I could already feel the sand between my toes, the sun beating down on my back. The sound of water lapping against the docks filled my ears, triggering a flood of memories. But wait? Something wasn't right. I squinted against the glare on the water, and then it hit me.

Dock, not docks. There was only one, not the two I was used to seeing. The beach seemed to stretch for miles without the second dock cutting across it and into the water. Faint rake lines traveled the surface of the sand, drawing my eyes to two canoes at the end of the beach, their noses touching the water. Closer to me, a line of smooth, blue-gray boulders formed a border between the sand and the lawn above it. Huh, those were new.

*BAM!*

Shit! I nearly jumped out of my seat, causing my still-buckled seatbelt to lock tight against my hips. The pounding intensified while I attempted to regain control over my breathing. A face peered through the glass, its pixie features outlined by wisps of wild pink hair. Karissa. She was talking to me through the closed window, but between the glass and my still-frantically beating heart, I couldn't make out anything more than garbled murmurs.

"Kris," I said as I cracked the window, "back up so I can get out." She stepped back, but not enough, so I hip checked her lightly with Burt's door.

"Oof," she cried. She clutched her hip and bent forward slightly, but quickly straightened back up and beamed at me.

"Sor—" As soon as I peeled my bare legs from the hot vinyl seats, Karissa launched herself into my arms, cutting my apology short.

"OhmyGOD! Could you have driven any slower? I was starting to think you would never get here."

I hugged her back with equal force, but loosened a little when her petite body tensed in my arms. "Sorry, chica. My mother would have gone crazy if she found out it took me less than three days to get here. Seriously, she probably would have flown cross-country to kick my ass and drag me back to North Carolina." We let go of our embrace.

"But if she did, what would you do with this stellar vehicle?" She gestured to Burt, a barely concealed smirk on her face.

"Hey," I scolded. "Don't mock Burt. You'll hurt his feelings."

"Burt? Seriously, you named this thing?"

But I wasn't listening anymore. A guy was walking toward us from the beach, his gait assured and confident. Even from our distance I could tell he was tall, over six feet. His long, wavy hair was pulled back in a low ponytail and was completely at odds with his clothes, which were meant to look casual—khaki shorts, faded blue polo—but screamed money. He had one of those faces you see on glossy magazine covers, usually attached to some well-known European heir. Add in the silver aviator sunglasses perched on his nose just so, and it was obvious this guy came from money. Probably a lot of it.

"Who's that?" I asked, gesturing to Rich Boy with my chin. The resort didn't usually have many guests this early in the year, and it's not the kind of place typically frequented by the wealthy.

Karissa glanced over her shoulder. "I dunno, but he's been here every day I've been here this summer."

"He's staying here? Which cabin?"

"Oh, oh. Someone's got it for the new guy. Oh la la," she sang.

"No, I—wait. The new guy?"

"Yeah," she said, putting on her patented I-know-something-juicy face. "He's not here for vacation. He must work for Craig."

Yeah, right. "No, seriously, where's he staying?"

"No, *seriously*, he works here. In fact"—she waggled her eyebrows—"he lives here. Right here, to be exact."

Now I knew she was making things up. Craig never hired new people. He only gave Karissa and Rory jobs because he wanted to make me happy. Of course, now he could barely manage a summer without them. "Very funny, Kris. You know what, whatever. It doesn't matter anyway."

Karissa smiled and stared pointedly at Rich Boy. I tried to be a little less obvious than my friend as he crossed the lawn, skirted around the parking lot without even a glance in our direction, and walked into the closest cabin.

My cabin.

"Okay, what the hell was that?"

Karissa sang an, "I told ya sooo."

I had to talk to Craig, to find out what was going on.

With one last look at my cabin—his cabin, the cabin, whatever—I spun on my heel and started to march to Craig's office. But I went nowhere—instead, I slammed into something. Or, rather, someone.

I didn't even see him come back out of the cabin; the guy made no noise when he walked, I swear. A deep laugh rumbled in my ear and vibrated my face. Which was still pushed up against his chest. Why hadn't I moved it yet? Who stands there with their face smashed against some random chest? Weirdos. Stalkers. Freaks. Oh, god, I was a weird stalker-freak, wasn't I? The laughing continued, and I forced myself to peel my face away from the soft cotton of Rich Boy's shirt, noticing he'd lost the polo in favor of a worn t-shirt. Trying to control the heat rising in my face, I looked up to apologize, and—

"*Rory?*" I was so surprised to see a familiar face that I almost forgot about Rich Boy—who was apparently still hanging out in my cabin—altogether.

"Good to see you, too, Laney."

You know how sometimes you see someone years after you did last? At first glance, there's no doubt who it is, but as you talk for a while, the person's facial features morph, and eventually you're left wondering how you ever recognized them in the first place. I'd had the feeling before, with elementary school teachers and old sports coaches. Never with someone I knew as well as I did Rory.

It was him, I could tell, but at the same time it wasn't. The longer I looked at him, the less he looked like the boy I knew. He'd grown probably three inches over the past year; my head could tuck under his chin perfectly. Sunlight shined off the curls in his dark brown hair. The awkwardness I had always considered inherently *Rory* was completely gone, and I could barely see the mark of the teenage acne fairy, which was so prominent last summer, beneath the golden tan he'd already built.

He smiled down at me, and in the crooked pull of his mouth, my best friend returned. I wrapped my arms around him again, squeezing with all I had, and I knew:

This was where I belonged.

# DAY TWO

MY PHONE BLARED DISGUSTINGLY early the next morning, jarring me out of my sleep. My hand slammed against the nightstand and groped the smooth surface until it found the offending device so I could turn it off. Ringer silenced, I dropped it back to the table and rolled over, pulling my puffy comforter to my chin. It was new this year, and a definite step up from the scratchy blanket that used to be on the bed. My eyes drifted shut again, and then I shot straight up.

"Shit. Crap, crap, crap." I grabbed the phone and mashed at the screen until it started to dial. She picked up on the first ring. "Mo—"

"Laney Madeleine, we had a deal." Her tone was even harsher than usual.

"I know. I'm so sorry, I—"

"You were to call me as soon as you arrived. I expect that was more than twelve hours ago. What was so important that you couldn't make a five-minute phone call to let your mother know you weren't slowly dying in a ditch somewhere?"

And she says *I'm* dramatic. Please, Mother. Like the call would have been any less than half an hour long. I nestled down into my pillows, trying to make myself comfortable for what was sure to be a monster lecture. "I'm sorry," I repeated. It was the only thing to do: apologize frequently, never argue, and don't bother trying to explain, no matter how many times she asks me to. Near daily *talks* over the last three month had taught me as much.

A door creaked, and I panicked slightly before remembering I had a neighbor now. It turned out Karissa was right and Rich Boy did live in my cabin. Well, not in *my* cabin, but close enough. Over the winter, Craig had cleaned out the storage area on the other side of the building and turned it into another living space. So now, rather than the quiet solitude I was used to, someone lived on the other side of my kitchen wall.

I peeled the covers back and made my way across the room to the window. Pushing the heavy curtain aside, I peered out and watched as Rich Boy crossed the parking lot and cut into the woods. Where was he going? There was nothing past the tree line but more trees.

"...worry about you all the time." My mother's voice cut through my curiosity and brought me back to our conversation. She was getting louder, which meant she was gearing up for her big finale. I let her rant for another minute or so, and then, sure enough, she sighed and said, "I don't know, Laney. I think this is a bad idea. Maybe you should come home."

My blood ran a bit colder, and I fought off a shudder. I couldn't show her my desperation, couldn't plead. She would view it as weakness, and I couldn't let her think for a second that I was too weak—too fragile—to stay. My voice threatened to waver, but remained steady as I said, "No. I'm fine, really. It was a stupid mistake, a lapse in judgment. I promise to call every week."

"Twice a week," she said.

"But I thought—"

Another sigh. She was beyond frustrated with me, and I could picture her face in my mind, the crease between her eyebrows—she swore it didn't exist—deepening by the second. "You broke our deal, Laney, and so now we have a new one. You can call me every Wednesday and Sunday, or you can come back home for the summer."

"You can't seriously make me come back."

"I am your mother, and I sure can. Until your birthday, you are still a minor. Dr. Patel is looking for a bookkeeper, and I think it would be great experience for you, Laney. It'll really prepare you for your classes, and he'll pay well enough to help you with college." The words she didn't say were shouted at me through her silence: unlike your father.

A job in the office next door to hers, where she could keep constant watch on me all summer. Right, like that was gonna happen. I suppressed the urge to whine, knowing exactly where the conversation would go if I did: I'd tell her she couldn't keep me away from my dad; she'd say she sure as hell could, he wasn't much of a father anyway; I'd bite my tongue before yelling that his lack of involvement was never his fault. Instead, what came out of my mouth was: "Okay. Wednesdays and Sundays. I promise."

"Thank you." Her voice held a little less edge to it now, but not much.

"Okay, but, Mom? I gotta go now. I'll call you tomorrow."

A pause. Then, "Where do you have to go at 6:10 in the morning?"

My mind searched for a lie, coming up with one way easier than it should. "Craig needs my help with something right away this morning, and I want to get a run in before."

"Oh, that's nice." The surprise in her voice was unmistakable. "I'm glad to hear you're running again, finally. I never understood why you quit when you had so much ahead of you still."

*Of course you didn't understand. You never listened enough to.* But I couldn't tell her that. I had to play nice, so I took a stab at stopping her before she became all weepy about the cross country scholarship I gave up by quitting the team right before state finals. "I know"—she kept talking, so I raised my voice to overpower hers—"Okay, I'm gonna go before I run out of time. I love you, Mom."

Her words stopped immediately, and her shock radiated through the phone. When was the last time I told her I loved her? I couldn't even remember, but she'd probably been counting days. Scratching them off on the wall of the bedroom she shared with *him*. "I"—she cleared her throat, and I fought to not be affected by the tears in her voice—"I love you, too, sweetie. Have a good run."

Tucked back in my bed, no matter how hard I chased it, sleep dodged my grasp, and I finally came to terms with the fact that I was up for the day. Five minutes later, I was geared up for a run, my familiar shoes hugging my feet like old friends. Because that's what my mother didn't realize: I never stopped running. Ever. Running was my lifeline, and I couldn't stop. The only difference was, before, I was running toward my future. Now I ran from my past.

✳︎  ✳︎  ✳︎

"Hey, kiddo!" Craig called as I jogged back into the

parking lot. He looked exactly like he did when I'd first met him five years ago—same dirty-blond curls peeking out from beneath the same beat-up hat he always wore. He stood with his hands buried deep in the pockets of his standard Carhartts, pushing his shoulders toward his ears. The stance made him look even bigger than he already was. A wide smile broke across his face, crinkling the skin at his temples until his eyes were nearly swallowed.

"Hi!" I pulled the earbuds from my ears and ran the last few steps to him. He wrapped me in his arms, his warm body enveloping mine completely. He smelled of dust and sweat and pine shavings, just like I remembered. "I missed you," I said.

"Missed you, too." Craig gave me a final squeeze before stepping back and holding me at arm's length. He studied my face—looking for what, I wasn't sure. But the expression that plagued his features was more serious than I'd ever seen him. "How are you holding up?"

I shrugged, attempting nonchalance. "I'm fine," I said. "Just moving on, ya know?"

He nodded, hesitantly. "Yeah, I know." He chewed on his lower lip as he thought, but then his concerned expression was replaced by another broad smile. "Sorry I couldn't be here yesterday. I'm so happy you're here, Laney."

"Me, too," I said.

"How'd you convince your mother?"

My mind flashed to her face the day she told me I couldn't go to the lake for the summer. The thinly-veiled anger as she tried to convince me it would be better for me to stay in Southport. "I don't know," I said. "All I care is that she did." Gesturing to my sweaty shirt, I continued, "You wanna come in? I need a drink of water."

Craig led me to my cabin door, holding it open for me to enter then following. He leaned against the kitchen counter and said, "I can't stay long—more meetings. But I wanted to say 'Hi' before I headed back to Missoula."

Filling a glass at the sink, I said over my shoulder, "You're having a lot of meetings these days, huh? Isn't that where you were yesterday, too?" I leaned against the counter opposite him and gulped at my water, thankful for the chill after my run.

He nodded and rubbed a hand across the back of his neck. "Yeah," he said, and just when I thought that's all I'd get out of him, he added, "we have some big things planned for this place. Quite a few changes." He waved his hand across my living area. "You like the new bedding?"

I forced another drink down my throat. "Yeah, I do." I hesitated. "So...um...what's the deal with the new guy?"

Craig looked at me quizzically, and I jerked my head toward the wall connecting my kitchen to the room on the other side, where Rich Boy was staying.

"Oh. That's Weston." I gestured for him to continue. "He's here for the summer, helping out."

"Helping out doing what? Where's he from? He can't be local if he's staying here."

My father shook his head. "No, West isn't local, you're right."

"So...what's his job?"

"He's—" A long groan escaped Craig's mouth. "I can't really tell you. Not yet."

"Okay...?"

"I'll let you know at the staff meeting next week, okay?" His face lit up like a little boy's. "It's a surprise."

"Oh come on," I said, dropping my now empty glass into the sink. "That's seriously all you're gonna give me? I promise not to tell anyone else." My voice took on a singing plea.

He shook his head again. "Nope. My lips are sealed until the meeting." He winked and mimed twisting a lock over his mouth and throwing the key over his shoulder. As his arm came back past his face, his eyes caught hold of his watch. "Oh, shoot, kiddo. I really gotta go. But...why don't we plan on dinner together later this week?"

"Definitely."

# DAY THREE

AFTER MY RUN THE NEXT MORNING, I made my way behind the cabins to the old stables. My first summer here, Craig was so proud of his stables; they were to be the shining star of his luxury resort. Nowhere else on the lake could one both sleep and book a guided horse ride. That was five years ago, and to my knowledge, the only people to touch the horses had been me, Craig, and Rory. No guided tours. The guests probably didn't even know the stables existed. Not that it bothered me. Aside from the rec lodge, the stables were my favorite part of the resort, and since they're so far out of the way, they were the perfect place to hide out for a couple hours.

The familiar comfort hit me as soon as I stepped into the building. Hay, musty and sweet smelling, lined one wall, and the sound of hooves hitting the floor—accompanied by snorting and the occasional whinnied plea for attention—was music to my ears. Each of the horses received a quick pat as I walked by, but they had to wait for any quality time. First, I had to see my girl.

As I approached the stall, I heard it. Another voice, humming and nickering. I wasn't as alone as I'd expected. A few more steps, and I turned the corner. There he was, Rich Boy, standing at the head of the stall, one hand stroking the chestnut mare's neck. For a second, I considered backing out of the stall and coming back later, but before I made up my mind, it was too late. Rich Boy—Weston, I reminded myself—turned to face me.

"She's a beautiful creature," he said, and OH MY GOD HE HAD AN ACCENT. British, maybe Australian? I didn't know, but for a brief moment, my resolve slipped. What was it about hot guys with accents that could completely undo me? He quirked an eyebrow, and I realized I'd been staring way too long. At least my mouth wasn't hanging open. I hope.

"Um, yeah, she is," I managed to sputter. "She's mine."

"Ah, then you must be Craig's daughter I've heard so much about."

"Yep. That's me."

He turned back to the horse and asked, "What's her name?"

"Epona." Why did I sound so breathless? Would he have believed me if I blamed it on my run?

Weston cocked his head to one side. "That's an...interesting name."

"Rory named her." Craig gave me Epona the summer after we met. He'd bought a new horse shortly before my mother and I came up to visit, and a few months after we left he noticed she was a lot heavier than she should be. It was winter, so he didn't think much of it. One day in the early spring, he went out to the stables and found two horses where there was once only one. That summer he told me the foal could be mine. Every little girl's dream: a pony from Daddy. I just got mine a few years late and from a man I barely knew.

"The protector of horses. Right?" Weston said. "And the goddess of, er, fertility." I stared at him. "The name. It's Celtic, right?"

"Actually, I think Rory named her after the horse in some video game."

"The repair guy?"

"Yeah, he used to be this total geek, and when I got her and was having a hard time coming up with a name, he kept going on and on about Epona, and it eventually stuck."

"Huh." He turned back and ran his hand over her nose, clicking his tongue, and I stood there, awkward. After half an eternity, he finally turned to look at me. I tried not to glare. But really? The accent and the looks and charm were starting to wear off, and I wanted to be alone with my girl. He shuffled his feet. I fought against another sigh. Finally—FINALLY—he took the hint and headed toward the door. "Well," he said as he passed me, "I guess I'll go see if Craig needs any help in the office."

It was out of my mouth before I even knew what I was saying: "Hey, we're all going to town tonight. Kinda a kick-off-the-summer thing. You wanna come with?"

He smiled, and the crinkles around his eyes eased my irritation almost immediately. "Thanks. I think I will."

And then he was gone. I walked up to Epona and stroked her nose, loving the feel of warm velvet under my palm; even her prickly whiskers felt wonderful. "Hey, girl, how're you doing?" Snort. I took that to mean she missed me, too. I buried my face against her neck and let myself melt into her warmth. Her coarse mane rubbed against me, and I burrowed deeper, pushing past to the slick, silky fur beneath. Her pulse thudded beneath the surface, keeping rhythm, slow and steady.

Time ticked on. Who knows how long I stayed there, leaning into Epona, letting her ease away my pains and anxieties. She stood there, not judging, letting me hold her, no questions asked.

God, horses are so much better than humans.

"You did what?" Karissa spun on her heel and pointed her comb in my face. She had been standing in front of my mirror, fixing her makeup and hair, for the last twenty minutes. Why she didn't get ready before coming over was beyond me. Maybe she loved my tiny mirror and lack of counter space. Now, she stared at me, her face demanding.

"I—well, I invited West to go out with us tonight."

"West? *West*? What, you already have a nickname for him?"

"No." She stared at me more. "Well, I guess. It's what Craig called him."

"Whatever. Did you tell *West* this outing is a ritual? A Karissa, Laney, and Rory ritual? A non-West ritual?"

"Come on, it isn't a ritual. It's just something we do. Besides, it's never only the three of us. We always—"

"Oh, my God! You totally want him. That's why you are fighting so hard for this."

"Why do you need that thing anyway?" I gestured to the comb in her hand. "Your hair is only like an inch long."

She jabbed the comb at me again. "Don't try to change the subject. You want Weston to come because you want to hook up with him." She spun back to face the mirror. "Besides, my hair is way longer than an inch."

It was the perfect opportunity to let the subject drop and go back to what I was doing. But even before talking again, I knew that wouldn't be the case. It was like my mouth was an agent gone rogue, working directly against the orders from my brain. So while what I wanted it to do was keep quiet and make cookies, what it did instead was say, "No, I invited him because I thought it would be nice"—or because my damn mouth refused to listen anymore—"just like it would be nice for you to step away from the mirror and help me out in here."

She marched across the room and looked over my shoulder at the cookie dough. Picking up a handful of chocolate chips, she gave me a smirk before tossing them into the bowl and returning to her post at the mirror. "There, I helped. Now back to the subject."

"Right. And the subject is?"

She glared at me through the mirror. "We were talking about how badly you want *West*." She said his name like it was a dirty word. Not that she had any problem saying dirty words. "You're gonna get laid tonight. I can see it in your eyes."

Finally, my mouth was as dumbfounded as my brain. I stood silent, stirring chocolate chips into the dough. I shouldn't have been surprised she thought it. In the past, she would have been absolutely right about—well, about everything. I used to sleep with a lot of guys, so what? I wasn't like that anymore. I'd changed. I had to.

It hit me like a hungry zombie during the apocalypse,

taking my breath with it. This was my chance. I could tell Karissa everything I'd refused to talk about all those months. She was my best friend—I *should* tell her. Stir my cookie dough. Muster up some courage. Stir. Contemplate how to start my story. Stir some more. Finally, I opened my mouth—

A loud crash from the front porch stole our attention and stopped any words that may have made their way past my lips. Through the window, I watched as Rory fought to untangle himself from my fly rod. Apparently for all his growth over the last year, he hadn't gained any grace.

Kris and I laughed as he hopped on one foot, pulling at the fly line wrapped around his other leg. Losing his balance, he leaned against a stack of tackle boxes, sending them clattering to the ground. Finally, he straightened up, smoothed out his shirt, and crossed the rest of the porch to the front door, leaving a wake of destruction in his path.

When he reached the door, Karissa and I scrambled back to where we were. She stood in front of the mirror, pulling at her individual spikes for the fiftieth time tonight, while I busied myself forming little balls out of the cookie dough. As Rory entered my cabin—without knocking, as always—I realized how much we'd all changed over the past year. I spent so much time worrying about the changes I went through, how different I was, that I never considered Rory and Karissa may have changed as well.

Rory looked like a whole new boy—a new man. Karissa looked exactly the same, despite her ever-changing hair, but something lingered there, something screaming *change*. I struggled to pinpoint what it was.

"Hey, girls." Rory dropped into the chair by the door, draping one long leg over its arm. Neither Karissa nor I looked at him; instead we focused almost maniacally on what we were working on. The silence was heavy, pressing on my chest and shoulders. Since when was there this awkwardness between us? Never before had I been at a loss around those two, but now I stood in the kitchen, unable to think of a single thing to say. I waited for Kris, ever the loud one, to break the silence, but she simply stood at the mirror, checking her mascara and reapplying lip gloss.

Rory looked from Karissa to me then back to Karissa again, a puzzled look on his face. "What is with you two? I'm pretty sure I just heard crickets chirping in here."

I opened my mouth, but again it failed me, and nothing came out. Maybe I'd spent so much time over the past months being silent I'd forgotten how to have a normal conversation. After a few "ums" and "ahs," I held up my mixing bowl, hoping it would be explanation enough.

"Awesome! Cookie dough!" Rory leapt from his seat and darted to the counter, taking the whole room in two strides, and grabbed a handful of dough. He rolled half into a ball and dropped it onto the cookie sheet; the other half he shoved into his mouth.

"Hey, Kris! You want any of this?" He held up another chunk of dough, tempting Karissa away from the vanity with it. When she got to us, she reached out her hand to grab the dough, but he pulled it away and popped it into his mouth.

"Ass," she said, shoving him with her shoulder. "Move over."

We rolled cookies in silence for a couple minutes, Rory and Karissa eating nearly as much dough as they put on the sheets. Turning to put a batch into the oven, I said, "So how's the band, Rory?"

"Excellent! We've been practicing our brains out, trying to get ready for the fall."

"What's happening in the fall?"

Karissa laughed. "Oh my god, he hasn't told you yet? It's all he ever talks about, I swear."

Rory's face deepened to a muted red under his golden skin. "I got accepted to the University of Texas, and the guys are gonna move down with me. Dinosaur Dance Off is going to take Austin by storm."

"Dinosaur Dance Off?"

A wide smile broke across his face, and he ran his hand over his body in a very Vanna White way, showcasing his t-shirt. It was faded gray and worn looking, with two t-rexes screened on the front, tilting toward each other, tiny arms held up. *Dinosaur Dance Off*, it said beneath, letters jagged and misaligned. "Yeah. You like it?"

"It's definitely...unique," I said.

"If by unique you mean ridiculous," Karissa said.

Rory stepped back, hands clutched at his chest and a look of mock hurt on his face. "Whatever. You love it and you know it. You'll probably be the first official Dinosaur Dance Off Groupie."

Karissa scoffed, but her eyes sparkled and a small smile found its way to her mouth.

And just like that, we were back to the way things had always been. The three of us played around in the kitchen, waiting for the cookies to bake. The tension and awkwardness left the room, and it was like we were fourteen again—completely carefree. It's strange how when you are with people you have known for so long, people you know nearly as well as yourself, time stands still and allows you to be who you were in the past. Being there with Rory and Kris let me erase the whole last year, if only for a moment; the familiarity of their company overshadowed everything else, and I was again the girl they knew. The confident, brave girl I used to be.

As we packed up the cookies and got ready to leave for the night, I realized that not once did either of my friends look at me with the mask of pity I'd gotten so used to. Never did their eyes linger on my arm, trying to see the scars I kept so expertly hidden beneath my sleeve.

It was 9:45 by the time we left the cabin. Weston was sitting out on the porch swing, reading a book. As Rory shut the front door behind the three of us, Weston closed the book—his fingers inside to keep his place—and stood. Karissa tensed beside me.

"What's with the cookies?" West gestured with the book toward the plate.

"Oh. I make them the first night every year. For the bartender, you know, to make sure he doesn't hassle us." How long had he been sitting there? And how soundproof were the walls of my cabin? It wasn't terribly well built, and I wondered for the first time if it was as private as I'd always thought. "Why didn't you come in?"

He shrugged. "No real reason." Something in his voice was off, and I couldn't quite place it. I didn't know him well enough to tell for sure, but oh man, he heard everything Kris said, didn't he? "It's such a nice night," he continued, "so I figured I'd stay outside and enjoy it for a while. Besides, I wasn't sure you guys would want me...." He trailed off, and his eyes flicked to Karissa for a brief moment.

"Well, would you look at that!" Rory glanced at his bare wrist and chuckled uncomfortably. "We are running out of time. Let's go." He grabbed Karissa by the upper arm and started to steer her to the parking lot; she shrugged him off immediately and turned back to face us.

"Who's driving?" she asked, rubbing her arm where Rory had grabbed it.

I sighed, hoping a summer away from my mother would break me of the habit. "I can drive," I said, "but two people will have to sit in the back."

"Oh la la. Of course Laney would volunteer her car," Kris sang. Rory giggled like a school girl. Charming.

"I don't get it," Weston said, and his accent made my legs go a little squishy. Damn it. "What's so funny about Laney's car?" He was beginning to look like maybe agreeing to go with us wasn't the best idea in the world.

"Nothing, really. It's just that Laney drives an El Camino, and we all know what that means."

"It's a Ranchero," I mumbled.

"Er, no, I don't know. What's the big deal about the El—R-Ranchero?"

Rory laughed again. "There's this song that goes with the car. How's it go again?"

"El Camino," Kris sang, "El, El Camino."

"The front is like a car."

"The back is like a truck."

"The front is for a kiss."

"The back is for the—" They both broke off into a series of loud giggles.

"It's a Ranchero," I muttered again, knowing it made

absolutely no difference.

"Hey, don't feel bad, Laney." Kris threw one arm around my shoulder, stretching onto her toes to do so. "It's the perfect car for you."

"You know what? You two get to sit in the back. Weston can have shotgun, and y'all can think about what you did." It scared me how much I could sound like my mother if I tried.

Kris and Rory took off toward the car, skipping and dancing, hopping over logs and generally acting like children. Kris leapt into the back of the car in one swift movement; Rory followed, tripping over the lip of the tailgate and crashing on top of her. She cried out briefly, but her wail quickly changed to more laughter.

I looked at Weston, who was standing with his hands shoved deep in his pockets, his shoulders hunched up, causing the collar of his polo to touch his earlobes. "Hey, about that," I started, but he shrugged my explanation off with a quirk of his chin.

The drive to the bar took us all of five minutes. It would have been easy enough to walk, but we had to bring Burt. Small Town Bar Hopping 101: walk back home, leaving the car behind so you have some motivation to roll out of bed in the morning. Nothing like having to walk a mile and a half to your car to get you moving.

The Place looked exactly like it always had. Small town

charm mixed with grungy biker bar. A couple played darts in the corner, and an old man sat at the end of the long bar, watching the TV screen above his head. Other than them, the place was empty. Except for—

"Derek!" Karissa danced across the floor when he came out of the back room. Derek was a staple in Seeley Lake. He'd been tending bar at The Place for three years and hadn't aged a day since his first on the job, when he should have chucked us straight out, but didn't. Derek was the only black man in town, and I had no idea how he ended up there. As far as I could tell, he had no family there, he didn't move for a job, and didn't have any particular ties to the area. He was just *there*.

"If it isn't my favorite delinquents," he bellowed then looked over his shoulder to the room he'd left. He added, his voice a little lower, "I hope you brought me the right stuff, or I might have to toss you out." A grin lit his face.

Karissa handed the plate of cookies to him. He took them, capturing her hand in his, and asked quietly, "How's Megan?"

She stiffened and pulled her hand away. "Fine." Her voice was cold, her eyes steely. Derek heaved a sigh and rubbed a hand across the back of his neck.

"What happened with Derek and Megan?" I asked Rory, my voice low and my eyes on Karissa, hoping she wouldn't hear.

Rory angled his body to stand between me and Karissa. "I don't know details"—his eyes cut briefly to Derek—"but when she moved, she just stopped talking to him. Hasn't answered his calls and never called him. Not once."

"Holy fuck."

When Derek and Megan started dating two years ago, nobody was surprised. It was obvious they were into each other from the first time they met—I was pretty certain she's the reason he let us stay that first time we came here. They were always together, perfectly complementing one another. They were going to get married. No date had been set, but we'd all been expecting it.

I watched Derek now as he composed his face into its normal, happy expression. "Hey, listen, you guys," he said, pretending not to notice us watching his reaction. "I have a new boss, and he's a real hard-ass. I can't let you drink in here."

Weston stepped out from behind us. "I'll take responsibility for them," he said as he pulled his ID from his wallet.

Derek scrutinized the ID for far longer than necessary, thinking, no doubt, it was a fake. The new boss must have been a nightmare for him to be so careful—I couldn't even count the number of times he'd served us without even pretending to card. He handed it back over. "All right, man, I can sell you a bottle, but if they are going to be drinking, they can't do it here."

Weston turned to us. "It's your night. What do you guys want to do?"

"Get drunk and play pool," Karissa said, eyeing the table at the other end of the room.

Rory pressed his thumbs to her forehead, making a show of working her scowl away. "If that's what you want, we can go back to the lodge. What do you think, Laney?"

I shrugged. "That works for me."

Weston followed Derek to the bar, waving away our offers of money, and we headed back outside. The crisp night air exhilarated me, giving me a slight buzz before we even cracked the bottle open. It was great to be out in the woods with my friends. My worries and pain melted off me and into the open air. Finally, I could be myself again. I needed this.

Karissa yanked the bottle from Weston's hand, and he, to his credit, didn't seem to mind her rudeness. "How old are you anyway?" She twisted the cap off.

"Twenty-three."

"And what's up with the accent? Where are you from?" She didn't even try to act pleasant, and I cringed at the harsh edge in her voice. Thankfully, Weston took it all in stride.

"Actually," he said, "I was born in New York City, but I lived in South Africa most of my life, and did my undergrad at Oxford."

"Swanky." Kris took a swig from the bottle and passed it to Rory, obviously done talking to Weston. We walked in silence for a while, passing the bottle between us, none of us sure what to say. Should I ask Weston more questions, try to smooth over the bristles Kris left? I watched him from the corner of my eye. His face was smooth, calm. Maybe I was imagining Karissa's attitude because of our earlier conversation. Or maybe he was great at hiding what he's thinking.

"Hey, Laney," Rory said, passing me the bottle. "You remember the first year you were here when we thought it would be a good idea to climb that tree?"

"Oh, god. How could I forget." I took a deep swig from the bottle, cringing at the burn the alcohol left in my throat. "My mother was so pissed."

"I don't see why," Karissa said. "That cast was the best."

"What happened?" Weston asked as the bottle was passed to him.

"There was this tree," I explained.

"Still there," Rory chimed in.

"Yes, there *is* this tree. It's in the middle of an empty lot, all alone."

Karissa snort-laughed. "It just broke Laney's heart to see that tree so lonely."

"Shut up! You said it, too." My head was already

starting to spin, and suddenly the memory of that day was so funny I couldn't even begin to tell the story without laughing.

Rory stepped in to finish, barely able to contain his own laughter. "We decided to be the trees only friends. So we climbed up as far as we could. But then Laney fell out and broke her arm."

Weston started at us and took another quick pull from the bottle. He grimaced and handed it back to me. "That doesn't sound like it was very funny."

"Oh, it wasn't." But Rory, Karissa, and I broke into more laughter anyway.

By the time we got back to the resort, my mouth was numb and my fingertips tingling. We walked into the parking lot, and I jumped onto the long log that served as a parking block and used it as a balance beam, stumbling to the other side. When I reached the end, Weston was there, holding the bottle up to me. I tossed my head back and took a drink, liquid trickling out the corner of my mouth. The alcohol sloshed in the bottle as I lowered it back down, and I jumped to the ground, landing shakily just in front of Weston. He reached out to steady me, and his hand lingered on my waist a while longer than necessary, playing with the hem of my shirt, his fingers tickling the soft skin of my hip. Rather than flinching away from his touch, I found myself leaning toward him slightly, an old, familiar feeling igniting in me for the first time in months. I hadn't felt it in so long, and I was surprised at how much I missed it. A look into Weston's eyes revealed the same hunger there, along with something else. Uncertainty, maybe? Fear? A tingling grew in my lower abdomen, coursing through my veins and setting my nerves ablaze. I leaned closer—

And was knocked aside by Rory, who was frolicking his way through the parking lot, Karissa at his side. "Oops," Kris said in her sing-song voice as she snatched the bottle from my hand, "sorry, guys. I feel like flying! Don't you wanna fly with me?" She ran in zig zags across the rest of the parking lot and lawn, arms out to her side like a soaring bird, Rory keeping pace with his fumbling footsteps. Weston and I trailed behind them in awkward silence.

By the time we reached the rec lodge, Karissa and Rory were already at the back wall, pulling pool cues from the rack. I hopped over the jagged threshold to join them. Halfway across the room, I turned to Weston, who was still standing in the doorway, as if unsure whether or not to join us. "Hey," I said, "you coming?"

He shrugged and surveyed the room. I followed his eyes, willing the blurry features of the lodge to come to focus: rustic log walls peppered with news articles and old pictures of the lake, uneven wooden floorboards, the pool table propped up under one leg by a wood block. Weston's

34

gaze landed at the entrance to the next room. From my position, I couldn't see it, but I knew what he saw. Mismatched couches in front of a huge, ancient projection TV. The upright piano that stood in the corner had seen better days, but it could still be beautiful under the right fingers. Mrs. Endecott, who came for a week in early July, could make the old instrument sing.

I cleared my throat to catch his attention once again. He stared at me, bleary eyed, and I was certain he would leave. He looked more uncomfortable at the idea of entering the room than I'd seen him look all night. But then Karissa shouted, "You pansies coming or not? Rory and I are gonna wipe the table with you," and Weston shrugged and stepped into the lodge finally.

"All right," Rory slurred. "I'll rack 'em. You guys crack em."

In the end, Karissa was right. She and Rory destroyed me and Weston. We played four games and lost every one. "What can I say?" Weston shrugged. "One thing I'm definitely not is good at billiards."

"You can say that again," I grumbled. Snatching the bottle from its perch next to the table, I noticed it was almost gone. "Hey, Ror? Why don't you go see what's behind the bar there. I need more of a buzz if I'm gonna play y'all again."

Rory bowed dramatically and retreated to the bar area.

Karissa rolled her cue across the table, checking for straightness, as if she'd know what to do if it were crooked. Weston leaned back against the table, propping his elbows on the rail.

"Hey," I said, and my voice came out way louder than I intended. Weston rolled his head to face me. "Why'd you live in South Africa?"

"My father took a job there when I was really young," he said, and between the accent and his drunk-slur, I found myself straining to understand him. "He found this boarding school he liked, so he jus' left me there when he took the next job."

"No shit?" Karissa asked. "How old were you?"

"Five," he said. "Just starting kindergarten." He shrugged, attempting nonchalance, but his back was stiff and straighter than it had been just moments before.

Five years old. Who the hell just leaves their kid behind at five years old, no matter how good the school?

Weston's eyes pierced mine. "Pretentious assholes like my father," he said. Shit. Had I said that out loud? My face burned, and I scrambled to find something to say to fix my stupidity, but my brain would not cooperate.

Thankfully, Rory returned just then, holding a tray with four tall glasses on it.

"What is it?" Karissa asked, snatching one of the drinks. The tray lurched off balance, and the remaining glasses sloshed their contents over the edges a bit before Rory righted them again.

"You don't wanna know," he said. "I just found whatever Craig had. There's a shit-ton of that cherry crap you love so much, though." He handed me a glass, then Weston, finally grabbing his own and dropping the tray to the floor.

Pressing the glass to my mouth, I inhaled deeply. The drink smelled sickly sweet. And toxic. I pulled a sip into my mouth and forced it down my throat. The sharp burn of the alcohol battled against the overwhelming tang of artificial cherries. I sputtered a cough. "Oh my god, Rory, that's—"

"Fucking fantastic!" Karissa yelled. "I've only had, like, two drinks, and my buzz is already back. Let's do this!" She used her pool cue to gesture to the table.

Weston racked the balls, knocking them askew the first two times he tried to remove the triangle. Finally, the cluster of balls stood together on the table, waiting for Rory's break shot.

The game was a mess. It took us a full half hour to clear the table, and even then each team hit so many of the other's balls in the pockets that we couldn't tell who really won. Karissa dropped her cue onto the worn felt of the table then tossed the rest of her drink back in one quick gulp. She swayed slightly on her feet, pounding on her chest. A belch ripped through the air. "All right," she said, "who's ready to swim?"

"Yousurethatzagoodidea?"

Rory, Karissa, and I all three turned to stare at Weston, who was leaning precariously against the pool table. "Huh?" Rory asked.

Weston straightened his shirt and pulled a long breath through his nose. "Are you sure," he said slowly, putting shaky emphasis on each word, "that swimming is a good idea?"

"Why? Just because Rory tried to kill us with those drinks?" Karissa shrugged. "You'll be fine, champ."

My head was spinning, so it took me a few seconds to slide down the pool table to him. I leaned my weight against him—trying to nudge him with my shoulder, but unable to pull myself back upright. "Don't worry," I said. My voice sounded foreign in my ears. "We do it ev'ry year. The cold water will sober you up."

"Okay." He pushed himself to standing, and I slid toward the floor, barely catching a hand over the edge of the pool table before I landed face-down on the hardwood. "Sorry 'bout that," Weston said. I shrugged and straightened up.

Rory stood at the door, still holding his pool cue, face peaky. "Don't worry, man," he slurred. "Karissa is a lifeguard. She'll save you if you drown." He pushed away from the door frame and swayed precariously. "Let's go."

"Aren't you going to change?" Weston asked us.

Karissa danced across the room, surprisingly light on her feet for the amount of alcohol she drank. She pulled the string to her bikini out the neck hole of her shirt and waved it in Weston's face. "We came prepared," she said. "Go change, and we'll meet you on the dock."

Ten minutes later, Rory, Karissa, and I stood at the end of the dock, looking out over the water. Moonlight glinted off Rory's defined shoulders, and I was struck again by how much he'd changed. Part of me yearned to reach out and touch him, to run my hands over his new muscles, trace their lines, to make sure he was real. But he's Rory, and we don't do things like that. Even drunk, I knew that much.

The dock bobbed slightly, and I turned to find Weston walking toward us, peeling his shirt up over his head. I spun back toward the open water, averting my gaze before I could be caught staring at him for, what, the thirteenth time today? He eased up next to me, and my eyes drifted toward him of their own accord. Board shorts hung low on his hips, and the edges of a dark tattoo peeked out from beside his right hipbone. I leaned forward, pulled by an insane need to know what it was, how far the ink went. If he could just shift his shorts the slightest bit...

My finger hooked in his shorts and tugged slightly, and

I realized: WHAT THE HELL WAS I DOING? Heat ambushed my face, and I jerked my hand back, but not before I felt the shifting pull in the front of his shorts. My stomach lurched. It was a good thing I was standing on a dock over water, because I needed to go drown myself.

Sensing my embarrassment—or perhaps needing a quick dose of cold water—Weston dove into the water and emerged a few yards out, steam billowing off his shoulders and head. A second splash sounded, and I nearly jumped out of my skin. How did I totally forget there were more people on the dock? I turned to Kris, my only ally left out of the water. I couldn't make out her expression in the dark, but no doubt it was disapproving. She doesn't miss much; I'd hear all about my impromptu shorts dive later. No way she'd let it go.

"Are you two wussies getting in, or what?" Rory yelled then slapped the water, splashing our bare feet.

"Yeah," Karissa said, her gaze never leaving me, "Laney *can't wait* to get wet." And with that, she jumped in without even bothering to strip down to her bathing suit.

The hem of my shirt rolled as I worked it between my fingers. Four months since I'd last worn anything but long sleeves. Four months of being covered, protected. Could I break that now? Karissa dove in with her clothes still on; maybe I should do the same. But the thought of so much fabric weighing me down, clinging to my body and separating my skin from the water, made me cringe. I couldn't do it. My body ached for the water.

It was dark out; nobody would be able to see. I could do it. I could. Slowly, I pulled the shirt over my head and off my arms. Goose bumps erupted on my skin immediately as I was blasted with cold air. A second to adjust my multi-wrap bracelet to achieve maximum wrist coverage, and I was under the water. It pulled through my hair, rushed along my legs, embraced my bare torso. Holding me in a way no person ever could. If time had stopped right then, I would have spent eternity at peace.

Rory and Karissa immediately started racing the length of the dock. They did it every year, and every year Kris won about twenty-seven times, but it never stopped Rory from challenging her. Their laughter filled the night, and I let it envelop me as I treaded water, my face to the stars.

Ripples pulsated against me, the tiniest change in movement, and I sensed he was behind me before I could actually feel him. Then, there he was, his hands resting gently on my hips below the water. I mentally braced myself for the involuntary tensing. It would come eventually; it did every time a man touched me. Except, I remembered, on the walk home. Not with Weston. Heat from his hands spread through my body, and a need built deep within me. So foreign, yet so familiar at the same time. The pull below my navel brought back sensations I thought I would never feel again. For the first time since that night, I felt fully like myself again.

I turned in his hands to face him. His eyes were slightly unfocused, and he wore a grin that barely pulled his lips up on one side of his mouth, but his desire was clear. Alcohol still warmed my veins, encouraging me as I let myself relax into him. I could let down my guard, follow my instincts and urges again. Right?

His lips had been chilled by the air, and were cold when they touched mine, ever so lightly, but they warmed up quickly when I pressed my mouth against his in return. He slipped one hand off my hip and wrapped his arm around my back, pulling my body against his. God, I fit in there so well. Urgently, but still gently, he pushed my mouth open with his own. His tongue played against mine, and desire roiled beneath the surface.

I have no idea how long we stayed like that, intertwined in each other's arms. The thrill of kissing Weston was even more intoxicating than the bottle Derek sent home with us. Each brush of his lips excited me more, setting my nerve endings on fire. The water caressed my skin, tickling my back, as we bobbed there in our own little world. I couldn't get enough. I pressed myself tighter and tighter against his slick skin until the tingle in the pit of my stomach grew into a silent roar. Finally, there with Weston, I was alive again.

He stroked his hand along my back as he kissed me even more deeply. He traced the line of my shoulder blade and down my arm. Then he reached my wrist, and his mouth froze against my own. His fingers played against my scar. And as quickly as things built up, they fell down again. His hand on my wrist brought the last four months crashing back, and the intensity swelling within me died out instantly. I pulled back and swam off to join Karissa and Rory, leaving Weston standing chest-deep in the water. I turned once to see him still watching me, but he never made a move to follow.

Smart boy.

# DAY FOUR

T-SHIRTS I'D SEEN RORY WEAR since I got to the lake:

1) The soft gray knit one I smashed my face against. Bold letters proclaimed **CAUSTIC ENCOUNTER**.

2) A plain white tee, with a bright blue silhouette of a man with hair that made Einstein's look tame, and the words, *Electrode Lickers*.

3) The *Dinosaur Dance Off* one he wore out to The Place.

And today he wore:

4) A deep brown V-neck with a white llama on the front. *The Young Alpacas*, it read.

As soon as we sat down, he dove right in. "So what was that I saw in the lake last night?"

"I have no idea what you're talking about," I murmured, taking the menu the hostess offered me. "Could I get an iced tea, please?" I asked her. Then buried my face in the menu and used it as a shield as I struggled to force the blush from my cheeks and neck.

A finger hooked over the top of the plastic-cased menu book; my arms stiffened against the pressure, but I eventually relented and allowed Rory to lower it. He stared at me with one eyebrow cocked and his crooked grin plastered across his face.

"Nice try. You practically devoured the new guy."

I shrugged.

"So...are you into him?"

"No," I said, way too fast. I pulled in a deep breath. "We were drunk. It was a mistake."

"You sure about that?"

"Yes," I snapped. He opened his mouth, no doubt to push further, but snapped it shut again when I glared at him.

We studied our menus for a few minutes then gave our orders to the waitress. We sat there, not talking, and I stared at his shirt until I just couldn't anymore without some kind of explanation. "Rory," I said, trying to pull his attention away from the TV above the bar. He didn't move even a little bit. "Rory!" I yelled, and he snapped his head to face me. "So nice of you to invite me out to lunch so we could commune with the TV."

"I'm sorry." He blushed, and my gaze shifted to the TV, where two hulking men in spandex were throwing each other around a spotlighted ring. Lasers swept across the background, and a strobe light threatened to send the whole audience into seizures.

"I never pegged you as a big WWE fan," I said, quirking an eyebrow at him.

"I-I'm not," he stammered. "I...well, I...what did you want? We could talk about Weston some more, if you'd like."

"God, no," I groaned. "What the hell is the deal with your shirts?" I waved my hand at his chest, and he bent forward, rounding his long back so he could look at the llama more closely.

With his shirt held out between his hands and a sliver of tan stomach showing, he said, "What? You don't like it?"

"The Young Alpacas? You do realize that's a llama, not an alpaca, right?"

The shirt dropped, and he stared at me with a fallen face. "You're shitting me, right? How can you tell?"

Great. Leave it to me to open my big mouth and spout out some random trivia nobody else cared about. Probably the shirt had some big significance to Rory, and I'd crushed him by being a know-it-all. He continued to stare at me with a scolded-puppy look, so I explained, "It's the ears. See how those are really big and kinda shaped like bananas? Alpaca ears are smaller and straighter."

"How do you even know crap like that?"

"I...I dunno, I just do." How could I tell him I'd become such a recluse that I spent my Saturday nights doing things like learning the differences between alpacas and llamas? Even I could tell how pathetic I would sound.

He leaned back and slouched down into his chair, his arms crossed over his chest, covering the llama. "And here I thought The Young Alpacas would actually stick."

"Stick to what?"

He shrugged, a slow, full-bodied movement. "Our band. We're doing great, but we can't decide on a name."

"Wait—I thought y'all were called Dinosaur Dance Off?"

"We were," he said, "just like we were called about sixteen names before that."

"And you make a shirt for each name?"

"Of course. How else are we going to know how it will look on merch?"

I had to give him credit for his optimism. The Rory I

left behind at the end of last summer wasn't even sure he could ever be a real drummer; now here he was talking about making it and selling merch. It was like we'd switched places over the school year. He gained all the confidence I had ripped from me. And I was left...well, I was left like this.

After lunch, Rory and I headed toward Karissa's house. Rory and Kris lived on the same street, three houses away from each other. They were practically siblings as kids, one of them always at the other's house. We walked in silence, passing the familiar sights on the way: a gas station, Derek's apartment, an old church, the tree I fell out of. I started to turn up the sidewalk at Rory's house, but he continued walking by without even a glance.

"Hey," I said, "aren't we going to say hi to your mom?" We always stopped to chat with his mom when we came into town.

"Nah. She's probably not even home. She's been gone a lot lately, taking the girls to camp and stuff."

So we continued down the street to Karissa's. The moment we stepped off the gravel shoulder and onto her cracked sidewalk, I knew something was wrong. Nothing was out of place, no signs of anything abnormal, but the air had a charge to it, a crackle that made my arms tingle and the hair on the back of my neck stand at attention.

Phantom ants marched along my skin, their tiny feet tapping a cadence of *not right, not right, not right, very wrong.*

My hand shot out and grabbed Rory's arm, jerking him around to face me. Sensing my apprehension, he stilled completely, his head cocked to one side, listening. At first nothing happened—we stood there like idiots, unmoving on the side of the road. Then we heard it. Yelling. Loud, violent yelling, the owner of the voice obviously pissed. *Mr. Goodman,* Rory mouthed. My face must have shown my disbelief, because he grabbed my hand and yanked me down the street toward his own house.

"Mr. Goodman?" Doubt rang heavy in my voice. "Seriously? I've never even heard the man speak more than two words at a time." And those words he spoke so quietly I could scarcely hear him.

"It's gotten bad this year," he explained. "He's out at The Place almost every night now, and I never see him during the day anymore. It's like when Megan left, something in him snapped. This isn't the first time I've heard him yelling like this."

"Shit. What does Karissa say about it?" My arm threatened to leave its socket as Rory tugged me down the road.

"Nothing. I tried to bring it up once, but she totally shot me down." We crossed the lawn to the front porch. The crooked planks were littered with sports equipment:

dirty soccer cleats and tiny pink shin guards, a football, a lacrosse stick, and a beat up pair of ice skates, still hanging out from winter. I wasn't surprised; with five kids under twelve years old, Rory's mom and step-dad were totally burned out. We lowered onto the wooden bench, which loudly protested our weight. Rory continued, "I'm worried about her, Laney."

"Kris?"

"Yeah. Have you noticed anything weird about her?"

"No—well, yeah, I guess I have. Yesterday, I asked her how Megan was, and it's like I told her I thought she looked fat or something. She totally freaked on me, told me she didn't want to talk about Megan. Then she left. She didn't even finish her lunch first." I thought back to the day I arrived, the tightening of her body when I hugged her. Was it possible?—no, I was overreacting. Seeing things where there wasn't anything to be seen. "Should we...should we go over there?"

Rory shook his head, his curls flopping across his forehead. "I did, once. I was walking by and heard him screaming, so I knocked on the door and pretended I needed help with my homework. Kris swore he was just upset and that it was no big thing, but I could tell how pissed she was. She wouldn't talk to me for almost a week after."

"Wow. Do you"—I paused to track down my voice,

which had seemingly run away—"do you think she's trying to hide something?" Rory stared into my eyes, trying to read my meaning. I spelled it out for him: "Do you think he's, you know, doing more than yelling."

"What? No. I think she's just embarrassed by him."

I wanted to believe him, but something didn't feel right. My mind fought to accept what Rory was saying, but my body refused to. Tiny demons clawed at my stomach, fighting to break free. I had to do *something*, rush to her house, make him stop, *something*. I jumped from the bench, but Rory's rough hand grasped my own and jerked me back to sitting. My elbows bashed into the back of the bench, and a splinter worked its way into my thigh, dangerously close to my ass.

"What the fuck?" I screamed as I jerked my hand out of his grip. I rubbed my elbow.

"I'm sorry, but you can't go storming in there."

"Like hell I can't." I made to stand again, but Rory's arm pressed across my hips, holding me to the bench. Anger bristled within me, and I had to fight myself to keep from punching my friend in the neck. I knew he meant well, but the pressure of his forearm across my body felt like a violation, causing my skin to crawl. I struggled against him, fighting to find any maneuver to throw him off from this position. Despite everything I'd learned in all my self-defense classes, I bucked my hips against his arm.

Rory jumped up off the bench and stood in front of me, his hands held up at his shoulders in surrender.

"Whoa," he said. "I'm sorry. Just...calm down, okay?" Like fuck I would calm down. I started to stand, but he rushed back to talking. "Trust me. Karissa will hate it if you go over there right now. Been there, done that, remember? I'll send her a text and let her know we're down here. Ask her to come watch a movie or something, okay?" My body dropped the rest of the way back to the bench. Rory pulled his phone out and went to work on the tiny keyboard. "There. Sent. See, we can get her out of there without causing a big scene." He sat back next to me, careful to stay on his side of the bench, to not touch me.

The unspoken questions rolled off his tense shoulders in waves, hitting me over and over again. Rory was my best friend—I was completely safe around him, so why the freak-out? I told myself it was because of my concern for Kris, that I'd gotten too worked up about her dad's yelling, but deep down I knew better. I was broken.

"I'm sorry," I began. Out the corner of my eye, I could see him watching me, a look of apprehension painted on his face. "I—I shouldn't have freaked out on you. I just...I can't stand knowing something is wrong and not be able to do anything about it."

Disbelief painted Rory's face. He knew there was something more going on, but the great thing about Rory was that I could trust him not to push too hard. I leaned into him and let my head drop to his shoulder. The ice melted off me, and my muscles relaxed one by one.

Just then, Karissa came up the street, the gravel crunching beneath her feet and flying out in front of her every step. "You two sure you want me busting up your party?" She called out, but her normal light, joking tone was dull and lifeless.

"Heck yeah! You know it's not a real party unless I've got at least two girls with me."

"Right. You keep telling yourself that, Chief." She leapt up onto the porch, much lighter on her feet already than she was on the walk over, and launched herself across our laps. "So, what movie were you losers gonna watch?"

"Um—" My mind went totally blank. Movies had been my whole life over the past few months, my only companions through long, sleepless nights. But still I was unable to think of a single title to tell her. I searched into the recesses of my internal database. "*Attack of the Killer Tomatoes*?" Of course my voice would squeak.

Rory shook next to me, and little bits of his ill-suppressed laughter snorted out his nose. Karissa's whole body stiffened on top of mine, and before I knew what was going on, she was off the bench and at the bottom of the porch steps, staring daggers at us. "So you heard."

"Heard what?" Wow, Rory was the worst at feigning

innocence. A toddler could have seen through his little *heard what* routine.

"Oh my god, Rory! I told you to stay the hell out of it. Why can't you mind your own shit and leave mine alone?" Upon closer inspection, I could see how red-rimmed her eyes were, glistening with tears I knew she was fighting to keep from falling. "Just"—she drew in a shuddering breath—"leave me alone!"

She ran back toward her house before either Rory or I could even try talking to her again. My body longed to chase after her, so strongly I could feel the familiar tingle of my muscles warming up for a run. But I knew better now. I'd seen firsthand what Rory had been trying to tell me was true. Karissa didn't want my help, and I had to respect her choice. God knows I'd been the one refusing help in the past. I had to hold to that feeling and remember how badly I hated when anyone tried to force help upon me. I could give Karissa what everyone back home had neglected to give me: a friend who would be there for her when she was ready, and who wouldn't demand anything until then.

# DAY SIX

CRAIG'S LOFT SMELLED DELICIOUS, like spaghetti and garlic bread, with an overtone of something sweet—pie, maybe?

"Knock, knock," I called, pushing the door open and stepping inside. His place wasn't much—an apartment over the main office—but I loved it. It was homey and comfortable. The summer after I met him, I came to spend my whole school break with him for the first time. I was only thirteen, so I wasn't old enough yet to stay in my own cabin and had to sleep up in the loft with Craig. I thought it was going to be super awkward, but I felt right at home instantly.

Now, he came out of the kitchen with a ladle in his hand. "Hey, kiddo! Go ahead and make yourself comfortable. I'm about done in here."

Craig's couch was one of those ancient relics that tried to swallow you whole when you sat down and made you feel like an arthritic old lady when you attempted to extract yourself from its jaws. I gathered up everything I might need—magazine, blanket, remote controls—and lowered myself onto the cushions. Sinking a full six inches farther than it looked possible, I thought I may never get off the couch again. At least I was comfortable.

Craig bustled back and forth setting the table, and guilt tugged at me for letting him do it alone. "Hey," I called out, "what can I help with?"

His head poked around the wall dividing the kitchen and living room. "Don't worry about it. I'm just about done." Proving his point, he carried a heaping bowl of noodles to the table and waved me over.

The spaghetti was every bit as good as it smelled. Craig was a great cook, maybe even better than Martin the Narcoleptic—husband number two. Though, to Martin's defense, I didn't care for much more than hot dogs and chicken nuggets at that age, so I never tasted any of his fancier dishes. But he was a chef, so they were probably delicious. As we ate our meal, I found myself wondering what things would be like if my mother had never gotten her first divorce. Would Craig have ever bought Leisure Lodge? Somehow I didn't think so. I twirled my noodles around my fork and let the daydream of the life I missed take me over.

Craig's voice jerked me out of my fantasy. "So, how's it feel to leave high school behind?"

"Oh my god, so amazing. I couldn't wait to get out of that place."

His hand froze, garlic bread hovering halfway to his mouth. "I thought you liked school."

Crap. "I did. But..." I shrugged, and his eyes flickered to my covered wrist. Briefly, but long enough for me to notice.

I knew my mother wrote to tell Craig what had happened. She might have done everything over the years to keep him out of our lives, even ignoring his existence over the past few years except for when I was at the lake, but there was no way she could let that one slide. He called as soon as he got the letter, but I wasn't ready to talk. A week later, I received a beautiful letter, telling me he was concerned, but as long as I promised to take care of myself he wouldn't push me to talk about it.

Now, he coughed, and my attention jerked back to him. He was obviously uncomfortable. Was he about to break his promise? Things were different now that I was at the lake; he'd want to talk things out, make sure I wouldn't cause him any trouble. I stared at my plate, appetite suddenly dead. He ate in silence for a few more minutes before he coughed again. So fake.

"Craig?"

"Yeah, kiddo?"

"You need some more water?"

His face turned pink, then deep red.

"Or maybe," I said, "there's something you want to talk about?"

"Am I that obvious?"

"Painfully so, I'm afraid."

"Well...here's the thing...." His gaze fell somewhere near my left ear, my forehead, my lips, but never my eyes. I was right. This was it. He was worried about me, thought I was going to be a burden this summer, too much for him to handle. I was certain of it. He was going to send me back to my mother and *him*.

"Craig," I said, "I promise you don't have to worry about anything. I'll be fine this summer."

"Huh?" His face screwed up, making him look like a little kid trying to figure out multi-variable calculus. "What are you talking about?"

"You mean you're not about to tell me it would be better for me to stay with my mother this summer?" The bite of my accusation stung my ears.

He stared at me for a second then burst out laughing. Not a little chuckle, either, but full-bellied guffaws. He struggled to regain his composure, almost succeeded, and then cracked up all over again. Finally, he calmed himself down, but not before tears were streaming down his face.

"Sorry. Your problems aren't funny. It's just"—he giggled, actually *giggled*—"that was about the furthest thing from my mind."

"Oh. Okay, what's up then?"

"It's...well, I invited you over tonight because...I just—"

"Craig," I interrupted, "spit it out."

"Okay. Laney, I'm getting married, and I'd love for you to stand with me." He said it all in one breath, the words tripping over each other in their rush to escape his mouth before he ran out of air.

My mind blanked—a vacuum thrived where my brain should have lived. It was so far from anything I'd imagined he would say. I knew he was married to my mother, but even so, I'd always pictured Craig as the eternal bachelor, running his little mountain paradise. Dating around from time to time, but never settling down. Maybe it was his shaggy hair and the mountain-man stubble he always had, but I couldn't picture him at the front of a church promising himself to some woman I'd never met.

I must have let my silence go on too long, because eventually Craig said, "I mean, it's okay if you don't want to. I thought it'd be nice to have you there with me."

"No. That's not it. I—you took me by surprise is all."

"I guess this is kinda out of the blue, isn't it?"

"Yeah," I said. "I'm used to the other parental unit

getting married. I didn't expect it from you, too!" I winked to let him know I was teasing. He smiled at me, his cheeks back to their normal shade of tan.

"So, what do you say, kiddo?"

"I say, when do I get to meet the lady who tamed you?"

He beamed at me. How had I not noticed the change before? Craig was clearly a fool in love. "Well," he said, "Weston is going to Missoula to meet her for lunch tomorrow. You could go with him if you want."

"Uh—" I'd been successfully avoiding Weston, spending as much time as possible at Karissa's and Rory's houses, not ready to face him after what happened in the lake.

Craig looked at me expectantly. "I dunno," I said. "There's a lot of stuff I should probably take care of around here, isn't there?"

He waved my concern off with the side of his hand. "Don't worry about it. The season hasn't even started yet, and I want you to go and have fun. Plus, if you do say yes, Angie has strict instructions to take you to pick out a dress."

Great. Dress shopping with Weston. Things were so not going the way I wanted them to. But I couldn't exactly say no to Craig. Not with him looking so excited, which is probably why I found myself saying, "Sure. It sounds like fun."

# DAY SEVEN

HE WAS WAITING OUTSIDE MY cabin when I got back from my run. In the time I'd been avoiding him, I actually managed to forget how breathtaking he was. The sun played with the golden hints in his hair, and I wondered briefly if what happened the other night was such a bad thing. Right up to the end, it was a pretty amazing, actually. "Hey," I said, "what's going on?"

"Craig told me you wanted to come to Missoula with me today." Have I mentioned the accent? My god it's hot. "And I wanted to let you know I'm leaving at ten." He shuffled his feet and purposefully and obviously avoided my eyes. So he *did* remember. Fantastic.

I didn't know Weston well enough to know how this would play out, but I knew enough guys to know it would go one of two ways: 1) He'd play it cool, pretending the other night was no big deal, like he hooked up with random girls all the time, so why would there be anything special about me? He definitely wouldn't be the first to bring it up. Or, 2) He'd expect something from me. Want something more. A relationship? Regular meaningless hook-ups? He'd think he had some sort of in because I was foolish enough to get drunk and let my guard down for one night. He'd be wrong.

He was still running the toe of his beat-up Vans—such a stark divergence from his Ivy League look—across the dirt, gouging a line between us, abjectly refusing to look at me. Fine. I could wait until later to decide how things were going to work out. We'd have plenty of awkward time in the car for that. "Ten?" I said. "Sounds great. See you then." Even I was taken aback by how cold my voice sounded, but whatever. I sidestepped Weston and headed into my cabin without giving him a second—okay, third—look.

When I slid into the passenger seat of Weston's car three hours later, the scent of musk and vanilla air fresheners assaulted me. I leaned back in my seat, inhaling deeply and closing my eyes. I could feel a wide grin tugging at my lips.

Weston's door clicked shut. "What's so funny?"

"What? Oh, nothing. It's not funny. It's just this

smell—"

"Yeah," he said, sounding embarrassed. "Sorry about that. The car's kind of old, you know?"

"No, it's not that. I love this smell."

He laughed, light and melodic. "I don't think anyone really loves this smell. I love this car, and I still don't love the smell."

"No, really," I said, remembering. "When I was five, my mother married Steve. He had an old truck that smelled just like this. I loved that truck."

"All right then. Feel free to take an air freshener when we get back. You could string it around your neck and bring this delight with you everywhere."

"You are a dork," I said.

"That's me. Any preference for music?"

"Whatever."

"Okay," he said, drawing the word out, "you aren't one of those people who has some strange aversion to The Beatles, are you?"

"Are you kidding me? Do such people exist?"

His face lit up with a smile, and heat flared in my cheeks. Damn fair skin; it's a dead giveaway every time. One more thing to thank my mother for. The squealing roar of an airplane engine filled the car, followed by the frantic drumbeat of "Back in the U.S.S.R."

We rode like that for about half an hour, nothing but

the sounds of the CD keeping us company. But the longer I listened, the harder it was to ignore how many of the songs were about love. Or sex.

"Hey, West?" I yelled over the music.

"Can we talk?"

He turned the music down. Slightly. "Yeah. What about."

I froze. The words were there, somewhere in the back of my mind, but I couldn't make them come out. "Um..."

"We could talk about how you've been completely avoiding me?" His cheeks jumped as he fought his grin into submission.

"Was not!"

"Please. We practically live together. You think I didn't hear it every time you crept out as soon as I got back in?"

"Okay, fine," I relented. "Maybe I've been avoiding you a little bit. Are you happy now?"

"Thrilled. Let me guess. You didn't know how to talk to me after what happened in the lake." He watched me out of the corner of his eye.

"Exactly!"

"I understand. It must have been terribly difficult for you. You could have broken the ice with something witty. Like, 'hello.' Or maybe, 'Good morning.'"

"Right. As if it's ever so simple."

"It is." He flicked on the blinker and zipped into the

other lane. A pair of headlights shone in the distance. He pressed his foot to the floor, and the old car stuttered before flying around a minivan. We darted back into our own lane just before the other car flew by, horn complaining loudly.

Weston laughed. "Calm down, Laney. We were fine the whole time." My left fist unclenched under protest, and I uncurled my stiff right hand from around the *oh shit* handle. Because, holy shit. He laughed again, and even his laughter had an accent.

"Shut up," I yelled. "You drive like a maniac!"

He shrugged. "What can I say? It's one of my many flaws."

"Many, huh? You sure you want to own up to that?"

"Of course. It's all part of the plan."

"Plan?"

"Yup. If I admit a bunch of faults right up front, then I'm covered. Whatever you discover about me won't be nearly as bad as you're expecting, and you'll be totally smitten in no time."

Right. Scenario B it was. I sat silent, taking some time to figure out what to say. How to let him down gently. I couldn't give him my normal morning-after brushoff—not if I had to work with him all summer. For the briefest of moments I let myself entertain the idea of *not* turning him down.

Weston laughed again, but where I would have used an uncomfortable chuckle, he threw his entire being into it, a more musical version of the deep throaty laugh Craig gave me last night. "I wish you could see your face," he said once he was calm enough to talk. "Relax. It's fine. I don't expect anything from you."

"Really?" Curse you, squeaky, pathetic voice.

"Really. We were drunk. Things happened. It's okay, but we can't let it happen again. Deal?"

"Sure."

We rode in silence for a few more miles, both of us sneaking glances, neither of us admitting to doing so. Finally, he spoke again: "Can I ask you something?"

And...here it came. I rubbed my scar with the thumb of my other hand and braced myself. "Shoot."

"Why were you so worried about it anyway?"

Oh. "It's just...I'm not the kind of girl who does that. Get drunk and throw myself at some guy." Okay, so I used to be exactly that girl, but I wasn't anymore. I was different.

At least, I thought I was.

✳ ✳ ✳

The first thing I noticed about Angie was how beautiful she was—the kind of jaw-dropping, eye-popping beauty I wasn't sure existed outside of Photoshop. Deep, rich chocolate hair fell in soft waves halfway to her elbows, framing the profile of her face perfectly. Even with only one side of her visible, I could see how striking her features were: strong eyebrows and a straight nose, high cheekbones accentuating deep eyes.

Then she turned toward us, and I fought to keep my gasp from being audible. A scar cut across the right side of her face, from brow to jawline. Its edges were puckered where it crossed the soft flesh of her cheek, and even through her olive skin I could see the angry red color proclaiming the scar *new*. A second, smaller and less-noticeable scar traced her forehead near the hairline, smoother than the first, but still red.

Weston placed his hand on the small of my back and gently nudged me forward. I hadn't even realized I'd stopped. Without him there, I probably would have never found the courage to walk to the table. When we were halfway to her, Angie stood to greet us, and my stomach fell out my butt.

Her belly led her from the table, round and swollen, sitting on her small frame like it had been strapped there with a harness. A sour taste bit at the back of my throat.

"Weston," she called out. "So great to see you again." She pulled him into a hug, and I stood awkwardly by their sides. As she let him go, she turned toward me. "And you must be Laney. I'm so happy to meet you. Your dad talks about you all the time." She beamed at me.

Heat crept up my neck and into my face. After way longer than was appropriate, I managed a small, "Hello." I forced myself to look at her face.

Her skin deepened, and she broke into a wide smile. I couldn't help but notice how her scar moved with the expression. "Let me guess," she said with a chuckle, "Craig didn't tell you about the baby?"

"Yeah, not so much."

She rolled her eyes playfully. "Well that's exactly like him, isn't it? Craig isn't so great with the touchy-feely stuff." We walked to the table and sat.

"No," I said. "He sure isn't." Which was one of the many reasons I couldn't wait to get to his resort this summer. "I think he was so terrified to tell me he was getting married that he couldn't bring up the baby."

"Why would Craig be scared to tell you he's getting married?" Weston asked from behind his menu.

"He was probably concerned I'd have an aneurism if I had to attend one more parental wedding," I said. He stared at me, one eyebrow cocked higher than the other. I sighed. "My mother's been married about a million times, and it drives me crazy. He probably thought I would go postal on him when he told me or something."

"But you didn't," Angie interjected.

"Nope. Craig's nothing like my mother. It took him

almost eighteen years to find you. I don't think he'd jump into this without thinking things through."

"Thank you, Laney." Her eyes misted over, and she placed a hand on her belly.

Our food came, and we ate in silence for a while, enjoying our meals, before Angie broke the silence: "What are your plans for the fall, Laney?"

I focused on chewing my pizza slowly, stalling. Finally, I swallowed and said, "I'm not sure. I got accepted to the U back home, so I'll probably go there, but..." For the first time, I considered voicing what I'd been thinking the past few weeks.

"But..." Weston prompted.

Okay, here it was. Truth time. Somehow it was easier to say it to this woman I'd barely met than to even consider telling my mother. "I was thinking maybe I would take a year off before college. Take some time, you know? But my mother would freak."

"You should do it," Weston said. "My gap year was incredible."

Angie smiled at me, and I caught myself staring again. "I agree," she said. "I took a year off, and it's the best decision I ever made. Aside from marrying your father, of course. Now, I'm stuffed to the gills. I'm gonna nip into the restroom for a sec, then we can go shopping, okay?"

"Sounds good."

As soon as she was out of sight, I leaned across the table toward Weston, who was absentmindedly sliding the handle of a fork underneath the leather cuff on his wrist, in and out, in and out. "Hey," I whispered, "I don't wanna be rude, but..."

"You want to know what happened?"

"It's like you read my mind."

"It's a talent," he said then slid the fork into his shirt pocket. Weirdo. "Let's get through an afternoon of shopping, and I'll tell you on the way home."

"Deal."

Angie came back from the bathroom, flipping her hair behind her shoulder as she walked to the table. Eyes followed her all the way through the restaurant—not just the men, though they definitely stared, but the women as well. She held her shoulders back and her head high, as if she was completely oblivious to the attention she commanded. I couldn't see how that was possible.

"Okay, you two, ready to shop?"

"Thrilled," Weston dead-panned.

She grabbed her purse from the table and fished out her wallet. "Very funny. Tell you what—if you can survive a day in the shops with us girls, I'll get you a treat at the end." Her eyes sparkled.

Weston turned to me, a sly grin on his face. "She thinks I'm seven, apparently," he said with a shrug. The waitress came back with the bill book. Angie held a hand out for it, her wallet still clutched in the other, but Weston reached out and intercepted it before she could grab it. Faster than seemed humanly possible, he whipped his wallet from his back pocket, slid a credit card into the faux-leather holder, and handed it back to the waitress.

Angie glowered at him. "You don't have to do that *every time*."

He shrugged and dropped his wallet onto the table then leaned back in his chair, stretching his lean torso even longer. "It's no bother." His hands rested together at the back of his head, and he looked like the definition of ease as we waited for the waitress to return with his card.

After signing the receipt—Weston left the server a huge tip, I couldn't help but notice—we headed back to the parking lot. "There's this fabulous little boutique over on Brooks I think you'll love, Laney. We can start there and head to the mall if we need anything else."

We piled into her car, Weston taking the back so I could sit up next to Angie. I watched her from the corner of my eye as she navigated through the city, carefully dodging the other cars. A trip through Missoula was like navigating through a battle field. Drivers paid next to no attention to lines and traffic flow, and streets intersected with one another at odd angles. We pulled up to a stoplight—the car in the next lane raced through, well after the light turned red—and she gave me a small smile.

"So," I began, turning in my seat so I could see both Angie and Weston, "how do y'all know each other?"

They shared a quick look, and the intensity of it shocked me back in my seat. Angie returned her gaze to the road, her knuckles whitening slightly where she gripped the steering wheel, and said, "I had a business conference in Philadelphia—"

"Which is where I'm schooling," Weston interjected. Angie nodded.

"What do you do?" I asked her.

"I was a Child and Family Services agent for several of the reservations in the state." She smiled sadly and accelerated back into traffic. "I'm not with them anymore."

"Okay..." I wanted to ask her why, but the look on her face kept me from prying. Instead, I said, "So you two met at the conference then?"

Angie shook her head, her small smile fading into a frown. "No. It was one night after the conference..." Her voice faded away, and she shifted in her seat. I waited for her to continue.

Finally, she opened her mouth, but Weston's voice cut in from the back seat, shaky. "I was out...we just bumped into each other and got to talking."

Angie's eyes flashed to the review mirror for a brief moment before a smile graced her face again.

The familiar clicking of the turn signal sounded, and Angie pulled the car to the side of the road, stopping just behind a dark blue BMW. I looked out the window to see a storefront painted in a distressed turquoise. A wooden sign hung from an iron bracket, swaying slightly in the breeze. As it swung back, I caught the name painted in bright pink. *Fusion.* The windows were filled with soft, silky fabrics, woven throughout with twinkle lights.

"We got along well," Weston continued, "so when Ang told me about the job at the resort, I couldn't turn it down."

I turned in my seat to face him. "Yeah? And what job would that be?"

He laughed. "Nice try. Your father warned me about that."

Angie's soft laughter mingled with Weston's, and she pushed her door open. "Craig is all about the surprise on this one. You know your dad."

"Yeah," I groaned. "I know." I looked at the front of Fusion again. "Well..."

"Let's get this over with," Weston finished for me, and we piled out of the car and onto the sidewalk.

The inside of the store was just as colorful as the outside. The floor was sealed concrete, with a painted yellow arrow stretching from the front door to the back wall, several diagonal stripes cutting through its shaft. To my left stood a long, sleek counter covered with scarves and belts, the occasional jewelry rack rising above them. The right side of the store was filled with racks of dresses, skirts, and flowing shirts. A young girl with choppy black hair and wearing a loose tunic over calf-length leggings called out to us, "Welcome to Fusion. I'm Kat. Just holler if you need help with anything, okay?"

Angie said, "Thank you," and made a beeline to the closest rack of dresses. She rustled through them, pulling three hangers down and draping the fabric over her arm before turning back to me and Weston. "Well," she said, "are you two going to stand there like you've never been in a store before, or are you going to come over here and pick something out?" Weston made a face, and she continued, "Okay, fine. West, there's a chair back by the fitting room. I know you've got a book tucked away somewhere. Laney, let's find you a dress."

Shopping with Angie should've been considered a full-contact sport. She worked her way through the rack, flinging unwanted items to the side and tearing the *maybes* into her arms. Every few minutes, she'd hold something up to my body before deciding whether to keep it or shove it back onto the rack. She didn't make small talk, only murmuring occasionally about my complexion and hair color. She was a woman on a mission, and I wasn't about to get in her way. I could get used to this. My mother's version of shopping involved full-day outings, painstakingly analyzing every article of clothing—sometimes loudly criticizing them—before deciding which few items to take to the fitting rooms. This process would continue at store after store after store until I was sure my head would explode if she held up another item. I much preferred Angie's form of retail therapy.

After about fifteen minutes, we made our way back to the fitting room. Weston sat on a puffy armchair just to the side of the curtained doorway, leaning back with one ankle resting on the opposite knee. He was so into his book that he didn't even notice our approach until Angie dumped the pile of dresses in his lap. He jumped and stared up at us, bug-eyed. "What?—"

Angie lowered herself into the chair next to Weston and pulled a dress from the top of the stack. Tossing it to me, she nodded toward the curtain and said, "Better get started."

"Shouldn't I take more than one?"

She shrugged. "If you want. But those rooms are tiny."

I grabbed the pile from Weston's lap anyway and made my way into the fitting room. Angie was right—the room was barely big enough to turn around in. Still, I didn't want to have to showcase each dress I tried on in order to get the next one. I took some time to hang everything on the two tiny hooks protruding from the wall, and then I peeled my clothes off.

The first four dresses were horrible. Nice on the hanger, but not great on me at all. They were immediately shuffled into the No pile. The fifth was okay—nothing special, but would work if none of the others ended up being better. And then I stepped into the sixth dress.

"I think I found the one," I called through the curtain. The dress was simple: ice blue with a swishy skirt and tube top. Two thick straps attached at the waist and extended for several feet. I played with them, pulling them over one shoulder then twisting them together into a halter-top style before finally criss-crossing them around my torso several times, creating a textured bodice. I spun in the mirror, admiring how the jersey fabric clung to my frame.

"Come on out, sweetie, and let us see."

I stared at myself in the mirror again, so exposed. The double-wrap hemp cord on my wrist barely covered my scar. A few adjustments made it better, but I still was not used to so much skin showing. Not anymore. Pulling a deep breath through my nose, I pushed the curtain aside.

"I think maybe it needs a shrug or something," I said, my voice timid.

Angie stood and grabbed my hand, pulling me closer and turning me so she could look at the back. "Oh, no, you don't want to cover this up. Why don't we just get some accessories?" With that, she pulled me from away from the fitting room and toward the long counter up front. Weston, who never even looked up from his book, stayed behind.

When we reached the display, Angie headed straight for a rack of sparkly necklaces. The black-haired sales girl walked up behind the counter and said, "You girls still finding everything okay?"

I nodded, but Angie said, "Actually, we need something to go with this dress." She gestured to me.

Kat's face lit up. "That color looks fabulous on you! Really brings out your eyes." She was already spinning the necklace display, her fingers running over the strands, as if she were searching for the perfect piece by touch. "You'll want Aurora Borealis for that dress."

"The Northern Lights?" I could feel my face wrinkling in confusion.

Kat's giggle was like a bell, such a stark contrast to her fairly deep voice. "No. Well, kinda, I guess. It's a name for a kind of jewelry. We just got a couple vintage pieces in last week." She went back to her search, finally taking her eyes from us and looking at the necklaces before her. "Ah," she nearly yelled, "this one is perfect."

My jaw dropped as she handed the necklace across the counter to me. I draped it across my fingers and examined it. Five strands of clear beads stared up at me, each slightly longer than the last. I twisted my hand, and as the light caught the beads, they all shimmered in myriad colors. It was as if a rainbow had been captured and forced inside the glass, only to show itself when the light hit exactly right. The strands met together at each end with a decorative silver bar, the clasp on the other side. It was one of the most beautiful things I'd ever seen.

"Go on," Angie said, "put it on."

I handed it over to her and pulled my ponytail up so she would have access to my neck. My breath froze in my chest as I waited for her to clasp the necklace. The weight of the beads across my collar bones felt foreign, but when I looked in the mirror behind the counter, it was forgotten. The necklace looked like it was made for this dress, the two complemented each other so perfectly. My fingers played with the beads at the hollow of my throat. "Wow," I breathed out.

"You want matching earrings?" Kat asked.

Almost in a trance, I fingered my ear lobe. "Not pierced," I said, "but I could use a bracelet if you have anything that'll work." I waved my hemp cord in the air, bringing attention to how drastically it clashed with the rest of the outfit.

She actually clapped. It made her look like an excited school girl in an anime series. "Perfect!" she squealed. "That actually came in with a bracelet and earrings, so we have exactly what you're looking for."

The bracelet was almost exactly like the necklace, but somehow not. It had three strands of beads, chunkier than the ones on the necklace. And, where the necklace was a crystal clear sky, colorless but for the subtle rainbows, the bracelet was overcast. The glass beads were darker, almost silvery, but they held the same hints of color. The clasp matched that of the necklace, and I fastened it around my wrist, pushing my hemp cord out of the way. It covered my scar perfectly.

Kat held a pair of earrings up. They were simple, a silver drop with a single glass bead at the end of each. "You sure you don't want the whole set? There's a parlor down the street that can pierce you." She grinned mischievously.

I shook my head and turned to Angie, noticing she wore earrings. "You should wear them," I told her. "They'd look great on you." She looked startled, so I hastily added, "Unless you already have your jewelry picked out, I mean."

"Oh, no, I don't." She looked at the earrings for a moment. "That'd be wonderful. Yes, we'll take them all," she told Kat.

With all the jewelry in order, Angie pulled me to a small wall of shoes. Thankfully, we were able to find the perfect silver ballet flats in almost no time at all. Now, dressed up in my full wedding ensemble, Angie and I returned to the fitting room.

"So," she called to Weston, "what do you think?"

He held one finger up and pulled his book slightly closer to his face, reading frantically for about fifteen seconds before dog-earing his page and closing the book. I felt like an idiot standing there waiting for him, like I needed his approval or something. Finally, he raised his head to look at us.

His eyes widened and his mouth dropped open. It was only a second before he composed himself into a neutral expression, but I'd seen it, and, judging by the glimmer in her eyes, Angie had as well. "It's, er"—he cleared his throat—"it's nice. I think I have a tie that color. I could wear that for the ceremony."

Angie said with a laugh, "Oh, sweetie, I'll get you a tie for the wedding. You don't have to worry about it."

"It's not a problem," Weston insisted. "Really, I think I already have one close to that color."

"I'm gonna go change back into my clothes." I removed the necklace and bracelet and handed them to Angie.

"You aren't going to try the others?"

I shrugged. "I only need one."

"But what about the rehearsal dinner? Will you have something to wear to that?"

Weston squirmed in his chair, obviously not thrilled at the idea of waiting through more dresses, and I picked at my bracelet and shrugged. "This one can be worn, like, twenty different ways. I can just wear it both nights."

"You don't have to do that, sweetie. I'll get you another." She craned her neck to look out at the racks. "If you don't want to try on any more, there's one just like that in a gorgeous green. It would be amazing next to your hair."

"You really don't have—"

"It's no use," Weston interrupted. "She's not going to back down."

Angie scowled at him. "Right. Like you have any room to talk, Mr. I Have To Pay For Everything." Weston gave a little half shrug, and Angie turned back to me. "So, what do ya say? You want to try some more on, or should I go get that green one?"

I looked from Angie, her face beaming at me, to Weston, who just smirked and reopened his book. It was obvious I was leaving with more than one dress. I groaned. "The green one, please."

Angie darted back to the sales floor, and I stepped behind the fitting room curtain, Weston's laughter trailing behind me.

A few hours later, having said good-bye to Angie, I was again greeted by the familiar scent of Weston's car. He shoved all my bags into the back seat—Angie insisted on buying me not only the dresses, jewelry, and shoes, but also a new swimsuit, plus a shirt and tie for Weston—and I watched through the window as he hugged Angie then kissed her on the cheek before she climbed into her own car.

We hadn't even made it back to the highway before I couldn't bear to wait any longer. I reached forward and turned the music down. Weston looked over at me.

"What's up?"

"I"—I sighed, hating how much I sounded like my mother—"I was wondering...I wanted to know..."

"You want to know where Angie got her scars?"

"Yes!"

He took a deep, shuddering breath, and his eyebrows lowered, shading his eyes. "It was about six months ago," he started, "and Angie came to Philadelphia for a business conference. She was out late one night, walking back to her hotel, and she got attacked. It was ugly and scary, but she's doing well now."

"Wow." I couldn't think of anything else to say. Inside, I was reeling. I couldn't imagine someone like Angie, so confident and in control, being attacked. She seemed so strong this afternoon, and my mind struggled to reconcile that image with the one of her beaten down.

"What are you thinking about?" Weston asked.

"Nothing," I whispered back.

"Liar."

"Really," I said, "it's nothing." Except it wasn't nothing, and Weston was right: I was lying. I was thinking about Angie and how carefree and happy she was, even though only a few short months ago, someone had cut her up. And about me and how I'd closed myself completely off and lived the last months in such darkness. My scars were so much smaller than hers, so why couldn't I let go of them and be happy again?

"Okay," Weston said. "I'm getting tired. We've got to talk or something."

"I could drive if you want."

"No."

"It's not a big deal. I'm not tired at all, and you can sleep on the way home."

"No," he repeated.

"Why not?" I pressed.

He sat silently. And sat some more. Finally I said, "Never mind. You don't have to tell me. What do you want to talk about?"

More silence as he tapped out a beat on the steering wheel. I waited.

"This car was my Uncle Luke's," he said. "During my gap year, I was here in the states to help him restore it. He always said when we were done, he'd sign the title over to me. It made my father so angry. 'No kid of mine will ever drive an old beater,' he kept saying. Our big goal was to get the major parts done by the end of the summer and finish the details during breaks from Oxford. I was so proud of all the work we did. I couldn't wait to finish."

He stopped talking abruptly, and his hands tightened around the steering wheel. His shoulders hunched up around his ears for a moment then he let all his tension go with a huff of breath.

I waited for him to continue his story, but it was like the well had run dry. "So now that you're back in the states, are you two working on it again?"

"No."

"Why not?"

He ran a hand over his face. "Luke died."

"Oh, my god," I said. "I'm so, so sorry."

Weston slammed on the brakes and swerved to the shoulder of the road. My stomach dropped through the seat, and I grabbed the *oh shit* handle again. We skidded across the gravel, the back end of the car jumping to the side slightly, and my heart skipped about four beats.

"West," I yelled, "what's going on?"

"I need a minute," he said.

His hands were shaking; he took three slow, deep breaths then slammed them on the steering wheel. I about jumped out of my skin. "Sorry," he said.

I shrugged, shakily. "It's okay."

More deep breathing. When he finally spoke again, his voice was so low I had to strain to hear it. "I did it," he said.

"Did what?"

"I killed him. It's my fault."

I gasped. It wasn't on purpose, and I'm sure it didn't help the situation, but I still gasped. Weston dropped his head to the steering wheel; his shoulders rose and fell in a slow, steady rhythm. I reached toward him, pulling my hand back once, unsure, before pressing on. He didn't notice, or didn't mind, the intrusion, so I laid my hand on his shoulder. Heat pulsed through his shirt, and his shoulder shook slightly beneath my touch.

"I fell asleep," he said.

"What?"

"Luke and I went to this concert at Club Sound. It went into a third encore, so we didn't get out of there until late. Luke had a few beers, and he was probably fine to drive, but he gave me the keys anyway."

I waited for him to go on, feeling his breathing grow jagged and then steady again. When he didn't continue, I said, "What happened, Weston?"

"I fell asleep. It had been such a long night, and I was exhausted. One minute I was driving along, listening to some tired radio show and watching the street lights blur by. The next I was jerking awake. I saw the headlights and tried to turn away from them, but I wasn't fast enough."

"Oh, my god, I'm so sorry." I was beginning to sound like a broken record, but what else could I say?

He shrugged, and I pulled my hand back into my lap. "The truck barely hit us," he said, "but it pushed the back of Luke's car enough to send us spinning off the side of the road. I don't remember much after that." He raised his head off the steering wheel. The expression on his face broke my heart; suddenly my problems didn't seem so big anymore.

"West—"

"I know," he cut in, "you're so, so sorry. So is everyone else. Everyone is always so very sorry, but it doesn't change the fact that Luke is dead and it's my fault."

I stared at my hands and picked at the cord around my wrist. This was so far outside my bubble of comfort. I had no words for him.

"Laney?" His voice was soft, tentative.

I shrugged my acknowledgement.

"I'm sorry I snapped. I've just heard the same thing over and over again, and I know you mean well, but I can't hear it again. Okay?"

I thought back to all the sympathetic looks I'd gotten from my mother and my friends back home. I remembered how everyone at school tiptoed around me the months leading up to graduation. How much I'd hated it. "I get it," I told him.

"Really?"

"Yep. Totally understand. I'm not sorry, and that's my final offer."

Weston visibly relaxed beside me. "Thank you."

"You're welcome."

We pulled back onto the highway, the hum of the tires quickly growing to cover the music. "Laney?"

"Yeah."

"Can I ask you something?" Crap, he sounded serious. My mind flashed back to that night in the lake, his fingers grazing across my scar. My pulse sped up, and a familiar whooshing sound filled my ears.

My silence was obviously enough of an invitation, and he opened his mouth to ask his question. My stomach flipped. "What's your favorite color?" he asked.

"What?" Was he kidding me?

"Your favorite color. What is it?"

I was so shocked by his totally normal, out-of-the-blue question that I couldn't even think of what my favorite color was. I couldn't even think of what color meant. Weston laughed. "All right, I know it's a tough one, but you can't cop out with some answer like rainbow or clear or something like that." He laughed again, totally carefree, as if nothing had happened on the side of the road.

What would it be like to be able to bury things so effortlessly?

# DAY NINE

"YOU KNOW WHO I MISS?" Karissa and I lay on our towels over the hot sand, enjoying our last afternoon of freedom before the season started and we were officially employees again. Rory sat in a lawn chair above us, a copy of Rolling Stone open on his lap.

"Who?" I asked.

"Larry," she said.

"The nail-biter?" Larry was husband number five, and his marriage held the distinct position of being my mother's shortest. Not counting Craig, of course. "You've never even met him."

"I know, but your stories were the best. What was wrong with him again?"

With a shrug, I said, "I dunno. Why does she leave any

of her husbands? That's just what she does." Truth? Larry wasn't my favorite step-father, and I didn't really care when he moved out. Of course, maybe by that point I was so numbed by the constant stream of men coming through my mother's revolving nuptial door that my opinion of him was skewed. Still, he was much better than the current option.

A shadow fell across us, and I looked up to see Weston setting his own lawn chair up next to Rory's. Lowering himself into his chair, he asked, "Is that really what you think?"

"About what?"

"About your mum? That she actually likes getting divorced?"

"Sometimes I do." Why else would she keep doing it?

Rory rustled his magazine and turned to face us. "That's pretty bogus, Laney. Nobody likes getting divorced."

"All I know," I said, "is the only thing I could see wrong with Larry is he bit his nails. Which is no reason for a divorce."

Weston shrugged. "I'm sure she had her reasons. Nobody gets divorced for no reason."

"Five times!" I hated how shaky my voice sounded. How vulnerable. "She's been divorced five times. If it had been only once, even twice, maybe I'd believe you. But five times? I'm not buying it."

"I don't think it's the divorce she likes." Karissa, who had been unusually quiet this whole time, propped herself up on her elbows. "It's the love."

We all stared at her. A boat passed our beach, sending a family of ducks into flight. "If it's all about love, why all the divorces? That's not very loving."

"Exactly. She's in love with being in love. It's all about the rush of a new relationship, the excitement and butterflies. She gets so caught up in the newness that she doesn't ride it out long enough to see if there's a real relationship there before she walks down the aisle." She sipped her lemonade, a smug grin on her face.

"Wow." She actually had a valid point. "You should take over my mother's job. You'd make a way better relationship counselor than she does."

"How does she keep her job, anyway?" Rory asked. "Isn't there some kind of governing board that says you can't counsel others about their relationships if you've had five failed marriages yourself?"

"I don't know," I said, "but there should be."

An hour later, I was well on the way to my first sunburn of the season. Rory had headed off to band practice, and Karissa was fast asleep on the towel next to mine, blessed with skin that probably wouldn't burn until she was standin ng on the surface of the sun. I watched the water for a while, until the silence picked at my nerves and made me want to crawl out of my own skin. Turning onto my side, I propped my head up on my hand and looked at Weston.

"What are you reading?" He didn't respond, so lost in his book that I almost went back to tanning without an answer. But I craved his company, his conversation. Ever since our trip to Missoula, Weston had taken to asking me random questions about myself whenever we crossed paths. Who was my kindergarten teacher? Did I play sports growing up? If I could only have one thing to eat for the rest of the summer, what would it be? He would pop up out of the middle of nowhere, ask a random question, we'd talk for a few minutes, and then he'd be off again, doing whatever work Craig had been giving him to keep him busy day and night.

I reached over and tapped his thigh. The book dropped from his hand and into the sand, and for a moment, I thought he might jump out of the chair and hit me. Running a hand over his face, he said, "Sorry. What'd you say?"

The laugh refused to stay out of my voice when I said, "What are you reading?"

After dusting the sand off the cover and shaking it from between the pages, Weston held the book up so I could read the title. *Pet Sematary*. Classic. "So, the King got your spine tingling, eh?"

"Don't mock. This book is terrifying. It's not nice to sneak up on people."

"I didn't sneak up on you. I was here before you were, remember? Admit it, you're a total wuss."

"I admit no such thing." He pressed the corner of one of the pages over to hold his place and rotated his chair toward me. "So, what's the deal with you and your mum?"

"What do you mean?"

"I mean, why are you so angry? I know it's not only her divorces. There's something else there. What is it?"

Months of practice. Perfecting my cool exterior, keeping my face calm when my heart and mind were anything but, covering up my past. I'd thought I'd mastered it, kept any traces of what happened locked away and covered up. And it took Weston all of—what? Three conversations? Four?—to see right through. Despite the sun on my skin and the heat radiating from the sand, an icy chill took hold of me. Bumps rose over my skin, and I rubbed my arms in a violent, futile attempt to force them back down. "Nothing. There's nothing going on. We don't get along, that's all."

"That's shite, and you know it. There's something deeper." He pierced me with a stare, the sunlight bringing out green flecks in his otherwise gray eyes, and suddenly I felt completely naked. I clasped my bracelet between my fingers, letting the rough hemp cords pull me back to myself, a tangible reminder of who I was now. As long as the bracelet stayed safely on my wrist, I could actually be naked, and it wouldn't matter. I would still be covered.

The sun beat down on us, and heat pulsed up from the sand as if I were sitting on a towel draped over the mouth of hell. Sweat trickled down the small of my back, creating a trail across the top of my bikini bottom. The hot summer air pressed in on me from all sides, suffocating me with its weight, and I had to fight the urge to gasp for breath.

Still, Weston stared at me, his eyes peeling back my defenses, layer by layer. Part of me wanted to swoon directly into those deep pools of his. But a bigger part wished to slink into the lake, never to surface again. My stomach knotted in on itself, and my lunch pressed up toward my mouth. "I"—I gulped against the lump in my throat—"I have to get ready for the staff meeting." I scrambled off my towel and ran to my cabin, stumbling on feet that felt detached from the rest of my body.

Weston's stare pressed on my back the whole way.

✳ ✳ ✳

"All right," Craig started, the same way he did every summer. We all stood in a lopsided circle around the fire pit. "Let's make this summer our best yet. We have a full schedule—we're booked solid through Labor Day, so we need to run like a well-oiled machine." I'd heard this speech enough times by now I could recite it in my sleep, so I zoned out and turned my attention to the lake. It was still early in the season, and the water was nearly empty. A lone boat at the far end of the lake pulled a group of kids on a tube. I savored the look of the empty lake for as long as I could; before long, the water would be filled with boats, happy vacationers enjoying their days with sand, sun, and coconut-scented sunscreen.

Craig continued on, reminding us of our jobs this summer, as if we didn't already know: Karissa was the lifeguard, and as such needed to keep the boat house clean and orderly; Melinda and Josie, the housekeepers, would only come in once a week to change the cabins over between guests; Rory was Craig's right-hand man, taking care of the grounds and fixing anything that broke. And I would spend my days in the office, repairing all the damage Craig had managed to cause with his paperwork over the past nine months. I had the spiel memorized, so it wasn't until Craig stepped forward and clasped a hand on Weston's shoulder that I tuned back in.

"And now, I want you all to meet Weston Beaumont. Weston just finished the first year of his MBA at the Wharton School, and he's agreed to come here for the summer to be my business manager. Weston's experience is in image repair and luxury resorts. He's here to guide us as we make the resort what it deserves to be. He'll help us pull this place up to par, and I trust him completely. Weston, do you want to give us an idea of what we're going to be doing around here?"

Weston stepped forward, but Karissa spoke up before he had a chance to start. "Wait. Beaumont, as in...?"

"Yes, Beaumont as in Beaumont Hotels," he said with that delicious accent of his. "I spent summers during my youth with my father as he turned struggling hotels into luxury destinations."

"So you're, like, crazy rich then."

"Karissa," Craig warned.

"I don't mind. Yes, Kris." Karissa seethed beside me at his casual use of her nickname. "I did grow up with a lot of privilege. I was very lucky. But, no, I am not rich. Anymore. Now, does anyone else have any questions before I get started?"

We stared at him, nobody uttering a sound. Probably not even daring to blink. I wasn't.

"All right. I've been doing a lot of planning since Craig and Angie asked me to come help, and I think we have some great things going for us here. This is a beautiful location, which is the most important thing. With some rebranding and a lot of hard work, we can bring this place up to its full potential." He took a deep breath, moving his entire being, before diving in again. "First things first, we are changing the name. You are no longer employees of Leisure Lodge. From here on out, we are Mountain Lake Lodge. We have a graphic designer creating promotional materials, and the new sign is being delivered later this week."

"Mountain Lake Lodge?" I asked.

His gaze shifted to Craig briefly. "We believe the new name better portrays the kind of resort we want to become. Now, with rebranding underway, we need to start turning this place into what the name suggests. All the cabins will be restored and updated with luxury appliances and furniture. Once we reach that point, we will update the stables and start a trail ride program. We aim to have it up and running the summer after next." He turned around and grabbed a box from the log behind him. "We have new uniform shirts for everyone. Please wear these any time you are on duty so our guests can easily identify you." He tossed a polo shirt to each of us from the overflowing box. An embroidered outline of a mountain adorned the left side of the chest, *Mountain Lake Lodge* underneath.

"Hey, what about me?" Karissa asked.

"I'm sorry, Kris. Since you'll be in the water a lot, we didn't think you'd like to wear a polo. We're having some t-shirts and tank tops made up for you. They should be here any day now."

"Thank you." I smiled as she warmed up to Weston.

Slightly.

"No worries. Now, as our first major order of business, I would like to announce we are closing the recreation lodge, effective immediately."

"What the fuck?" I yelled then clamped my hand over my mouth at Craig's glare. "I mean, why?"

Weston shuffled his feet, appearing nervous for the first time. "Our reasons are threefold." Who the hell actually talks like that? Not even the accent could save him now. "The lodge doesn't generate enough business from the guests to justify keeping it open. We've found our guests would prefer to spend their time on the beach or in the water, exploring the area, or together in their own cabins. We could offset the cost of operation by opening the lodge to local residents for banquets and events, but that isn't in line with the image we want for Mountain Lake Lodge. And finally, the building is not structurally sound enough to be deemed safe for operation. We will close it for the time being and reevaluate the situation down the road."

He wanted to close down the best part of this place because it didn't fit with his happy little image? Like hell. "What *exactly* do you mean by reevaluate the situation?"

"I mean"—he cleared his throat—"we'll decide whether we want to restore the building, or if it would be a better option to demo it and clear the grounds."

Demo as in..."No! You can't come in here with your

fancy clothes and prestigious education, throwing around all your *experience* watching your father destroy people's hard work to make another million bucks, and start tearing down—"

"Laney." The words died in my mouth. Never before had I heard Craig be sharp with anyone. He shook his head, signaling I'd gone too far.

"It's okay, Craig," Weston said, and I wanted to strangle him. To take all those conversations, all the time spent building a friendship, every instance of me swooning over his damn accent, and shove it all down his rich, pretentious throat. "I understand Laney's frustration. Change is never easy, especially when it's something you love so much. It's a natural reaction."

"You don't understand shit," I muttered. Rory clasped my hand in his; I squeezed back, putting all my anger and frustration into the move.

"Great. That's all settled then." Craig clapped his hands exuberantly, reminding me of the coach in a bad football movie. That trait right there? Probably the reason my mother made him notch number one on the great divorce headboard. "Now you kids all have fun before I find something for you to do."

I knew it was coming, but tried to escape it anyway. "Laney," Craig called out. "Can I talk to you for a minute?"

The scene I caused

replayed in my mind as I crossed the fire pit to where he stood. Weston backed away before I reached them, leaving me to face Craig alone. "Sorry," I said as soon as I got to him. If there was one thing my mother had taught me, it was that a quick apology went a long way. Even if it wasn't sincere.

"Laney, I know things are going to be different around here. It may be hard for you. But I need to be sure you can handle this."

"I'll be fine."

"Are you sure? Because I need you to be able to put aside these outbursts and work alongside Weston this summer."

"Alongside him?"

"Weston is my business manager, kiddo. All the business decisions need to be passed through him, including the bookkeeping. You'll have to figure out how to make it work."

Lovely. Maybe the job with Dr. Patel wouldn't be such a bad idea. Could I handle working with someone who wanted to take away all the things I loved about the resort and turn it into something completely different? Someone whose friendship and closeness I desired with every bit of my being, but who I also wanted absolutely nothing to do with?

All I knew was that I had to try.

# DAY FOURTEEN

"OKAY, WE'VE HAD ABOUT enough of your attitude."
Karissa and Rory burst into my cabin. I sat on my bed,
reading, which is what I'd planned to do for the whole
evening.

"I don't know what you're talking about," I said, not
looking at them.

"Nice try." Rory plopped onto my bed, nearly
bouncing me off the edge. "You can't avoid him forever,
you know. What have you even been doing in here this
whole time?"

I gestured vaguely toward the kitchen counter, where
my laptop stood open, a pile of notebooks and receipt-filled
boxes beside it. The first task on Weston's list for bringing
Leisure Lodge—Mountain Lake Lodge—up to speed was

digitizing our records. Which, thankfully, was something I could do in the comfort if my own cabin, without having to be in the office at the same time as him.

"Hey, we get it," Karissa called from the kitchen, where she was rummaging through the meager pickings in my fridge. "We don't want the place to change, either, but Weston's kinda got a point."

"Seriously? I thought you practically hated the guy, and now you're on his side?"

She dropped onto the end of the bed and tossed a grape into her mouth. "I'm not on his side. But don't you think it would be nice if your dad could pull in some more business? Maybe charge a bit higher rates and make some real money?"

I hated that she had a point. "They don't have to close the rec lodge to do that," I grumbled.

"Agreed. But"—Karissa hopped back off the bed—"there's nothing we can do about it right now, so instead, we're going to go out and take our minds off it."

A groan rose in my throat. "Where? Can't we just hang here?"

"No," Rory said. "You've seen entirely too much of this cabin."

Karissa tossed a pair of denim shorts on the end of the bed. "I already talked to Derek. The big boss man is out of town for the night. Get dressed. We're going to The Place."

"Another round?" Derek set a tray of drinks on the table then slid into the chair next to Karissa. Was this round five or six? Seven? I couldn't remember. My head was spinning slightly, and everything around me seemed to be moving in slow motion. I sipped at my new drink—something fruity and sweet—and tried to listen to the conversation across the table.

"...again tonight," Derek said.

Karissa's face grew red. "What...say?" She took a gulp of her drink, shaking the alcohol down.

Derek shrugged. "...usual...you know...Megan."

I leaned forward to hear them better, and suddenly the floor was coming toward my face.

"Whoa there," I heard a deep voice say, and then I was being held by a pair of huge, rough hands. The man set me straight, making sure I was stable on my feet. But then he didn't let go. Why was he still holding me? His thumb drew soft circles on my upper arm, and acid climbed up my throat.

"Leggo," I slurred.

"What's that, pretty thing?" His breath reeked of stale beer and cigarettes.

"Issad leggo." I tried to jerk away from him. My head took a violent twirl, and I swayed toward the ground again. The man's grip tightened.

Panic clawed at my throat, and I pulled back once

more. When he wouldn't let go still, I swung my knee upward. My aim was off, and I felt like I was pulling my leg through quicksand, but my hit was effective enough. The man yelled and let go of me. I pitched backward, hitting the high-top table with my shoulder before falling to the ground. Cold liquid poured over my head, and the sound of shattering glass came from my right.

"What the hell just happened?" Derek was standing beside me, hovering over the drunk man.

"Nothing, man. I was just trying to steady her, and she went ape shit. Chick's got problems."

I watched the mans boots as he walked back to the bar. Suddenly, Rory's face was in front of mine, his eyes bloodshot. "What's wrong?" he asked, reaching toward me. I batted his hand away then put my own fingers to my face, shocked to find tears trailing down my cheeks.

"Nothing," I managed to say. "Just...I wanna go back home, okay?"

Rory nodded. "Okay." He helped me to my feet and turned to Derek. "Hey, about the glass—"

Derek waved him off. "Don't worry about it. It happens sometimes. You just get her home safe, okay? And make sure she gets lots of water."

"Will do," Rory said. "You ready to go, Kris? We've got quite the walk ahead of us."

As we reached the door, I turned back to survey The

Place through bleary eyes. Everything seemed so normal, just like it had every other time we'd come here over the years. So why did I feel like the building was going to crush me? Rory pushed the door open, and a cool blast of air hit my face, sharpening my focus. My gaze found the man I'd kneed sitting at the bar. He took a long pull from his beer bottle, staring at me with open confusion on his face. I shrugged at him and attempted a small smile, anything to let him know I was sorry for overreacting, but I couldn't.

Not when I could still feel his hands on my arms.

# DAY FIFTEEN

THUD. THUD. THUD THUD. THUD. Thudthudthudthudthud. The pounding of my feet kept time with the pounding in my head. What had I been thinking last night? Obviously I hadn't been after about drink three, or I wouldn't have had drinks four through six billion. Two weeks at the lake and I'd slipped right back into my old ways. I was like the girl in the after-school special who made a huge mess of everything, and everyone was *oh so disappointed* in her. But don't worry, because by the end of the thirty-minute block, she always finds a way to fix everything and tie her life up with a cutesy little bow.

Unfortunately for me, I was never very good at bow tying. I always had to have my mother tie the ribbons on packages, because if I did it myself, it would look like the bow had been tied by a chimpanzee. With its feet. While having a seizure. Trust me—my bows are never neat, always sloppy.

Just like my life.

I ran faster, my muscles stretching and flexing and screaming against the alcohol still working its way out of my system. Maybe if I ran fast enough, I could leave last night—the last two weeks, the last year of my life—behind. Everything could be erased with the soles of my shoes against the asphalt. Then I wouldn't have to deal with Weston and the way even the thought of him pulled me in opposite directions, causing a small war to be fought between the two halves of my soul. I could make it all go away. If only I could run fast enough.

My phone rang, and I struggled to pull it from my sports bra. Rory decided we couldn't let Karissa go home last night as drunk as she was, so she crashed in my bed. She was still out cold when I left; she was probably calling to bitch at me for heading back to town without her. The thudding in my ears decreased slightly as I slowed my run to a brisk walk and answered my phone.

"Hey, Kris. I'm almost to town. I'll bring you back—"

"Laney?" Not Karissa. My blood turned to ice, and my feet were suddenly glued to the ground. I couldn't move, couldn't speak. Couldn't even think. The forest sounds all stopped, leaving me in a vacuum of silence, kept company by only my own erratic heartbeat. Slowly, a muffled buzz grew in my ears, like I was listening to a boat cruising on the lake from beneath the surface of the water. I was drowning on solid ground.

"Laney?" The voice repeated. "Your mother was calling you, but one of her clients rang in on her cell with some kind of emergency. She'll be back soon."

Sound came back to me all at once, assaulting my ears and trying to split my head in two. The phone connection crackled. He breathed in my ear from more than two thousand miles away. I couldn't breathe at all.

"How's the lake?"

Small talk. How could he possibly think I would be able to make small talk with him? My mind couldn't fully comprehend what he was saying. More silence. He sighed. He must have picked that up from my mother. He was waiting for me to respond. I could be strong; I could do this. A deep breath, and I opened my mouth.

"..."

Finally, clattering came through the receiver—he was obviously passing the phone off, thank god—and another sigh greeted me. This one I recognized—my mother was upset.

"Laney." That was it. My name, nothing more.

So I replied, "Mother."

Another sigh. It was a regular old sigh-fest in that

house. "Honey, I don't know if it was such a good idea for you to go out there. I think you should come back home and work for Dr. Patel. It's not too late."

"What! Why?" My mind scrambled to account for the past two weeks. I never missed a call, never let on to her that things here weren't as I wanted them.

"Craig—"

"Whoa. Did Craig call you?" Shit. He freaked out because of my performance at the staff meeting. He didn't think I could handle myself this summer, so he was going to ship me back home? My throat closed off.

"No, honey, Craig didn't call. We were talking about it, and we think it's too much to ask Craig to do this. You know, with the way things are. He's not well equipped to handle things if...something happens."

*Right. And he is? Please.* Out loud I said, "Everything is going to be fine, I promise. You don't have anything to worry about."

I could hear *him* talking in the background. Open communication and all the shit she taught her clients. Finally she decided to take her own advice. Too bad it was with the wrong, wrong, *wrong* man.

"I don't know, Laney. Mike thinks it would be best for you to come back home for the summer."

Acid rose in my throat, a bitter reminder of last night, and I struggled to force it back down. Never would I puke where my mother could hear it. She'd have me on the next flight back home before I even had time for a breath mint.

Once I trusted myself to open my mouth again, I said, "It's not up to *him* to decide when I come home. *He* is not my father. Craig is, and I'll stay here."

Sigh, sigh, sigh. Would she rise to my anger or not? I could practically hear her thought process. On the one hand, I was being rude to her, and as my mother she shouldn't put up with it. On the other, if she were to argue with me now, she would be openly admitting to herself—and to *him*, as if he didn't already know—that we didn't have the picture perfect mother/daughter relationship she prided herself on. Not that we'd had it in months, but she didn't want the rest of the world knowing things weren't all *Gilmore Girls* between us anymore.

"All right." Her voice held a false calmness—who was she trying to kid? "You can stay. But you will uphold our deal."

"Every Wednesday and Sunday. Like clockwork. Promise."

"You will take care of yourself, and I will check with Craig to make sure. If I hear of you hurting yourself at all, I will have you on the first plane out of Missoula."

"I drove here," I interjected.

"Don't get smart with me, Laney. You try anything, and I will fly you home. End of discussion. That car of yours can rust in Montana for all I care." So much for keeping up her calm front.

"You don't have to worry about me," I said in the least abrasive voice I could muster. "I'm okay. Really."

His voice cut in again, muffled enough by the distance that I couldn't hear what he said, but not muffled enough to keep my stomach from flipping. She sighed one more time. "Well, I'm still not—"

"Mother. I have to go. We've got a lot going on around here, and I need to get to work. I'll call Sunday."

"Well...okay. I'll talk to you then. I love you, honey." She was still worried—her voice dripped with it. But I couldn't let it get to me. I wouldn't let her worry bring me down. Couldn't. I shoved my phone back into my bra and went back to my *busy* day—running to town, picking up coffees, and lounging on the beach for the entire afternoon. I settled back into pace. thudthudthud.

My skin still crawled with the sound of his voice.

# DAY NINETEEN

"SO THEN THIS KID WALKS OVER to me all devil-may-care and asks me to take my top off! And his parents are, like, ten feet away. I would have punched him in the face if I wasn't afraid of chipping my nails."

"Or jeopardizing your job," I said.

"Or not being able to reach his face," Rory added. "What are you now? All of four foot five?"

"Haha. Very funny. I'm serious, you guys. What happened to raising nice, polite young men who know how to treat a lady? Who don't act crude, and who don't break up with their girlfriend because she has the balls to get a summer job?"

"Speaking of not being crude," I said. Karissa's boyfriend of six months called that morning to tell her he didn't want to be alone for the summer, and since she was working so much they should take a break and see other people. She'd been on a tirade all morning, and now all the other diners at The Place for the lunch rush were staring at our table, watching the spectacle of the spunky half-Korean girl with the hot pink hair.

"I think," Derek said, dropping our plates onto the table. He lowered himself into a chair and grabbed one of my fries. "Feminism happened."

Karissa stared at him. "Sure, Derek, why don't you join us? You can eat our food and explain to us why you have a problem with women being equal to men."

"I don't," he said around another fry, "but I do have a problem with women insisting they do everything for themselves, that they are the same as men, and men are worthless and unnecessary, but then turning around and bitching when men don't treat them like princesses. I get sick of women who say it's insulting when a man opens a door for them, but still expect us to know when it's okay to step up and be gentlemen."

Karissa's face burned deeper and deeper shades of red, and Rory pulled the drink menu up in front of his face. I wished I had something to hide behind, too. Karissa could be scary when she was pissed. "You can't be serious," she yelled. If any of the diners weren't already watching our table, they definitely all were now. "Women fight and fight for our basic rights—to be taken seriously and to be looked at as more than men's playthings—and now you are criticizing us for it? You are a pig."

Derek held his hands up, palms forward in standard surrender pose, but he failed to keep the grin off his lips. "That's not what I'm saying at all. I'm all for equal rights. I'm simply saying you can't expect us to be gentlemen if you are yelling at us for being chauvinistic. Pick one and stick with it."

"Hey, Derek! You gonna work today?" One of the cooks stood at the entrance to the kitchen, plates of food lining his arms.

"Saved by the lunch special." He jumped up and strode toward the kitchen, leaving Karissa's rebuttal to fall on his empty chair.

"Well," Rory said, lowering the menu at last, "how about those crazy guests, huh? There's a subject I can roll with."

And Karissa went right back to ranting about the crazies on the beach, having completely forgotten about her fight with Derek. The girl was passionate, but she had the attention span of a goldfish.

After we paid for lunch, Rory headed to band practice, and Karissa and I walked through town to the ice cream shop. Now, we sat on a swing set, me with a root beer float and

Kris with a banana split the size of her head.

"How can you possibly eat so much ice cream? You just ate your body weight at The Place."

She shoved a huge spoonful of her dessert in her mouth and rolled it around her tongue. Melted ice cream dribbled down her chin. "Whatever. Don't be jealous. You know us Asian chicks have hollow legs to store our food in."

"Yeah, because you're a regular Yunjin Kim."

"Shut up. My mom's Korean."

"And your dad is about as white as they come."

The smile slid off her face immediately. "He doesn't count," she said, her voice barely above a whisper. The bowl in her hands shook slightly, and even her spikes seemed a bit droopy. Her eyes glistened with tears I knew she didn't want me to see, so I focused on the wood chips surrounding the playground equipment.

The memory of her face two weeks ago swarmed my mind. She had been so angry at us for even knowing what was going on; I couldn't imagine what would happen if I were to bring it up. But could I sit there while she was obviously hurting and not say anything? I had to try.

"Kris," I started, my voice soft. When she didn't immediately lash out, I pressed on. "What's going on with your dad?"

"Nothing." The words weren't even fully out of my mouth when she answered, her voice colder than the ice cream we were eating.

"Come on, Kris. We're best friends, and I know you better than that. What's going on? Has he...has he hit you?"

She jumped to the ground, leaving the swing twisting in the air behind her. Just when I thought she was going to leave me sitting in the park alone, she spun back around, slipping a little on the wood chips and knocking the cherry off the side of her banana split. She always saved the cherry for last—it was her favorite part.

"Best friend?" she screamed. "You're seriously going to pull the best friend card now? How about four months ago? Was I your best friend then?"

"Of course—"

But she was going again before I could finish. "Bull shit. Bull. Shit. If you thought we were best friends, you would have called me. You wouldn't have ignored all my texts and phone calls. Did you ever think maybe I needed my *best friend* this year?"

"Kris, I'm—"

"Of course you didn't! You just thought about you and all your little problems living in your huge house with everything you could possibly want. Why would you bother to talk to us little people?" Finally, she came to a shuddering stop. A single tear dropped from her eyelashes; she wiped it away with the back of her hand then stared at me with steely eyes. Her whole frame quivered, and I waited for her to lose control and drop her ice cream altogether.

I felt like I'd been slapped. No, I felt like I'd been strapped to the back of a raging bull before it stormed the streets of Pamplona. My drink slipped out of my fingers and spilled all over my lap, the cold of the ice cream and soda barely penetrating the numbness setting in.

"Kris—" How could I even start? My throat threatened to close around my words, but I continued, "What happened when your sister left?"

"Oh my god, Laney. That's all you can ask? I don't want to talk about Megan. This isn't about fucking Megan!"

"Then what's it about?"

"Nothing. It's about absolutely nothing. I'm going home. I'll see you at work tomorrow."

And then she was gone, storming off across the park before I could even formulate words in my mind. I wracked my brain, sorting through memories I had spent so long locking away. Had she tried to reach out to me? And I ignored her? When did I get so wrapped up with myself and my problems that I couldn't tell when my best friend was crying for attention? I had to fix this, but how?

Karissa may have had a short attention span, but something told me she wouldn't forget this anytime soon.

# DAY TWENTY-FOUR

"HEY, YOU DECENT IN THERE?" Rory popped through the
door, eyes wide open, before I had a chance to answer. I
stood there in my official Mountain Lake Lodge polo—my
long-sleeved t-shirt safely underneath—and my underwear.
Rory's eyes bulged, and he spun away from me. "Crap!
Why didn't you stop me?"

"Oh, I don't know. Maybe because you were practically
on top of me already by the time you said anything."

"I...I—"

"Chill. You've seen me in way less than this. I've been
in a bikini every day this summer. Not to mention every
other summer."

"I know, but this is different."

"Why, because you think it's gonna bite you now that

there isn't a protective layer of Lycra there?"

Still he refused to turn around, preferring the company of my door. "Very funny. Now could you put your pants on already?"

"You're telling me you didn't come over at this fine hour to seduce me? Well, in that case, I suppose I'll get dressed." I made a show of putting my shorts on, trying to rustle the fabric as much as possible for his benefit. "There, all my scary bits have been thoroughly covered. You can turn around, wuss-pants."

In slow motion, as if he was certain I was trying to trick him, he turned to face me. As soon as he saw all was safe, he launched himself across the room and onto my bed. With his arms thrown back behind his head, he talked up to the ceiling. "What's the deal with you and Karissa?"

"Mffpt you toopuk avoot?" He sat up and stared at me, one eyebrow cocked, so I spit out my toothpaste and tried again. "What are you talking about?"

"You suck at playing dumb. You know that, right? I'm talking about the fact that I haven't seen the two of you together in days."

"I've been busy."

"Riiight. And I suppose Karissa was also too busy this morning, which is why she refused to come over here with me?"

A groan escaped my lips as I flopped onto the bed next

to him. "I pushed her about her dad."

His gaze cut into my skin. "I warned you. She hates for her dad to be brought up. I guess I kinda understand. How would you feel if Craig was acting like him and everyone knew?"

"It's more than that, Rory."

"I know what you're thinking, but I think she's just embarrassed by him."

"That's not what I'm talking about." Though I still wasn't completely convinced there wasn't more going on with Mr. Goodman.

I waited for him to ask me what I was talking about, but he didn't say a word, just watched me intently. Maybe I could pretend the conversation was over, that he wasn't waiting for me to spill my guts out on the bed. Maybe I was coward, but it was an appealing idea. With my eyes closed so I didn't have to see his judgment, I pressed forward. "A few months ago, Karissa called me a whole bunch of times. I had a lot going on and was so wrapped up with myself that I never called her back. She reached out to me, and I ignored her."

Tears prickled beneath my eyelids, so I scrunched my eyes shut even tighter, trying to force them back. No such luck. They rolled down my temples and into my hair. Almost imperceptibly, the bed shifted beneath me. Rory wrapped a hand around my arm, causing me to jump, and then pulled me into him. He held me tight, and with my face buried in his chest, I let loose and cried, releasing months of pent-up hurt with the sobs his shirt barely muffled.

Eventually, my sobs died out, and I was left hiccupping into the wet circle I'd left on Rory's shirt. He rubbed circles on my back with his knuckles and hummed lightly in my hair, his mouth pressed gently against the top of my head. I couldn't quite place the song, but something about it soothed me, and I found my muscles relaxing and my stomach untwisting. Rory's chest vibrated with his humming, and I turned my head so I could lay my ear above his heart. Soon the steady beat beneath the surface grew erratic, speeding up and skipping about.

His knuckles jerked, losing the steady cadence they had been rubbing, and he lowered his hand to the small of my back, where he rested it, shaky fingers spread wide. His breathing grew irregular to match his heartbeat. His chest rose and fell sharply, and then he was so still I was afraid I'd imagined it all. The shirt rustled in my ear as I strained my neck to look up at his face. Everything came in flashes after that.

The look in his eyes. Stormy and dark, but excited.

A hand running through my hair...

...Rubbing a stray tear from under my eye.

His lips parting slightly.

Mine following suit.

Goosebumps.

Butterflies.

Rory leaning forward, so close.

And a phone ringing, the shrill cry piercing through the moment. I jumped back, smacking my shoulder against the bedside table. Rory shoved his hand deep into his pants pocket, pulling the phone out lightning fast and shoving it to his face. "Craig, what's up?" His voice was about six octaves too high; Craig would know immediately what was going on. Never before had it crossed my mind that he might become a protective. Not even while I was kissing Weston.

"Yeah," Rory said after a few more seconds. "Okay, I'll be right there." He pushed his phone back into his pocket and faced me, his shoulders hunched dangerously close to his ears. "That, uh, that was your dad. Mr. Hinckler is having some issues with his plumbing I gotta look at." He ran the sole of one shoe over the top of the other. "So, I guess...I guess I better go." A deep glow crept up his neck and into his cheeks. His gaze dropped to my mouth, and he pulled his bottom lip between his teeth. His shoulders dropped back down, and he strode across the room to the door, rubbing one hand over my arm as he passed. Heat flared on my skin, following the trail his hand left. The door clicked shut, and he was gone.

What the hell happened?

# DAY TWENTY-SEVEN

THE TIME HAD COME. Today, I would finally have to suck it up and go back to working in the office. Since our staff meeting and Weston's big announcement, I'd successfully done everything I could possibly do using my laptop in my cabin, thankful that the conversion from hand-written ledgers to Quickbooks took so much time. Even so, I ran out of things I could easily do days ago and had been stretching myself to figure out tasks that didn't involve the office. But the stables *needed* to be cleaned, so it wasn't like I was completely avoiding things.

I used to be better at lying to myself.

I looked in the mirror for the hundredth time this morning. What I was looking for, I wasn't sure. It's not like anything had changed. Same pale skin, same red hair. Same slender nose, the only facial feature I inherited from Craig. Part of me wished the mirror would show me someone completely different. A perky, happy girl who hadn't spent the last several months destroying her relationships. That would be nice.

But I wasn't that girl. I was just me, and I was procrastinating. With one final glance, I left, sleeves grasped safely in my fists.

The walk to the office felt like a death march, each step weighing me down in the bog of my own misery. When had I become such a coward? Never in my life had I avoided someone I'd kissed. I was always the callous one, moving on with my life and pretending nothing happened. The boys were left feeling awkward and nervous, not me. Never me. But of course, never had any of those boys taken my whole world and turned it upside down within the space of one tiny staff meeting. Remembering the calculating, business-like way he announced he would be changing everything ignited the rage in me all over again.

I stomped the last few steps to the office door, channeling my anger through my flip flops and into the dew-soaked ground. For the first time this morning I hoped Weston wouldn't be here not for my sake, but for his own. There was no guessing what I would do when I saw his face. His pretentious, rich, snobby—

The door swung open, and Weston stepped out onto

the porch, his cell phone pressed between his head and shoulder. Oh, god, his face. His beautiful, swoon-worthy, kissable face. Why was I so pissed again? All my anger begged to be let go, to seep through my feet and into the porch. And then he looked up at me, and the shock on his face nearly knocked me over. I scurried past him and into the office, my stomach fighting its way into my throat.

As the door was closing, I heard him: "...bringing the new sign in this afternoon, then will look at the lodge and decide what..."

With a click, the door sealed me into the office, alone. Decide what? What the hell was he going to say? After a brief debate with myself, I dropped into my chair. It would be way too conspicuous if I were to burst back out onto the porch and listen to his conversation. Besides, the good bits were over by now anyway.

One look at my desk showed me the trouble I'd gotten myself into by avoiding this place for so long. Craig was as technophobic as they came, so there wasn't much beyond basic bookkeeping I could do on my computer. He hadn't even automated the reservations system yet, preferring to write everything in a ledger by hand. That would probably be the next thing to change under the reign of Weston the Hotel God.

Reservation slips fluttered to the ground as I tried to make sense of all the piles before me. This was going to take a week to work through. I cranked the music on my computer as high as it would go, and David Bowie's voice filled the room. With any luck, Weston would hate David Bowie. Too bad the speakers weren't louder.

✳  ✳  ✳

Four hours later, I'd run out of Bowie and could almost see my desk. And Weston still hadn't returned. Why did that bother me so much? Frustrated, I slammed my computer shut and stormed to the door. It swung easily with my shove, but then stopped abruptly and swung back, slamming me in the face.

"Shite!" The voice on the other side of the door stopped me dead; my hands hovered in the air, halfway to wiping the tears from my eyes. Of course he would come back right in time for me to make a total ass of myself. My eyes still blurry, I pushed the door slowly and peered around the edge. Weston was kneeling on the porch, raking French fries into a paper bag with his fingers.

Without looking up at me, he said, "This was supposed to be a peace offering, but it seems I've failed."

"No, it's my fault. I'm sorry." I squeezed through the door and helped him pick up the destroyed remains of our lunch. He'd brought me my favorite meal from The Place. How did he even know what to get?

Once we were finished, he pitched the bag in the trash

and wiped his hands on his pants. "Well, that's out. What do you say we go grab a hot dog at The Bay?"

"Seriously?"

"Yeah. I'm hungry, and I imagine you've not eaten yet, either?"

As soon as he mentioned it, my stomach yelled in affirmation. But I wouldn't give in to his charm so easily. I wished I could hit him with the door again. "You must have missed my tone there. I meant 'seriously' as in 'you think I am going to go anywhere with you?' Not likely."

"Well, yeah," he said, obviously confused. "I did think that."

"You thought wrong."

He sat on the step with his back to me. "So you're still mad at me. I get it. I'm sorry I upset you, but I'm only doing my job."

"You can shove your job up your ass."

"Are you right- or left-handed?"

"What? No, none of your stupid questions. I get to ask the questions now."

"All right"—he turned and locked his eyes on mine—"Ask your questions."

Here it was, my chance to ask anything I wanted to know about him, and my mind went completely blank. Not a single question. I grasped for anything to ask, but came back short every time. Weston motioned for me to sit down, and I found myself crossing the porch. Suddenly I was on the top step, so close to him I could feel his heat through my clothes.

"Truth?" he asked.

"Please."

"Your dad's in trouble, Laney."

"What? No he's not."

"Yes, he is. He doesn't want you all to know, but he's in deep trouble. This place has been pulling him down since he bought it. If he doesn't turn things around, he'll lose it all. He can't afford to keep operating like this. With Angie and the baby, he has to be able to make it work."

Time stood still, and my mind strained to comprehend what he was telling me. How could I have missed this? I was in charge of the books, the paperwork—I should have caught it. Craig needed help, and I was too dense to even realize it.

I asked the only question I could think of: "If he's so bad off, how can he hire you? Your family name is synonymous with *Luxury Hotel*. Not the kind of thing some poor guy with a failing resort can afford."

He coughed. "Well...I'm not being paid, actually."

"What?"

"Angie helped set it up so my work this summer applies to my MBA. I'm technically schooling right now."

"And I guess it's not like you need the money anyway."

He stiffened beside me, his back straightening. "That's...not entirely true."

"Oh, very funny. What, you can't get a new Masserati with your trust fund?"

"Shite, Laney, you are a piece of work, aren't you? My father cut me off when I took this job instead of working for him for the summer. I'm schooling on scholarship and fixing this place up because Angie asked me to. Sure, I have some money, but it's not like I'm a Rockefeller." He stood to leave, and my hand shot up to grab his before I even knew what I was doing.

"I'm sorry," I said. "I didn't realize."

"You don't bother to realize. Not everyone is against you. Someday you'll see that." He pulled his hand out of mine. "I've got work to do."

He was gone, and I was left on the front porch, the truth of his words seeping into me like a stain.

# DAY THIRTY-TWO

SINCE OUR FIGHT ON THE PORCH, it had been a nightmare in the office. Weston was barely civil to me, only talking when absolutely necessary for us to do our jobs and giving me one-word answers to my questions, totally rebuffing my attempts to smooth things over. So three days ago, I asked him a question. Completely random, the first thing that came to my mind. I'd hoped to disarm him, the way he did me the first several times he played the game, but he answered without hesitation, as if he'd been waiting for me to ask.

Since then, I'd learned about Weston: his favorite ice cream was lemon custard; he only had detention once in school, for sneaking to the girls' campus junior year; he loved sauerkraut, but hated raw cabbage; he had no siblings, because, as far as he could tell, kids interfered with his parents' social calendar too much; he once had a dog named Spock.

And now: "Who was your first kiss?"

For once, he seemed surprised by my question. We'd been carefully avoiding anything more personal than "Who was your fourth grade teacher?" up to this point, and this one cracked his cool exterior. I almost thought he wouldn't answer.

"Her name was Amy Vucasin. First grade. She trapped me in the kissing corner on the playground after lunch."

"That so doesn't count. Who was your real first kiss?"

A flash of something crossed his face, changing his features completely, and was gone again before I could properly digest it. "Funny story," he said. "It was Amy Vucasin. Summer after Year Eleven. We all went cliff jumping one afternoon, and it just happened."

"So what happened with Amy after that?"

"We dated for a couple years, actually."

"And then?"

He dropped his gaze to his lap, where his hands worked at the pen he held. Remove cap. Unscrew end. Drop ink cartridge out. Reverse, and repeat. I watched the cycle through three times before talking again. "Hey, it's okay if you don't want to tell me. It's none of my business."

"No, it's okay." He took a deep breath—not quite a

sigh, but close. "After Uncle Luke died, Amy tried to be there for me. She was amazing. Kind and supportive, wanting nothing more than to help me deal with what happened. I was in such a dark place that I didn't think I deserved her. It was my fault. How could she not see that? So I pushed her away. She tried to hold on, but eventually I shoved too hard, and she left. She's with someone else now. They seem happy."

"Wow, I'm really—"

"Don't say you're sorry. Just don't."

"I learned my lesson already." I winked at him. "What I was going to say was, 'Wow, I'm really not sorry, but you have to get over yourself.'"

"What?"

"What happened was not your fault."

"Laney, I fell asleep at the wheel. And he died."

"I don't care. Luke's death was *not* your fault. Stop making it about you."

Weston sat quiet for so long I was certain I'd pushed way past the bounds of our fragile friendship. Why couldn't I keep my big mouth shut and let him feel sorry for himself? "Hey," I said, trying to salvage what I could, "I shouldn't have said that. I'm sorry."

And then he reached across the desks and grabbed my hand. Slowly laced his fingers around my own and squeezed. "Don't be," he said. "I needed it. Thank you,

131

Laney. Really. Thank you."

Such a simple gesture, something I'd done with countless boys. So why did it feel now like my heart might punch a hole through my chest?

✶ ✶ ✶

I pulled my curtain aside and watched as Craig and Angie piled into her car and drove off toward town for their date. I'd overheard her telling Weston they were going to dinner at the steak house at the end of the lake, which meant the would be gone at least an hour. Pulling the door open just enough to fit my head through, I peeked out onto the porch. The swing was empty, and the windows to Weston's cabin were dark. I slipped out of the cabin and across the lawn to the office.

A light shone from inside, and I could make out Weston's silhouette through the thin window covering. Still working. I crept around the side of the building and made my way up the back staircase. Craig and Angie's door was unlocked, as always. I pulled it open a fast as I could, to avoid dragging out the inevitable creak the old hinges would emit. Once inside, I flicked on the inner hall light, hoping it wouldn't show too strongly through the windows.

I hated snooping in Craig's apartment, but I had to know the truth. Weston wouldn't have said Craig was in trouble if there wasn't some kind of problem. There wasn't anything in the official books, but if something was going on, surely I could find it somewhere in here.

The old file cabinet in the bed room was sitting open, stacks of paper piled on top of it. Without giving myself time to change my mind, I pulled all the lose papers into my hands and crossed the room to the bed. After flicking on the bedside lamp and settling into place, I pulled the first sheet to me. Then the next, and the next.

I stared at the numbers before me, the overdue notices, the warnings of court dates and collections proceedings. My mind scrambled to piece everything together. How could the resort books look so solid with all of this happening? I flipped through the papers again, tears filling my eyes.

We were going to lose the resort. I couldn't see how even Weston, with his Ivy League education and luxury-resort background, could pull us out of this hole. All the rebranding and image control in the world wouldn't help if Craig foreclosed on the property and lost the Forest Service lease on the land. Which, according to the papers scattered around me, was exactly what was going to happen.

A tear dropped onto the bill in my hand, and I jumped. I hadn't even realized they'd escaped my eyes. But once that first one fell, it was like the floodgates were opened. I wanted to tear the evidence to shreds, burn the bills and the collections notices. Make it all just go away.

Instead, I shoved everything off the bed and curled up on Craig's pillow and cried. Six years ago, I didn't even know this place existed. But now? Now I couldn't imagine my life without it. It was more than a fun place to spend my summers, more than just where my dad lived. The resort, the lake, even the tiny town, had all become a part of who I was, shaping my very being. Losing this place would be like losing a part of myself.

A soft creak made its way through my muffled sobs, and I bolted straight up on the bed. Shit. Papers were scattered all over the room, and there was a wet spot the size of a small planet on Craig's pillow. Pulling my sleeve across my face to catch the tears and snot, I tried my best to compose myself. There was no way to avoid being caught, but at least I could try to be presentable. With a deep breath, I faced the door and steeled myself for what was to come.

Weston rounded the corner into the room, a steaming cup in one hand and a small cupcake in the other. "Hi," he said softly. "I thought you might like some comfort food." He held the cupcake out to me.

"How—"

"I saw you coming up here. You want it?"

With a shaky hand, I took the cupcake from him. "So you just watched me sneak into my dad's apartment and what? Ran to town for treats?"

He dropped onto the bed next to me. "Yes."

"But why?"

"I knew what you would find. I thought you might need some cheering up."

I ran a finger through the cupcake frosting and popped it into my mouth. "Why didn't you just stop me?"

"Would you have believed me without seeing all this for yourself?"

Another tear slid from my eye, and I shook my head. Weston reached toward me, his hand jerking to a stop for a moment before continuing on. He brushed the tear away with the side of his thumb, lingering along my jawline. "I'm sorry," he whispered. Then he was gone, leaving a cold spot next to me. He set the cup on the bedside table under the lamp and set to work collecting up the papers I'd thrown to the floor.

I ate my cupcake then grabbed the cup. The hot, bitter-sweet chocolate slid down my throat as I watched Weston clean up my messes.

"Thank you," I whispered.

"It's no problem." He dropped the papers back on top of the filing cabinet and leaned against it, arms crossed over his chest.

"It is though. I was a total bitch to you. You should hate me right now. But instead, you show up with cupcakes and hot chocolate and wipe my tears."

His face softened, and he pushed off from the cabinet. "I don't hate you, Laney. I couldn't." He held a hand out to me. "We should get out of here before Craig and Angie come back, though."

I nodded. "You're not going to tell them?"

"There's nothing to tell. Now flip that pillow and let's go." He smiled at me and, for the briefest moment, everything seemed okay again.

# DAY THIRTY-SIX

"WE'RE ALMOST THERE," Weston told me.

"You've said that four times now. Where are we even going? I'm supposed to meet Rory for lunch."

"You'll be back in plenty of time for lunch. I promise."

As soon as I stepped into the office this morning, Weston grabbed me by the hand and led me back out the door. After a stop at my cabin to change into tennis shoes, he hauled me toward the woods. We'd been weaving through trees and around puddles left behind after a night of heavy rain for the past half hour, and I was beginning to think he had no clue where we were going.

"You're not taking me out here so it's easier to dispose of the body, are you?"

He hopped up on a log and spun to face me. "What?

Of course not. You know, for such a tough girl, you sure whine a lot."

"Whatever. You have some random dude lead you out into the woods without any explanation."

"Relax. We're here."

I looked around at the trees and ferns we'd been traipsing through all morning. "Okay...and here would be *where* exactly?"

With a flourish, he hopped down from the log and offered me his hand. When I stared at it without moving, he reached out and tugged me along with him, saying, "I found this spot while I was surveying the grounds a couple days ago. It's been gloomy in the office, and I thought some fresh air would be good for us. Now come on."

He led me over the log and onto another one, nestled between two bushes. Beyond the bushes, it was like entering a different world—in one stride, we put the forest behind us.

Sunlight bounced off the water, making each ripple glitter. The beach itself was only about twenty feet wide and completely surrounded by bushes, but the sand was pure and golden, as if nobody had set foot here before us. From where I stood, I could see no boats, no cabins, nobody but Weston. We were completely alone in the world.

Weston crossed the beach, his footprints leaving lasting

impressions in the perfect sand, and sat on a sun-bleached log. Wait. I recognized that log. I looked around again, and it came rushing back to me.

"Dead-Fish Beach," I muttered.

"Come again?" Weston was staring at me like I'd sprouted a third arm out the side of my head.

"Dead-Fish Beach," I repeated, louder. "The second summer I was here, Karissa, Rory, and I had a week-long competition to see who could catch the most freshwater clams. Kris and I worked our way through all the reeds and found this place. We totally won—there are so many clams out here."

Weston's shoulders slumped. Almost imperceptibly, but I noticed, just like I noticed his smile looked a little more plastic-y than it had a minute ago. Was he trying to show me something new?

He cleared his throat. "Why Dead-Fish Beach?"

"When we first found this place, there was a dead fish on the sand."

"Creative."

"Whatever. We were young."

"Excuses. You want one?" He pulled a granola bar from his pocket and tossed it to me before I had a chance to answer. I caught it barely before it hit the sand, silently thanking whatever power gave me decent reflexes.

"Thanks," I said, sitting beside him on the log. "I'm

starving."

We ate in silence, looking out over the lake. A pontoon boat trolled by, a party in full swing on the decks, women in bikinis laughing and tossing their heads back, hair shaking over their backs.

"A couple summers ago, Craig rented one of those," I said, using my granola bar to gesture to the boat. "He took us up the inlet, and we got lodged on a fallen tree."

Weston laughed. "How'd you get back?"

"We sat there all afternoon. Rory and I got so sunburned. Eventually, a group of fishermen came by and helped free us."

When we got home, exhausted and sunburned, we ordered a pizza and plopped ourselves on the couch of the rec lodge to watch movies for the rest of the night. My chest clenched at the memory, and I turned to Weston.

"Can I ask you something?"

He turned to me, his expression serious. "The fact that you didn't simply ask me makes me think you want to know something more than whether I prefer lobster or steak. Which, by the way, it's lobster."

"Good to know. But, no, that wasn't what I wanted." He indicated for me continue. "Are you really thinking about closing the rec lodge for good?"

"Er...yeah, we are."

"Why?"

"Like I said at the meeting, it's not in line with our goals for Mountain Lake Lodge."

"Great, another fucking sound bite. Did they teach you that at Cambridge?"

He cut me with a glare. "My turn. Why does it matter so much to you?"

A highlights reel of my past scrolled through my mind. Kris, Rory, and I playing arcade games; drinking Shirley Temples till we wanted to puke; sitting cross-legged on the pool table, a Ouija board perched between us; watching more campy horror movies than I could possibly remember. "It's my favorite part of this place," I told him, my voice hitching slightly. "All my best memories are tied to that lodge."

"I'm sorry, Laney, it's—"

"Why do you get to say 'sorry' when I never do?"

"Because this is something I'm actually responsible for. I have a right to feel sorry."

"So change it! You don't have to go through with this. Use your fancy business degree and figure out how to keep it open."

"Truly, I'm sorry, but I can't. Craig and I decided, and the lodge needs to be closed until we figure things out. We can't afford to do otherwise."

"Whatever." I hated that he was right.

Weston rubbed his hands on his pants and jumped off

the log. "Okay. You need to cheer up. I hereby declare we aren't leaving this beach until you find me ten clams."

"What?" He couldn't be serious.

"You were the one bragging about how many clams are out here. Prove it." The challenge was clear in his smile.

I kicked off my shoes. "Fine. You're on." I rolled my pant legs to my knees and stepped into the cool water, relishing the feel of the wet sand pressing between my toes. This was where I belonged; I could spend days standing in the water like this.

Seven clams later, the wind picked up. My hair blew around my face—why did I grow it long again?—and stuck to my lip gloss. My hands were totally covered with mud. After a few attempts at brushing the hair away with my shoulder, I admitted defeat and turned back to Weston. "A little help here?"

His shoes were already off, and he was rolling his pants up. He waded out to me, not stopping until he was much closer than necessary. Heat pulsed from his body, slamming into me with full force. He swept the hair from my face, his thumb tracing my cheekbone to my ear. My lips were happily hair free, but he didn't take his hand back. His eyes locked on mine, a familiar look of hunger brewing within them, and he cupped his hand around the back of my neck.

A flame flared in my stomach, licking at the bottom of my ribs and then traveling lower. Despite the heat tearing through my insides, my whole body buzzed with goose bumps. Could he feel it, too?

Weston lowered his head to mine. We stood there, forehead to forehead, for almost longer than I could stand. Each breath he took caressed my skin, and my body screamed for him. I lifted my head to finally take the kiss I needed so badly.

Our lips brushed, barely meeting—

And then it was over. His hand left my neck; I couldn't feel him near me at all. I opened my eyes to find him backing away from me.

"I...we better get back. You're going to miss your lunch date."

He grabbed his shoes as he crossed the beach back to our log, leaving me standing alone in the lake, the fire in my stomach replaced by a stone as cold as the water around my legs.

✳   ✳   ✳

Rory was strangely quiet during the trip to town. He sat next to me in Burt, wearing an acid green t-shirt with *Dorothy's Parker* stamped on the front, drumming his fingers on his thighs to the beat of the stereo.

"Hey." I turned the music down so he could hear me. Better get this out of the way. "About the other day..."

"Huh?"

Okay. Apparently this was all on me. "What happened between us was...well, it was nice, but I don't think—"

"What are you talking about?" The confused expression on his face melted away to surprise, then understanding. "Oh, that. It's fine."

Not for a second did I believe him. He was way too fidgety to be fine with it.

"Really, it's okay," he said, obviously perceptive to my skepticism. When I kept staring at him, he added, "I promise. Things were emotionally charged, but we're friends, Laney, no matter what. One morning in your bed doesn't have to change anything between us."

"Wow. You made that sound way sluttier than it was."

He flashed his lopsided grin. "Couldn't help it. Now watch the road."

Rory looked no less agitated than he had before. Great. We pulled up to The Place, and he bolted from the car and ran to the restaurant before I even got my door open. I followed behind him, slower, dragging my feet across the gravel parking lot.

Her voice reached me as the door began to swing open. Karissa came storming out of the restaurant, Rory on her heels. "...not your right!" was all I caught of her tirade.

He grabbed her by the arm and forced her to stop. I stood rooted to the spot, my feet unwilling to move any farther. Rory turned her to face me then pressed down on

144

her shoulders, as if he could dig her feet into the ground and plant her like a tree. "Okay, you two. I hoped we could all have a nice lunch and talk this over."

"Not happening," she said. I couldn't say a word.

"Enough. This shit has gone on long enough with you two. You've been friends way too long to let it fall apart over this. Karissa, Laney was concerned about you. No, don't. I'm talking now, not you. Laney fucked up, and I promise she knows that." He didn't have any idea how well I knew it. "Give her a chance to make it up to you, Kris. You can't even pretend you haven't been miserable the last few days."

"Humph," was all she said.

"Kris," I tried, "I am so, so sorry."

She stared at her feet. "I guess I am kinda hungry."

"Great! You two go in there and have a great time. Derek has strict orders to not let you leave until he sees you smiling."

"You're not coming?" As much as I wanted to fix things with Karissa, I was terrified by the prospect of facing her alone.

"Band practice. See you later!" He loped across the parking lot, leaving us to face off against each other.

Karissa glared at me, as if this were my doing. Like I would mastermind this whole thing and put Rory up to it. Silence overcame me; I stood too scared to even try speaking to her. Eventually, she said, "Well, I guess we better get to it."

I followed her back into the restaurant, absolutely thrilled when she didn't swing the door shut in my face. Progress.

"I'm sorry," I said as soon as we sat down.

Karissa glared at me. "You're really good at saying you're sorry, but I have a hard time believing it anymore."

Derek hovered by the cash register, watching us. My hands shook under the table. Closing my eyes, I gasped in a deep breath. "Really," I said, looking at her again. "I'm so, so sorry. You have no idea." Tears prickled my eyes. "I was going through a bunch of shit, and I had this huge fight with my mother right before you called. Life just sucked, so I didn't want to talk. Not just to you, but to anyone." Karissa's eyes bore into mine, demanding more. "I was selfish. I should have called you back. I'm sorry." A tear finally slipped out.

"Going through a lot of shit?" She threw my words back at me. "Yeah, me, too. But you don't see me trying to hide the scars on my wrists." She reached out and pulled on my bracelet, and I recoiled.

"I know. I should've called. I know," I said again.

"You want to tell me now?" she asked.

I brushed a tear off my cheek and gave my head a jerk. "Not really. Not right now." I pleaded with her with my eyes.

"Fine," she said, and a ghost of a smile crossed her lips. "Dammit, Derek," she called out, "we're talking. Can we get some food already?"

As we waited for our food, we sat awkwardly, trying to make small talk, but we couldn't keep a conversation going for the life of us. Finally, Derek dropped our plates in front of us. I watched his retreating back as he walked into the kitchen, then turned back to Karissa.

"Hey, can I ask you something and not have you rip my head off?"

Her hand stalled halfway to her mouth, French fry hanging in the air. "You want to know about my father." It wasn't a question.

"Yeah."

She dropped the fry back into the pool of ketchup on her plate and stared at her food, eyes buggy and unmoving. My stomach growled, but I was hesitant to move, to speak, to do anything.

Finally, without looking at me, she said, "He's always been like this. Volatile. The littlest things set him off."

"How could we not know about it?"

She shrugged and finally met my eye. "Megan. She was like some kinda drug for him or something. He'd get going, and she'd just swoop in and calm him down."

"But now she's gone."

"Yeah." Another shrug. "Mom and I can't seem to figure out how to handle him the way she did."

"Has"—I squared my shoulders and forced my voice to come out evenly—"has he ever..."

She jerked her head in a quick nod. "I know what you're thinking. He doesn't hit us. He's a dick, but he's not like that."I wanted to believe her, but something pulled at the back of my mind, telling me there was more that she wasn't saying. One look at her face, though, and I could tell pushing would be the wrong move. So instead, I said, "I'm so sorry. I was a bitch."

"You can say that again," she said, but a wide smile broke across her face.

# DAY FORTY-ONE

WESTON PULLED THE CAR OFF the dirt road and into the gravel lot, a cloud of dust choking through the open windows. "I saw you and Karissa talking after work. You two must have worked things out?"

I nodded. "Things aren't perfect, but they're...better."

"Perfect's boring anyway. You ready?" He grabbed his bag out of the backseat, and we got out of the car.

"What do you have in that thing?" The hike to Morrell Falls wasn't a long one, but he'd packed like we were heading into the wilderness for a week.

"Just the necessities."

"Necessities? For who? The queen?"

"Oh, funny. Let's make fun of the Brit. You know I'm not even British, right? If you must know, I brought us a lunch, a first aid kit, and a water purifier. And my book."

"You think you'll be doing a lot of reading on our hike?"

"Well, no, but I like to have it with me."

"Fair enough. Let's go."

As we reached the falls, I ate my own words. We rounded a corner, a light mist coating our skin, and I hit a tree root. One minute I was upright, walking and laughing with Weston, who sounded hilarious and totally asinine when he tried to talk with an American accent. The next I was on the ground, dirt in my hair, blood on my shin, and my ankle quickly swelling to the size of a softball.

Weston was on his knees by my side in an instant. Before I could sit all the way up, he'd ripped open his pack and was pulling bandages and Neosporin from the first aid kit. "I can clean up this cut," he said, "but it looks like you twisted your ankle pretty good. I don't know what to do about that."

"I'm fine. Nothing but a bruised ego." I rolled over and hopped back to my feet, my ankle immediately screaming to me that I was not, in fact, fine. I fell back to my knees.

"I got you, love." Oh my god, he called me *love*. In one swift movement he bent over, tucked an arm beneath my ass, and jerked me into the air. My legs moved upward so quickly I was terrified my head would fall back and smack the ground. I shrieked and threw my arms around his neck. I hated that I did it, but I couldn't take it back now.

As he carried me to the edge of the water, I muttered into his chest, "This is so humiliating."

"Don't worry. As long as you treat me real nice, I promise not to tell everyone how you needed me to swoop in and rescue you."

"You are enjoying this way too much."

He set me down on a rock, and I immediately missed the warmth of his chest pressed against my side. "Here, let's take your shoe off so you can soak your foot in the water. The cold should help with the swelling." He unlaced my hiking boot, one hand holding my calf, his movements so deliberate I wondered if he'd ever unlaced boots before. My leg burned beneath his hand. Frustrated, I reached down and yanked the boot off, crying out in pain as my foot tried to detach at the ankle and come off with my shoe.

"Why do you think I was being so gentle?" Weston's voice, while it had every right to mock, was instead laced with concern.

"I don't know. I thought..."

"What? That I got off by playing with your shoelaces? I'm not demented, Laney."

Well, no, I didn't think that. More like I was worried *I* would get off if he didn't remove his hand from my leg. You know. In case this whole experience wasn't humiliating enough already. I lowered my damaged ankle into the water. The cold bit at me, but took the pain of my injury away almost immediately. I tilted my head back, eyes closed, and enjoyed the sensation of the sun's heat warring with the frigid chill of the water.

Suddenly his hand was back on my leg. I kept my eyes closed, fighting against the urge to watch his every move. He brushed a wet cloth around my cut, cleaning away the blood and dirt. Electricity shot up my leg, radiating from the point where his skin touched mine. My stomach did a pirouette; in that instant, I lost to my desires. I watched as he finished rinsing the dirt from my wound. He leaned forward, his mouth so, so close to my skin, and blew softly across the cut, igniting a fire deep within me so strong even the waterfall couldn't extinguish it. If he didn't stop, I'd soon be laid out fanning myself like some over-dramatic actress in a daytime soap.

Mercifully, he pulled back just before my arms turned to total jelly and I fell backward. He pressed a Band-Aid to my shin, covering it completely with his hand, caressing the skin on either side. Slowly, he closed the gap between us and pressed his lips to my knee, above the wound. "There," he said. "All better?"

Oh. My. God. I gulped at the air, hoping to pull enough in to formulate a response. Every thought that came to mind ended with the words "throw me down and take me now." No way could I say it, no matter how strongly my body begged me to. Would he think any less of me if I threw him back and straddled him right here? A need built inside me, consuming all my common sense. I had to be near him, to touch him, have as much contact as physically possible. I felt like I might actually die without it.

"Laney?" His voice was soft, and he looked at me with caution, his fear that he went too far clear in his eyes. The look was enough to snap me back to my senses.

"You are never going to let me live this down, are you?" I pulled my leg away from him and hugged my knee to my chest.

"I wouldn't count on it. Now let's eat lunch. Saving your life has left me famished." He winked with those beautiful eyes of his, and I swooned all over the sandwich he handed me.

"Okay, this I *am* going to hold over your head for the rest of your life. I think you need to make me some kind of medal."

"And what would it say on it? 'Jerkface of the Year: Takes Pleasure in Others' Pain?'"

"Absolutely, but only if you make yourself a 'Damsel in Distress' award."

"Screw you. You can put me down now. I'm fine."

"Liar. We'll still be up here at Christmas if I leave you

to your own devices."

When we left the falls, I was fine. But about halfway down the mountain, my foot had swollen way beyond the confines of my tiny hiking boots and was threatening to turn gangrenous at any minute. I tried to hide my pain, but apparently I was "limping like a drunk pirate" and was in desperate need of help.

So now I was on Weston's back, being carted off the mountain like a toddler who couldn't make the hike on her own. There was no way to stay on without pressing myself completely to him, my chest to his shoulder blades, his hands gripping my thighs, my coochie barely touching his lower back, mere fabric between us. My body sang with the contact, and I resisted the urge to press myself even tighter to him in an attempt to fuse us together. My fingers itched to reach out, to trace the line across his collar bone and around his shoulder. To feel his bicep held firmly in my hand. I let my head dip forward so my cheek rested against the side of his head. The waves of his ponytail tickled the side of my neck, and I shuddered. A deep inhale. Somehow, there in the middle of Montana, he managed to smell like the ocean: all sand and salt and promise.

The backpack, which I now wore on my back, had been steadily tugging me toward the ground, and I suddenly found myself gaining momentum and slipping away from him at an alarming rate. "Shit!" I screeched like an owl. Weston readjusted his grip around my thighs and jumped, launching me higher up on his back, and I wrapped my arms around his neck more tightly. The backpack bounced against me, pressing my lady bits flush to his lower back. A shock zinged through me.

"Oh, my god," I yelled, "You have to put me down. Right. Now."

"But your ankle—"

"Now!" He lowered me to the ground, where I immediately dropped the backpack and sat on it. *Calm down, Laney.* I crossed my legs tightly, trying to force the heat between my thighs back into my stomach where it belonged.

"What happened? Is everything okay?" Weston dropped to one knee in front of me, and I covered my face with my hands in a futile attempt to hide my furious blush. "Hey," he said, voice soft and full of concern. His hands wrapped around my wrists and pulled gently. Once my eyes were visible, he continued, "What is it?"

"No-nothing." My breathless voice was a complete giveaway. He must have known what was going on; I sounded like the girl in a low-rate porn flick. "I just needed—I had to sit down for a while." I took a few deep breaths, willing myself to calm down.

"Is it your foot? We only have a little way to go. Come on, we can make it, love." He wrapped his arm around my waist, and mine looped around his neck. He slid his other arm beneath my knees, and I gasped.

Just then I heard the crunching of boots on the gravel-covered path. Great. Exactly what I needed, for someone to see me in full-on swoon mode here on the side of the trail.

"Weston, is that you?" Oh no, no, no. Of all the people to traipse by at this exact moment— "And Laney! What a joy to see you again." She very carefully avoided looking directly at us.

For a brief second, I rejoiced at the thought that she was alone, but then Craig rounded the corner and joined her. His eyes grew big for a moment then darted from my face—surely still scarlet—to Weston, to where his hand wrapped under my thighs. He'd never been a typical father, which wasn't surprising since he wasn't there to see me as a little girl, but this was probably too much even for him.

"Hi," I practically yelled, my voice all high and screechy. "We were...we, uh—" Why hadn't Weston moved his hand yet? Surely this would've been better if he wasn't still crouched beside me with his hands all over my body. I dropped my arm from his neck and nearly pitched backward off my perch on the backpack. A pathetic girly scream escaped my lips, and I grasped at his shirt to right myself. Heat rushed to my face again as my fingers brushed across one on his nipples. Great. Could this situation get more awkward?

"You were...what, exactly?" Craig's tone was light and joking, thankfully, but I caught a trace of something else under the surface—anger, maybe?

For the zillionth time today, Weston jumped to my rescue. His arm disappeared from under my legs, and, after steadying me so I wouldn't flip backward off the backpack and break my head open on a rock, he removed the one from around my waist as well. "Well, this is awkward," he said.

Angie chuckled, and Craig said, "Just a bit. What's going on?"

"Laney sprained her ankle." He gestured to me, like it was explanation enough for what they'd walked into. "I was trying to help her back to the car."

Craig was at my side in an instant, one hand on each ankle, feeling for differences between the two. "This left one is swollen pretty badly. How'd it happen?"

"I dunno," I said. "I slipped on a root or something."

"When?"

"Right before we got to the falls. It was all wet from the mist."

Craig cut a glare to Weston. "You still took her to the falls after this?" I'd never heard him sound so intense before. "What if she did something serious?"

The skin around Weston's hairline grew blotchy, and for once he was the one scrambling for words, and I got to jump in and save him. "It's okay," I said. "He thought it would be good to put my foot in the cold water. I think it helped."

Craig turned my foot from side to side, and I struggled to keep from crying out, not wanting everyone to know what a wimp I was. It was bad enough having Weston view me as helpless. I didn't need everyone else to see the same thing.

"It's pretty bad," Craig said. "Has it gotten worse with you walking on it?"

"No," I said. "It's fine."

"She's lying," Weston interjected, and I wanted to punch him in the throat. And then kiss it better, but that was beside the point. He continued, "She insisted on coming down by herself, and things got ugly."

"It wasn't *that* bad," I mumbled.

"Laney, you were walking like Hulga."

Craig, Angie, and I all stared at him. What did he just say? Angie braved asking first. "Who's Hulga?"

"Come on, you know. Joy Hopewell?" We continued to stare. "*Good Country People*?" More staring. "Flannery O'Connor? Come on, I thought she was one of the American greats."

"Where'd you learn that?" I said. "Oxford?"

"Well"—he shuffled his feet—"yeah."

"I quite like O'Connor," Angie said, "though I can't say

I've read that one."

Craig had been looking back and forth between us like he'd been watching a match of verbal tennis this whole time. "So, you're saying her foot is bad?"

"Yes."

Craig sat on the ground next to me and dug through his own pack. Never again would I mock someone for over-packing for a hike. He dropped a few things to the ground—granola bars, a half-empty water bottle, a baseball cap—before yanking an Ace Bandage out and holding it up triumphantly. "Take your shoe off, kiddo. I'll wrap it for you."

I considered arguing—we only had a couple hundred yards before we reached the car—but it would be easier to listen, so I went to work removing my shoe again. Slowly, this time. Once it was free, Craig set to work, wrapping and pulling the bandage around my foot and ankle like he'd done it a thousand times before. In a matter of minutes, I was outfitted with a mini, soft cast. I wiggled my toes and stretched my foot up and down then side to side. It seemed secure enough.

"Where'd you learn to do that?" I asked.

"Your dad was an athletic trainer in college," Angie explained. "He used to do this for the basketball team every day." She looked at him like he was a cup of gourmet Crème Brûlée that she wanted to dig into right there. It was like Weston and I completely disappeared when she looked at my father. Maybe I should have been grossed out by it, but my heart leapt at the sight of their obvious love.

Weston interrupted the love-fest. "We better get back." He turned to Angie. "Do you need my help moving your stuff in this weekend?"

She beamed at my father. "I'll come get you if we need you, but I think Craig and I can manage on our own." She patted Craig's arm.

He shook his head a little, bringing himself back to the real world. "You want help getting to the car?"

"No, sir," Weston said. "I can manage."

The thought of climbing back on Weston's back sent the blood rushing to my face so quickly I was afraid my toes would go numb. I couldn't get back up there in front of Craig and Angie. "Actually," I said, "help would be great."

Craig and Weston shuffled around me, one on each side, and pulled me up to standing. We worked our way around the last curve in the trail to the parking lot, the great five-legged creature, with Angie following behind us, Weston's backpack in hand. We made it to the car, and the two men maneuvered around awkwardly, trying to get me into the passenger seat. Finally, Craig stepped to the side, and I dropped into the chair. Weston lifted my legs into the car and shut the door. I watched through the window as he, Craig, and Angie talked. Then he shook Craig's hand, gave Angie a hug, and joined me.

As the car pulled out of the gravel lot and back onto the pitted road, Weston reached across the console and laid his hand gently on my leg. My breath caught in my throat. Tingles ran from where his skin touched mine and up into my stomach, where they exploded, setting loose a throng of butterflies to beat against my insides.

Slowly, so slowly I wasn't sure I was actually moving at all, I covered his hand with my own. He flipped his over and wrapped it around mine, lacing our fingers together. With a slight squeeze, he looked over at me, his eyes burning through me, and I tried to relax into the seat for the ride home.

# DAY FORTY-TWO

I WAS OLD ENOUGH TO HELP MY mother plan two of her five weddings. Both times she had a bunch of grand ideas, dozens of magazines with little Post-it flags marking every other page. Charts and schedules were made, and she would declare that *this time* everything would go perfectly according to schedule. Then the weeks would slip by, and we'd end up sitting on the living room floor at 4:00 AM the morning of the ceremony, frantically finishing up all the details.

Which is why when Angie showed up at my door this morning asking if I wanted to come help her make favors for the wedding—still more than a month away—I almost couldn't answer her. I'd stood in the doorway, staring like an idiot, until I was pretty sure she thought I was one.

Finally, I muttered something along the lines of, "Sure, sounds great," and hobbled back in to take a shower.

Now Kris, Rory, and I sat in the rec lodge with Angie, surrounding the beat-up pool table, making bell wands for all the wedding guests.

"Remind me how you guys roped me into this again?" Rory fiddled with his wire heart, failing to get the bells and beads to line up inside the loops. The pile in front of him was filled with crooked, loosely twisted wands with awkward little hearts at the top. A stray bell was on the table next to the pile, obviously detached from whichever favor it belonged to. He held up his latest sad attempt. The twist of the wand was uneven, and the heart perched at an angle on the top, causing the string of beads and bell to hit against the edge of the heart, even when Rory held the wand still. "What's the point of these things anyway?" he asked.

"We give them to the guests at the wedding," Angie explained, "and they all shake the bells at the end. Kind of like the old throwing of the rice."

"So why don't we throw rice? It'd be a lot faster than making these things."

"Because rice makes birds explode or something," Karissa said. Her pile was much bigger than any of ours, and each bell wand was perfectly formed. It was almost freaky how quickly she'd picked up on the process after

Angie showed us.

"No way! Really?"

Angie laughed at the two of them. "No, they don't explode. But it's not good for them, so no rice throwing."

"Besides," Kris said, "if we threw rice, we wouldn't be able to witness your stellar craft skills."

Rory held up a half-finished wand. "Whatever. You didn't tell me I was going to be a slave for the day."

I tuned them out and focused on my own pile of wands. They weren't quite as nice as Karissa's and Angie's, but they would work. Making them was actually calming; doing the same thing over and over allowed my hands to stay busy while my mind drifted back to yesterday.

Weston held my hand for the entire drive back to the resort, occasionally rubbing the sensitive area between my thumb and first finger. I, on the other hand, held my hand embarrassingly still, so stiff it might as well have belonged to a cadaver. Every time I thought I had gotten control of myself and considered making any kind of move, the butterflies revolted again, and all my energy had to go into not jumping him right then. Or throwing up. Whichever.

When we got back to the resort, Weston pulled the car to a stop in front of our cabins and gave my hand one last squeeze before letting it go to remove his keys from the ignition. He ran a hand through his hair, gathering it at the base of his neck, and turned to me. His eyes burned into my own, and in that moment I knew—I absolutely *knew*—he was going to kiss me.

So, of course, I panicked. The look in his eyes was too intense, brought back too many similar looks from too many other guys, and I couldn't handle it. I probably made some lame excuse, but I couldn't remember. Something about calling my mother, or maybe about having to take care of Epona. It was all kind of a blur. All I knew was I bailed out of the car, limping to my cabin. As I closed my door, I caught a glimpse of Weston's face—he stared at me through the windshield like I'd punched him.

Once I was safely in my cabin, I'd flung myself onto my bed and tried to burn the image of Weston's pained expression from my mind. I'd spent months carefully crafting my defenses, changing who I was and protecting myself, but somehow he had managed to scale all the walls I'd built. I was so certain I couldn't be touched, that I was beyond feeling, but suddenly I'd found Weston standing in front of me inside the fortress I'd crafted. And it scared the shit out of me.

"Laney?" Angie's voice broke through my memory, and my cheeks heated as blood rushed to my face.

"Yeah?" I racked my brain; what were they talking about? Maybe I could make up a response that would make sense. I looked at Rory's newest creation. "Oh, yeah. You're getting the hang of it. Looking better." I smiled.

The three of them stared at me, unblinking. It seemed like even the music lowered, it got so quiet. One minute Bon Jovi was wailing in my ears, and the next I could hear the birds outside.

"Um, thanks," Rory said. "I guess."

"Where were you?" Karissa asked. "You totally zoned out there."

"Yeah, sorry. What did you say?"

Angie's eyes sparkled, and I wondered if she knew exactly what I was thinking about. She'd seen Weston and me together yesterday; it wouldn't be surprising if she'd made assumptions about what was going on between us. Wasn't going on...or was? After the way I'd left things, I wasn't sure.

"I asked if you were hungry. Rory's going to get us some pizza."

Forty minutes later, we sat on the floor, leaned against the wall, each of us with a plate of pizza on our laps. I picked at mine, pulling the toppings off one by one and nibbling at them, my appetite completely missing. Karissa sat to my right, devouring her fourth slice, and Rory was to my left, a pile of uneaten crusts on his plate. Two crusts dropped to the ground as he leaned forward and across me.

"Hey, Ange?" he said, avoiding the elbow I threw at his side.

"Yeah?" A bite of pizza muffled her words, and she covered her mouth with her hand as she leaned out from Karissa's other side to look at him.

"How did you know Craig was the one?"

She popped her knees up and rested her elbows on them, crossing her wrists in front of her. She chewed her pizza slowly, a thoughtful expression on her face. Finally, she swallowed and answered, "He isn't the one."

My heart plunged into my stomach. What the fuck? I had to tell Craig.

Kris started yelling before I could even form a coherent sentence. "Are you shitting me? What's this whole wedding even about then?" My thoughts exactly.

"I love him." Angie looked right at me, her gaze drilling into my eyes as though she knew exactly what I had been thinking. "I don't believe there is only one person out there for each of us. You could spend your entire life looking for the *one* and never find that person. But if you allow yourself to believe in love and give yourself fully to the person you choose...well that is beautiful."

Angie's cheeks darkened. Her eyes, which remained trained on my own for her entire speech, misted and took on a far-away look. Probably, I should have been weirded out to know that thoughts of my dad put that look on her face, and maybe if our situation were different I would have been. But now I swelled with pride, my heart beating about a thousand times a minute, excited to know Craig was now with someone who obviously adored him. My face heated slightly with shame. I had been so quick to assume the worst about her.

"Is that...okay, Laney?" Angie's concern for me was palpable, and again I wondered if she could read my thoughts. I didn't trust myself to form any coherent sentences, so I nodded. She turned to Karissa and waited for my best friend's response.

"Okay, well, I guess that's cool," Karissa said. She stared at the floor. "Sorry I yelled at you," she mumbled.

Rory slid his plate away from him, and the rest of his uneaten crusts fell to the floor. He pushed his legs straight, rubbed his t-shirt smooth (burgundy with gray lettering: *Bones For Lost Mittens*), and folded his legs back up under him again. "What if," he said then stopped so abruptly it was almost like he hadn't spoken at all. He rubbed one hand through his shaggy hair before dropping it back to his side like it were dead. "What if," he repeated, "there *is* only one, and I—or whoever—never finds that one person?"

What if? Could there be only one person for each of us? Maybe that's why my mother couldn't stay married—she kept jumping into marriage with men who weren't the one. But then, what Angie said made sense. There were, what? Seven billion people on this earth now? What a cruel joke to have only one perfect match for each person. We could all spend our whole lives searching and never even come close to meeting the one.

"Rory," Angie said, and her voice was soft and comforting. "You are eighteen years old and living in a tiny town in the middle of Montana. It's okay if you haven't found love yet. You're moving on to more exciting things soon, and you'll find someone eventually. I'm sure of it."

He squirmed again. "How? You barely know me. How can you be so sure?"

Angie's smile lit the room. "I know enough about you to know that you will find love." The statement was so firm, so conclusive, it was impossible not to believe her, and I realized she could have been speaking to me, not Rory. Did Angie believe I could find love? I wasn't sure I did. Maybe some people were meant to be in love and others were meant to have fun, but ultimately stay alone. It's what I'd done my whole life, and for the most part it worked well.

Until Weston.

The idea rang in my head so loud I thought for a moment someone had said it out loud. I tried to push the thought away, but it persisted. Weston didn't know my history—he had no idea how many guys I'd been with, blatantly giving the finger to the idea of love and monogamy. He didn't know of my past and my ghosts.

And he...well, he made me feel things I hadn't felt in so, so long. Maybe even ever.

Could Weston be my one?

# DAY FORTY-THREE

I LEFT MY CABIN EARLY THIS morning, hoping to catch Weston before he ate his normal breakfast of yogurt, granola, and a banana. After my realization yesterday, I was equal parts excited and terrified to see him. If Weston was my one—or one of many possibilities, as Angie would insist—I wanted to know for certain. But...what if I was reading way more into things than were actually there? I was only seventeen years old. And he was a college graduate, a cultured business man already. Probably I was nothing more than a summer plaything for him, a way to pass the time before heading back east to school in the fall. Was I being completely stupid for thinking I had finally found someone who was with me for all of me, not only the physical parts?

I skipped up the porch with slightly less spring in my step and a hell of a lot more trepidation. Hesitating at the office door, I fought to bring back the hopeful, jittery feeling I got when I considered the idea that I might be falling for Weston—and him for me—but the only thoughts that came to mind were ones of me throwing myself at him and being humiliated.

Finally, I pushed the door open, taking a small step inside. The lights were off, and Weston's desk sat empty. Wow. I never beat him in—I was pretty sure he started work before the sun rose most days. The oscillating fan blew past me and fluttered a sheet of paper on my desk. I was across the room in two steps, snatching it up.

*Laney,*

*I had to go back to Philadelphia to take care of some school things. Sorry I didn't give you any warning. Things around here have been keeping me so busy I mixed the dates up. I'll be gone a week. Matthew got the new reservations system loaded on your computer, so take some time to familiarize yourself with the software. His number is below if you need any help. Once you get used to how things work, would you please input the reservations for the rest of the summer? I'll check over them when I get back to make sure everything is running smoothly. Other than that, business as usual. You know what you're doing.*

*Thank you,*

*Weston*

I blinked. Read through the note again, quickly. It was so cold and formal I was surprised he didn't use last names. I mean, he had typed the damn thing and printed it on the shiny new Mountain Lake Lodge letterhead. Had I upset him so badly the other day that all the familiarity between us was gone? I dropped the paper into the recycle basket. It swayed and fluttered on the way down, and the breeze of the fan caught it right before it hit the basket, flipping it upside down and sending it to the floor.

There, written on the back of the paper in blue ink:

*I'll miss you, love.*

My heart jumped, fluttering up into my throat. Love. I picked the paper back up and folded it gingerly, trying not to crease any of his words. After sliding it into my back pocket, I set to work learning the reservations system like a good little employee.

The new software was complex, but not terribly hard to learn. By lunch time, I was ready to put actual reservations into the computer. The reservations log sat on my desk, staring at me like an old horse that knew it wouldn't be ridden anymore. Every reservation since Craig bought Leisure Lodge—years of memories—was written in that book. As many times as I'd bemoaned the lack of any kind of computerized system, now that I had one, I was hesitant to use it. Craig's system was rustic, maybe even arcane compared to the systems at Beaumont Resorts, but I liked it. Once I was at the lake, I could leave the outside world behind. Now we would be plugged in all the time. It would be convenient, yes, probably it would even boost our reservation rate some, but it was still sad. Like we were leaving part of what Craig built behind.

Rather than inputting any reservations—they could wait till tomorrow, and the old leather-bound book could live to shine one more day—I set to work addressing the mailings Weston had left on my desk. Postcards for all our former guests, brochures for travel agents. Vouchers for free nights during the off season for our more loyal customers.

Time raced by as I stuffed envelopes, addressed postcards, and sealed brochures. Before I knew it, my stomach was growling, and I looked for the clock. It was after two already—I'd worked through lunch. But I only had a small stack of postcards left to do, so I decided to finish up before finding food.

Fifteen minutes later, I leaned back in my chair, stretching my hands over my head. I didn't dare count the number of items I'd just stamped. My hands were cramped, and I was beyond ready to be done. A small stack sat in the center of my desk—the ones I'd addressed after I ran out of stamps. I rolled my chair around to Weston's desk, in search of extra postage.

I found them immediately, sitting front and center in the first drawer I opened. Shoving it closed again, I made to push myself back to my own desk. But a slip of paper sticking out from the closed bottom drawer caught my eye, pulling at my curiosity, and I stopped. My hand reached for the drawer then dropped back to my lap. Seriously, I was going to be that girl? *Leave it alone, Laney.*

But the other side won out, and before long I was pulling the drawer toward me. It hitched on the track, and I almost quit, but then it let go and glided smoothly. A small, framed photo sat on top of the pile in the drawer; I lifted it out and studied it. Weston's hair was shorter, loose around his face, not quite long enough to pull into his standard ponytail. He wore a crisp button-up shirt and pressed khakis and held a mortar board in his hand, the tassel hanging toward the ground. His other arm hung loosely around the shoulders of a petite girl with lush black hair. She wore her graduation robe open over a fitted blue dress. Her high heels lay on the ground beside her, and she stood barefoot in the grass, beaming at the camera. She was beautiful, with dark skin and shining eyes. Amy. Who else could it be? I couldn't tear my eyes away from the image, not because of how beautiful she looked, but because of Weston. He smiled bigger than I had ever seen, so large his eyes almost disappeared in his face, the skin crinkling around his temples. His teeth glinted in the sunlight. But still, none of that was what held my attention. The way he looked at Amy, as if he was completely oblivious to the camera, despite the obvious pose, was captivating. Never had a man looked at me that way, and I coveted it.

For a full five minutes, I stared at the picture, finally putting it aside to look at the rest of the drawer. Three forks sat on top of a book and a couple papers, one of which was pulled at an odd angle, a crease from the door across its corner. I pulled the whole stack out, tipping the forks off onto the table. What was with this guy and forks? I made a mental note to ask him sometime, when I could work it in without making it obvious I'd searched his desk.

The creased paper was a printout of the new rental rates for after the renovations were completed. I scanned over them. Holy shit! Did he really think people would pay these kinds of rates to chill at a lake in Montana? All those years working with his father must have completely diluted his idea of what normal people were like. I threw the paper aside before it could enrage me further.

Below that paper was a letter to Weston. The letterhead proclaimed, *From the desk of Walter A. Beaumont.* Now I knew where Weston got his inclination toward typing letters that could—and in this case, should—be handwritten. I set it aside without reading it; Weston's relationship with his father was barely even civil, and this was a line I was not comfortable crossing.

Finally, I held onto the book, my fingers caressing the soft, buttery leather of its cover. I flipped it open and gasped. Staring up at me from the first page was a colored pencil sketch of the beach and lake. It looked exactly as it did the day I'd arrived, sun glinting from the water and the two canoes just kissing the shore. The detail in the piece was stunning. I turned to the next page.

Epona looked back at me from the edge of the page, her eyes soft and inviting. Each of her tiny whiskers was intricately penciled in, and it looked as though I could reach through the page and feel the velvet of her nose. The rest of the picture was filled with the stables. Or, rather, the stables as Craig had described them to me the first time he told me of his big plans, clean and straight, the paint fresh. They looked as if they'd just been built. The ground around them was open and clean, the normal forest debris completely gone, and a bare path led from the bottom corner of the page to the stable opening.

I turned page after page, absorbing the images before me: cabins with straight rooflines and new facades. Bathrooms with claw-foot tubs or Jacuzzis. Freshly manicured lawns. Potted flowers hanging from porch awnings. Each picture was drawn with the precision of the first two, the colored pencils marking details I couldn't even imagine. They were beautiful.

When I reached the last page, my fingers tightened

around it involuntarily, crinkling the edges in my grip. He would know I looked at it now, but I didn't care anymore. The picture was beautiful, like all the ones before it, the details immaculately crafted. The water in the background seemed to shine off the page. Each tree had a life of its own—every needle and leaf had been placed carefully. It belonged in a gallery, not shoved to the bottom of Weston's desk drawer.

As beautiful as it was, though, I wanted to tear it to shreds and leave the pile on top of the desk for Weston to see when he got back from Pennsylvania. Because in the middle of the drawing, where the rec lodge should have stood, was a wide expanse of grass, with no indication a building had ever been there.

*Calm down.* I tried to convince myself I was overreacting, that this was only one option, not the future of the resort. Maybe Weston loved to draw—he was certainly good at it—and the level of detail in the piece had nothing to do with the importance of the idea. Unconvinced, I forced everything back into the drawer, not even bothering to make sure it was in the right order anymore. I shut down the office early, knowing I wouldn't see any guests anyway, and headed to the stables.

Maybe some time with Epona could clear my mind.

# DAY FORTY-FIVE

I NEVER WOULD HAVE TOLD HER had the call not caught me completely by surprise. I was standing by the side of the road as Rory added oil to Karissa's beat-up old Civic, which burned oil faster than gas, when my phone started tap dancing in my pocket. I yanked it out and answered without even a glance at the screen.

"Laney, honey." My mother's voice was falsely sweet. Crap. It was way too early to deal with her.

I lowered myself to the ground, not caring about the dirt I was probably collecting on the back of my shirt as I leaned against the car. "Mother. Hi."

"My god, Laney, I know I taught you better than that. What a way to answer a call."

A dandelion blew in the wind, tickling against my bare

leg. Without a thought, I plucked the flower from the plant and pressed it into my thigh, forcing yellow dye onto my skin. I cleared my throat with exaggeration. "I'm sorry, Mother. What can I help you with today?"

She heaved the mother of all sighs, and she was so easy to visualize, forefinger and thumb grasping the bridge of her nose as she fought to calm herself before speaking. "Laney, something came up. I got to the office today, and Dr. Patel was waiting for me. It seems that mindless twit he hired when you refused to be sensible and come home decided to elope over the weekend. Like that'll last." *Like you have any room to talk, Mother.* "Her new husband is in some sort of travelling show, a circus or something equally silly."

"Okay." I could see where this was headed, but I still silently begged for her to not go there. No such luck.

"I checked up on it, and we can get you on a plane back home as soon as tomorrow morning. The Missoula airport has more options than I would have guessed."

Now I squeezed my own nose, a scarily close replica of the version of my mother I saw in my mind. "No. I don't want to work with Dr. Patel. I won't be home until the end of the summer." My voice was dull, lifeless. Would she even hear my words, or was she already completely set in her idea?

"Don't be ridiculous, Laney. This is a wonderful

opportunity, and it will go far toward getting you ahead in your degree. I let it slide earlier, but it's no coincidence the job is open again. How many other girls will get a chance like this? You will start college ahead of the game, with some real experience under your belt. Don't waste this chance so you can play around in Montana."

"I hardly think filing papers and answering phones for Dr. Patel will count as real experience."

"It's more than the other students will have. You will be immersed in the office of a working psychiatrist. Amit is too professional to breach any patient confidentiality, but I am certain he will share with you about the process and philosophy of his job. It will be so much more than phones and paperwork, honey. The Psychology Department at State loves stuff like this."

It was out of my mouth before it could even take a lap around my brain: "I'm not going to be in the Psychology Department, so I don't care what they love."

Silence. Dead, eerie silence. The phone was so utterly quiet that my heart gave a little flutter at the hope we'd been disconnected before my latest case of verbal diarrhea. It was something I'd thought of before, obviously, but only to myself. I hadn't even had the guts to tell Rory or Karissa. It'd been my plan since I was thirteen to go to State and major in Psychology. Saying out loud I didn't want that future anymore seemed like a betrayal to everything I'd worked toward thus far. Judging by the small huff of breath that finally sounded in my ear, it was also a betrayal to my mother.

"What do you mean," she said, her voice steady and calculated, "you aren't going to be in the Psychology Department?"

"I don't know. I'm not sure psychology is the best route for me to take." Except, as soon as I said it, I *did* know. It didn't matter what had been planned for so long. If the past year had taught me anything, it was that things change. Plans fall apart, and lives veer off course. Sometimes we can't control or stop the change—it is thrust upon us, forced, despite our protests. I hated that kind of change. But this? This felt right, and suddenly it didn't seem so much like I was giving up. It was my life and my choice. I squared my shoulders, forcing my spine straight as I sat in the gravel and dust. "Sorry, I lied. I *am* sure. Psychology isn't what I want to do."

More silence. Rory offered a hand to pull me from the ground, his expression equal parts concern and bewilderment. I tried to climb into the backseat, but his arm snaked around my waist and gently pulled me back. He squeezed through the gap between the front seat and the door frame, his legs spidering up to his face. Rory had insisted on me sitting shotgun this morning, despite the fact he had to turn himself into a contortionist to get into the cramped backseat, and he wasn't dropping his stubbornness now.

My mother's next words came out cold, her control slipping. "What. Exactly. Do. You. Plan. On. Doing. Then?"

This part, I couldn't tell her. I had a hard enough time telling myself what I was thinking. So I retreated, dropping onto the worn bucket seat and closing the door. "I—I don't know," I said, my voice sounding small.

"Figure it out, Laney. You are too old to keep floating along in life. You need a plan, and unless you come up with something soon, you'll be in the Psychology halls come fall." Her voice reeked of frustration and disappointment.

It was no use reminding her I was only seventeen. I wasn't even a legal adult—a fact she would be more than happy to use to her advantage if I were to push the issue too far. So rather than telling her what I wanted, that this was my life and I needed to live it how I saw fit, not how she dictated, I said, "I will."

"You better." Her words were clipped, and a clear image of her face popped into my mind. Mouth drawn into a thin line, eyes slightly squinted. Blotches of red beginning to show on her creamy skin. It was a face I'd rarely seen growing up, but had seen nearly every day over the past months. The face she made whenever the distance between us reared its ugly head. It was the same face she used to wear when she would talk on the phone to her friends, lamenting her latest failed marriage or frustrating client. Disappointment. Irritation. Anger.

I'd hated seeing that look the first few times she showed it to me, but I'd seen it so much by now I could scarcely remember my mother with a different expression.

We wrapped up our phone call with some false pleasantries, both of us obviously uncomfortable and fuming, and I threw my phone into my purse on the floorboard. I leaned my head back and closed my eyes, focusing on my breathing to stop the panic from taking me over. For years, my mother and I had been a pair. A team, working toward the same thing my whole life: my future. State, majoring in Psychology. Then a Master's degree at Stanford. I would do it the right way, not like her. Education would come first, before boys and babies. I would not struggle to make ends meet all through school. No matter our differences, we'd always been together on that.

It had been the plan for as long as I could remember. Even before I decided to go to State—a decision spurred by their excellent Psych program and top tier cross-country team—we knew the rest of the journey. My mother had started putting a chunk of her paycheck aside each month as soon as she was making enough money to spare any.

The Stanford Fund, tangible proof I was headed in the right direction. It was my mother's dream, and for years, I thought it was mine as well.

I felt Rory's hand as he gently laid it on my shoulder, all his warmth and concern pressing through my thin shirt and onto my skin. With a slight squeeze, he asked, "You wanna talk about it?"

My breath rushed out in a great huff, rustling some papers on Karissa's dashboard. "No," I said with a shaky voice, "not right now."

"Okay. But we'll be here to listen when you decide you're ready." He patted my shoulder a couple times then removed his hand, leaving a trail of cold where his heat had been.

I did want to talk about it, terribly. But not now, and not with Rory. He was my best friend, but he wasn't who I should go to with this. It scared me how badly I wished Weston was there. Maybe it was the fact that he could relate to the feeling of disappointing a parent by wanting your own life. Maybe it was that he didn't know the old me. He had nothing to compare me to—all he knew was the person I was this year. His view and opinion wouldn't be tainted by who I was and what I did in the past.

Or maybe, it was that, despite all reason, I was falling desperately in love with him.

The realization struck me so hard I found it hard to

breathe. Never before had I considered actually loving someone. Hell, I'd spent most of my life thinking love was a ridiculous idea, made up by people who couldn't take responsibility for their basic sexual desires. Could you blame me? It wasn't like my mother had shown me any fine examples of love. She lived her life hopping from man to man, bed to bed, marriage to marriage, switching husbands as soon as she got bored with the last. She always claimed love, but how could it possibly be? No, love was a joke. Humans were meant to have fun, which is what I'd always done: had fun with no strings attached. Until it wasn't fun anymore.

But this thing with Weston? It was different. I didn't intend for it to be—I didn't intend for there to be a thing with Weston at all. But it happened, and now I was quickly losing control. Life would be fine if things were purely physical—I could handle that—but this was so much more. It would be a lie to say I didn't want him, physically, that I didn't fantasize about being wrapped in his arms, my legs circling his hips as he slowly buried himself in me...but even without that, I longed for his company. These days without seeing or talking to him were torture, and that scared the shit out of me. Is that what love is—the pain that being without him brings?

"Bull shit," Karissa cut in, her cold voice jerking me from my longing.

"Huh?" I shook my head to rid the images I'd conjured of Weston in my bed.

"That's crap, Laney," she said. "This is what I've been talking about with you. There is obviously something wrong, but you're, what? Too good to tell us? I thought we were supposed to be your best friends."

"Hey," Rory said, "it's—"

"Shut up. Don't make excuses for her. She's a big girl."

Rory sank back into his chair and studied the passing scenery. He knew—we all knew—not to push Kris when she got like this. The worst part was she was right. She and Rory were my best friends, so why did I keep shutting them out? I bit back a sigh.

"I'm sorry," I said. "You're right."

"Thank you. So what's the deal with you not doing psychology anymore? I thought that was what you always wanted to do."

"I don't know. I mean, I did always want to do it, but I'm starting to realize maybe it's what I wanted because it was what my mother wanted, you know?"

"Okay. So what do you want now, then?"

"I...I don't know."

She looked at me, keeping her eyes from the road for a frighteningly long time. "You don't actually think I believe that, do you?"

My skin tingled, and all I wanted was to be out of the

damn car. I squirmed in my seat. "What do you want to hear, Kris? I don't want to be like my mother, giving advice about something I obviously have no fucking clue about. The woman has five failed marriages. Five. Who the hell decided she could counsel others about their relationships? I won't be a total hypocrite."

Rory's voice was tentative coming from the back seat, like he was afraid Karissa might castrate him for speaking up. "Um, you're not your mom."

My voice caught in my throat, choking me and sounding way too much like a sob. "I know," I squeaked out.

It was the truth—I wasn't my mother, and thank god, but I wasn't any better either. For years, I thought I would specialize in grief counseling, helping people work through the things they'd done and had done to them. It excited me, the idea of helping someone who needed relief so badly. But the past months had taught me one thing with absolute clarity: I failed at handling my own grief. How the hell was I supposed to help others if I couldn't deal with it myself? If I did, I would be exactly like my mother, a hypocrite with a job I had no right to do.

"Lane." For once, Karissa's voice was soft, caring. "It's us. Tell us what you're thinking."

It was so simple, the way she said it. *Just say it.* Easy peasy. So why was I struggling so hard to admit to them—and to myself—what I was thinking? I took a deep breath and let it out, throwing all the words into a single huff, slurring them together so quickly I hoped she wouldn't understand them. "I was kinda thinking I could go into hospitalities and do hotelandresortmanagementorsomething." Heat rose up my neck and invaded by cheeks.

"Huh?" Rory had obviously gotten lost in the jumble of words.

"Hotel and resort management?" Karissa's eyes were tiny slits. "As in, exactly what Weston does?"

"No. Well...no. He's a business guy, with the MBA and stuff. I thought I could major in hospitalities." I added in a tiny voice, "It's not the exact same."

She stared at me, her eyes still tiny and still very much not watching the road. She'd driven this stretch into Missoula about a thousand times, but I still clutched the edges of my seat, wishing she would look ahead, especially now that traffic was starting to pick up on the outskirts of the city.

"Right," was all she said. Such a simple word, but in it I heard all the things she didn't say: I was being exactly like my mother after all, changing my life for some guy I'd known for only a handful of weeks. How many times had I bitched to her about my mother changing the decor of our house, or her favorite restaurant, or her cocktail of choice, her clothes, her haircut, even the way she spoke...all based on whichever husband she was with at the time. Even when my mother and I were still close, more friends than mother and daughter, it was something I'd hated about her. It was like she was unable to stand as her own person—her style and opinions were totally fluid, ever changing to meet the views of her current lover. And here I was doing the same thing. At least, that's what Karissa *didn't* say.

I wanted to explain it was the work of ushering the resort through all these changes, and not Weston, that led me to this decision. But what if she was right? What if I was lying to even myself, and I was no different from my mother? Weston loved his job so much, and his excitement was infectious. Was it the job that had wooed me, or the man?

"Whatever you decide, I'm sure you'll do great at it. You'll have your first couple years to spend figuring it out anyway." Always the peacemaker, Rory reached around the side of my seat and gave my arm a soft squeeze. I turned to Karissa. Her features had softened some, but the smile was still tight. I couldn't decide if it was better that she hadn't said what she was thinking or not.

After picking up about a hundred things for Craig—all the random stuff he couldn't find in town—we headed to Sergeant Pepper's, an indie record store near the university.

Rory and I flipped through the classic rock vinyl, silently showing each other any particularly awesome finds. Karissa never made it past the front counter, which she was now leaning over, flirting shamelessly with the clerk. I couldn't hear what she was saying, but she ran her fingers over the back of his hand, coaxing blood into his cheeks. And probably other areas.

Rory nudged me and dropped the album he'd been looking at onto the stacks in front of us. The Beatles' *White Album*. My mind flashed back to my last trip to Missoula, with Weston. "Maybe you should give that to your friend," Rory said, not unkindly. "I swear he's listening to this album every time he's in his car."

"Yeah." A couple weeks after our trip, I'd asked him about it. The *White Album* had been his uncle Luke's favorite album, and listening to it was the only time Weston didn't miss him, as if listening to the music brought Luke back to him. I ran my fingers lightly across the silky cardboard sleeve.

Rory gently pulled my fingers into his hand. "You miss him, don't you?"

A shrug pulled at my shoulders, my well-practiced indifference coming through. He squeezed my fingers. "It's okay to miss him, Laney."

"I know it'd be okay," I snapped, "but why would I? He's only been gone two days." A vice grip closed over my heart. I hated lying to Rory, but I wasn't ready to tell him how attached to Weston I'd already become. I couldn't let him know I already missed him so desperately after only two days that all my anger over that damn sketch had already dissolved, and that I couldn't even imagine what it would be like after a full week.

"Truth," Rory said, staring intensely at me.

I shrugged.

"Okay, well how about I tell you *my* truth. Laney, your entire demeanor changes when you're around Weston. Shit, even when you're just talking about him. It's like this dark veil is pulled off your face, and you are light and happy again. I love watching you with him, and I love when you tell me stories about him. Because when you do, you're more like the girl you used to be."

Tears assaulted my eyes, and I fought to keep them from spilling out. It felt like he'd taken his hand, wrapped it around my throat, and squeezed until I couldn't force air into my lungs anymore. Again, I was drowning on solid ground.

I shook my hand out of his and rolled my shoulders, forcing myself to calm down. "I don't"—another deep breath, a struggle to keep my words from breaking apart—"he didn't know me before. He can't compare this me to the old me. It's easier, I guess, being with someone who can look at me without all my past shit clouding the view." Now the tears did fall. Fuck.

"Laney, what happened last year?"

My eyes went wide. Instinctively, I grasped my shirt sleeve into my fist. "Nothing." Cold. Clipped.

"Stop it," he said, and then he reached down and jerked my hand up to eye level. With his other hand, he pulled the sleeve up to my elbow, gently, but still forcefully. My bracelet, so carefully wrapped this morning just like every other morning, covered my scar, but even I couldn't pretend not to know what he was talking about. He dropped my arm back to my side and stared at me.

My defenses rose automatically, a feeling I was so, so familiar with. I'd become so accustomed to shutting everyone out that it happened without my consent now. Wasn't this what I'd been waiting for all this time? For someone to ask me what happened, for someone to want to find out rather than assume they already knew? I'd longed for my mother to ask; I had silently begged for my friends to force it out of me. And now there was Rory, his eyes soft and concerned, and my proverbial walls were rising. I gulped down a breath and forced myself to break through.

"It was the night of regionals," I said, and even I was shocked by how small my voice sounded. My words didn't even make it all the way to the floor I was staring at. Rory's hand brushed my chin, lifting my face to look at his, his calloused fingers simultaneously rough and comforting. I inhaled deeply—

And was assaulted by the smell of dirt and motor oil, still on Rory's hand from our stop on the side of the road. In an instant I was back in my room on that night, the same smell on *his* hands as they pressed against me, pushing my face, forcing me to watch him. My stomach threw itself against my throat, and I jerked away from my best friend, flinging a hand over my mouth to stop my lunch before it ended up on the tile floor. Wheezes filled the room as I gasped for breath, dizzy and lightheaded, black spots clouding my vision.

With what strength I had left, I pushed past Rory, shoving my shoulder into his chest, and ran. Karissa's hand brushed my arm as I passed her, but I couldn't stop. I shrugged her off and pushed the door open.

The brilliant sun took the rest of my vision, and I bent over, my hands on my knees. After a few more gulping breaths, I staggered to the car, fighting with every step to not hit the pavement. Finally, I made my way, and everything broke loose. My body racked with sobs, and the tears flowed freely now. I could only hope to be back in control by the time Karissa and Rory got to me. He could have the front seat this time.

I jerked awake to the sound of the car door slamming. The sun burned my eyes, which were puffy and chapped from crying. I slurped drool back into my mouth and sat upright.

"Good morning, Sunshine," Rory said.

"Ugh. Morning," I said, my voice raspy.

Karissa cranked the key, and the Civic's engine coughed to life. She turned around in her seat and stared me down. "What the hell happened in there?"

"Nothing."

She slapped the steering wheel. "Enough, Laney."

Rory reached across the console and dropped his hand to Karissa's shoulder. She tried to shake him off, but he held firm, squeezing her shoulder lightly. "Shhhh," he whispered before turning to me. "I'm sorry for whatever I did. You wanna talk about it?"

I shook my head. "No, I don't." Karissa seethed in her seat. Trying to ignore her, I said to Rory, "Don't be sorry. You didn't do anything wrong."

"But—"

"It's fine," I snapped. "Just let me sleep."

Anger rolled off Karissa, washing over me, and I watched as Rory soothed her, sliding his hand across her shoulder and to her neck. He ran his fingers through her hair until she finally relaxed and pulled the car out of its spot. I curled in on myself and tried to fall back asleep for the drive home.

# DAY FORTY-EIGHT

WESTON COMES HOME TOMORROW.

It was the first thought I had when I woke up this morning. Followed closely by, *since when do I think of the resort as home?* I didn't know when the shift happened, but this was home now. Not the cabin, furnished with all Craig's things, or even the resort I loved so much. But the feeling of contentment, of belonging, of love. That was home to me now.

So I guess maybe Weston wasn't coming home tomorrow. He was bringing home back to me.

# DAY FORTY-NINE

I DIDN'T SLEEP LAST NIGHT. Not at all. So I was up before the ass crack of dawn, ready to go for my run before the sun even rose. I crossed the room to where my running shoes were sitting in front of a chair. On the chair was my outfit for the day, a v-neck, long-sleeved t-shirt that highlighted my collar bone and a pair of denim shorts. My best pair, actually, the ones that made me look like I had legs for days and an ass to kill for. I'd spent half the night trying to decide what the perfect outfit would be for when I finally saw Weston again, and the other half of the night bitching at myself for being the girl who tried so damn hard. I'd never been that girl before. I'd never had to be.

With my shoes laced tight and my hair pulled back, I strapped my iPod to my arm and set out. Running so early was liberating. Nobody to see me, nobody to stare. I wore capri running pants and a tank top. My bracelet lay coiled on my bedside table, ready for me to wrap it on when I dressed for the day. For this one hour, I could let myself be bare, and as I ran, I could pretend I was whole again, that the past year never happened.

The cabin door shut at the same exact time my heart slammed into my ribcage. My feet stopped moving so fast I almost pitched off the porch and into the dirt and pine needles scattered on the ground. Uncle Luke's old car sat parked right next to Burt. And on the swing, Weston sat in a pair of gym shorts and a fitted t-shirt, his hair tied at the base of his neck.

"It's about time you made it out, love. I was beginning to think you'd stopped running." My stomach plunged and my heart sang. Oh my god, how could I have forgotten how beautiful he was? All my daydreams and fantasies while he was gone paled in comparison to the real thing. Goosebumps rose over my whole body, and my skin felt electrically charged. All it would take was one touch, and I would explode.

He was staring at me, his eyes hungry, waiting for me to say something. I reached to pull my shirt into my fist and froze when I realized it wasn't there. In my tank top, with no bracelet, he could see everything.

"I, uh"—I backed toward my cabin, my wrist pressed

flat against my thigh—"forgot something. I'll be right back." The doorknob rattled in my sweat-slick hand. Why wouldn't the damn thing turn?

"Wait." In one swift movement, Weston was out of his seat and across the porch. He covered my hand on the knob and linked the fingers of my other hand with his. My heart played hopscotch across my ribcage, and my head swam. "Please," he said, "leave it uncovered." Slowly, he pried my fingers from around the door knob and pulled me toward him and into a tight hug. "You look fantastic." He pressed his lips to my forehead, and I melted all over the front porch.

We stretched together in the dew-covered grass, the moisture clinging to our limbs, and then set out for my normal morning run. Each step, every thud of my feet hitting the pavement, sent a zing of electricity up my spine. My skin crackled with the charge of being so close to Weston. Being here next to him, our breath intermingling in the crisp morning air, was more sensual, more erotically charged, than any of the nights I'd spent in some guy's bed. His arm brushed against mine, so lightly I may have been imagining it, and I chanced a glance at him. Sweat was beginning to bead up around his hair line, and the stubble on his cheeks glistened in the rising sun.

"See something you like?" he asked between deep breaths. The side of his mouth tugged upward, highlighting his dimple, and he watched me out the corner of his eye. I turned back to the road, thankful that, for once, my face was already hot and would mask the furious blush his scrutiny incited.

We made it to the bridge, and I started to turn around, like I did every morning. Weston stayed on the path, heading straight to the other side. With a slight stumble, I corrected my turn and followed him. "Come here," he said and grabbed my hand, leading me off the road and into the tall grass. We slowed our pace and picked a path down the hill to the river's edge. He led me across the muddy shore and partway back up the hill, to where a flat rock sat under the bridge, completely hidden from the road. He sat on one side of the rock then pulled me down next to him, close enough our legs pressed against each other.

"What?—"

Weston shushed me and leaned back on his elbows. I followed suit, positioning myself so our shoulders were touching. My body sang with the proximity, my shoulder and leg nearly burning with the intensity of the contact. I opened my mouth again to ask what we were doing, but he beat me to it: "Relax and wait, love. It'll be worth it."

The water in front of us was nearly as smooth as glass, only the occasional ripple indicating the slow-moving river was alive at all. Here, so close to the lake, was its widest point, and the faster currents and rapids had all calmed.

Reeds at the shoreline swayed in the light breeze. For more than five minutes, we sat completely still and silent, and then Weston tensed beside me and sat up.

A crashing came from our left, and I shot upright. Weston held one finger to his lips and motioned with his head for me to look past him. A second later, I saw it. Lumbering down the hill, no more than fifty yards from where we sat, came a moose. Directly behind her, two babies frolicked into view, careening through the grass and splashing into the river until they were submerged up to their hackles. The mother gingerly stepped in next to them and lowered her head to drink. The sun crested over the mountain, lighting her fur ablaze. The calves threw their heads back and forth, spraying water everywhere, the droplets catching the morning light and glistening in the air.

"It's beautiful," I whispered.

"I know."

"How did you know they would be here?"

"I come every morning," he said. "I don't sleep much, so I started canoeing. I found this place my first week here."

"Wow. Are they always here?"

He nodded. "They come right around this time every day, for a few minutes."

"Wow," I repeated.

"Yeah." He looked down at me, want clear in his gray

eyes.

"Um..."

"..."

"..."

He lowered toward me. My chin raised in response. He brushed his knuckles across my cheek and around my jaw then cupped the back of my neck in his palm.

And then his lips were on mine. Softly at first, almost as if he was afraid I would push him away. More urgently as he laid me back against the rock. His tongue slid between my lips, tickling them open to invite him in. I nipped at his lower lip, and he responded by pushing himself against me, making his desire clear. The pressure awoke something inside me, the part of me I'd kept in hibernation for too long. I hitched a leg over his hip, giving him closer access.

With a moan, he pressed his full weight into me, our bodies fused together. His fingers wrapped around my ponytail, tugging gently. A gasp escaped me, and I thrust my hips up into him. A low, guttural growl grew in his throat, and he met my movement with one of his own. We rocked together, the heat between us intensifying. Building. Threatening to overcome me.

I broke away from him and gasped for breath. His mouth dropped to my jaw, and then my exposed neck, where he pressed his lips lightly before playfully nipping at my skin. My nipples tingled, and I wondered, distantly, if he could feel their excitement through our clothes. The heat between my legs rushed through my whole body before centering where he rubbed against me with an intensity I almost couldn't handle. "Oh, my god," I panted.

Weston pulled his mouth from my collar bone and hovered above me, still for the moment. "Do you want me to stop?" he asked, concern filling his eyes.

I wrapped my arms around his neck, twisting his hair between my fingers the way he had done mine, and smiled at him. "No." I shook my head and repeated, "No. Don't stop."

His mouth crashed back to mine, and my chest rose to meet his as he lowered himself back down. His free hand caressed the side of my face, ran down my arm and across my hip. Sliding up the soft flesh of my stomach, he cupped my breast, his thumb grazing across my nipple, and I wished I could tear my sports bra off. My hips bucked up into him; I had to feel him against me, to have the building pressure released. His hand traveled back over my ribcage, ticking across my side and eventually cupping my hipbone. He guided me as I rocked into him, frantically at first, and slowly, sensually as he worked me closer and closer to the end.

The hand in my hair tightened, pulling my chin up, my mouth away from his. He dropped his mouth back to my neck and brought both hands to grasp my shoulders.

With another moan, he crashed his pelvis into me once more.

I bit down on Weston's shoulder to silence my scream as I exploded.

# DAY FiFTY

I PRACTICALLY FLOATED INTO the office the next morning. Weston sat at his desk, working on the new reservation system, a pair of black-rimmed glasses perched on his face. Following the breeze, I crossed the room and dropped into his lap. The rolling chair glided toward my desk as I kissed him, our passion from yesterday still roiling in me. Weston froze for a moment then pushed me abruptly from him.

"What the—" I started as I heard the toilet flushing from behind the wall. "Who's here?"

"Ah, Laney," Craig said as he rounded the corner back into the main office. "Exactly who I was looking for."

"You"—I cleared my throat, trying to get rid of my obvious surprise—"were?"

Weston shuffled the papers on his desk and pushed his

glasses up his nose. A splotchy redness was making its way up his neck and into his face. Thankfully, Craig was totally oblivious to the awkwardness permeating the room.

"We have a couple young ladies who were hoping to rent some horses," Craig explained.

"Okay?"

"They went to KP's up in town, but he had a huge reunion booked today, so all his animals are out. He called and asked if I had any he could use."

"Right, so why does this involve me?"

Craig looked at Weston, who was pointedly avoiding my gaze. Shit. What in the hell did he tell my father?

"Well, Weston thought this would be a good opportunity to have a trial run of sorts for our own trail guide program, so we told them we'd take them."

"We, as in..."

"Nobody knows the trails around here as well as you do, Laney." Weston still wouldn't meet my gaze.

"Hello? What about Rory? He grew up here. He knows them."

"Mr. Evercott has some plumbing issues. You know," Craig said with a smirk. Mr. Evercott was an eighty-year-old widower who came up for a few weeks every summer. He was always eating Grape Nuts and would tell anyone who would listen about the importance of a high-fiber diet. A sweet old man, but he had more plumbing problems than

206

the rest of our guests combined. Rory was at his cabin at least three times a week. Secretly, I thought he was lonely and did what he needed to in order to have some company.

Craig continued, "There's two of them, so you'll only need to saddle up Epona for yourself and two others. I think Zeke and Joker would be the best."

My gaze darted from Craig—all confidence and oblivion to my unwillingness—to Weston, who still stared at the floor to my left. Why the hell wouldn't he look at me? A breeze came through the window, bringing the sound of giggling with it. I looked outside to see two women, in their early twenties, standing in the grass at the edge of the parking lot. How had I missed them on my way in? The wore nearly identical outfits: straw hats with colorful bandanas tied around the brims, tank tops—one blue and one brown—with thin western-style shirts tied below their boobs. Tiny denim shorts that barely covered their asses were followed by tanned legs stuffed into brand new cowboy boots. Their outfits screamed of a western-themed dance at a sorority. They talked to each other, laughing and twirling their perfectly styled hair every few sentences.

Turning back to Craig and Weston, I said, "Fine. I'll take them. But when they get saddle sores in their coochies, I'm not treating it."

Craig's face flamed red, and he mumbled something

incomprehensible. Weston motioned me to the door. As soon as it opened, Muffy and Fluffy, the fake cowgirls, stood at attention, hips popped and chests on display.

"All right, ladies," Weston said, "you are almost good to go. This is Laney, and she'll be guiding you today. Laney, Casey and Lindsay. They're in town for a friend's wedding."

"Awww," the one on the left—Lindsay, I think—drawled out, "I thought you were gonna take us, sugar." She pouted at Weston.

He rubbed his neck and pushed his glasses back up his nose, a gesture I was quickly recognizing as a nervous tick. I stepped forward before he could say anything. "Sorry, y'all," I said, my North Carolina accent turned up full force. Maybe Lindsay would drop her fake drawl now. "West here barely knows which way to face a saddle." Not entirely true, but I wasn't feeling terribly generous right about then.

We made our way past the cabins and toward the stables. Lindsay and Casey mumbled and groaned behind me as we picked our way through the forest. "Sorry," I said. gesturing to the branches covering the way. "We weren't really planning to lead tours yet, so we haven't prepared the paths to the horses.

"Oh, we know," one of the girls replied. I could practically hear her flipping her hair over her shoulder.

"Weston told us all about how this place is trying out some new things and improving. It's about time, if you ask me. Do you remember how horrible it was last year?"

"Oh my god, I totally forgot about that!" This one must have been Casey. Her voice was about two octaves higher than Lindsay's, and nasally. "We stayed here last year," she explained, apparently to me, "and our toilet, like, exploded on us. It was so nasty."

"I bet," I mumbled, trying my best to ignore her. We stepped into the stables, and I turned to the girls. Casey's nose wrinkled in disgust at the musty hay smell, and she picked her way toward the horses, high-stepping and watching her foot placement like one wrong step would result in a serious maiming. Please. I'd cleaned out the stables last night before I let the horses back in from pasture.

"Oh," she shrieked, and the horses jumped and let out a collective huff of displeasure. "I want this one." She reached a hand out to Epona, who—good horse she is—snorted and pulled away.

"Sorry," I said and wedged myself between her and my horse, "but this one is mine. You'll be on Joker." I motioned to a stall across the aisle, where the black gelding stood tall and proud.

"Isn't Joker a little big for her?" Lindsay asked as she fanned the air away from her face with her hat. The smallest hint of pleasure coursed through my veins at the sight of her flattened and sweaty hat-head.

Casey stared at Joker like he was going to tear out of his stall and crush her at any moment.

"He's big," I said, "but he's the most gentle animal we have. Epona"—I jerked my head back to my horse—"is still a little spitfire."

Lindsay shrugged and placed her hat gingerly back above her curls.

A quarter of an hour later, I had the horses saddled and was getting pretty great at tuning Muffy and Fluffy's voices out. I swung onto my saddle and turned Epona to face them. "I was thinking we could take the trail to Morrell Falls," I said, and my face burned as the memory of my hike with Weston invaded my thoughts. "It's not too long," I continued, "and the views are spectacular."

"We want to go to the lookout station," Casey whined. "That's where that other guy was going to take us."

"Weston?"

"Oh, no, not him. But, damn I wish he would." Her eyes sparkled, and I killed the flippy feeling working its way up my throat before I had a chance to identify it. "That KP guy. I guess it's one of his regular trips."

Lindsay led her horse over to the edge of a stall and climbed onto the saddle. The grace with which she mounted Zeke was impressive; my assumption that she had no idea what she was doing may have been premature. She'd been on a horse before. Probably many times. Casey, on the other hand, had obviously only seen them from a distance. I dismounted and went to help her.

"We can go to the lookout if that's what you want," I said as I guided her foot into one of the stirrups, "but it's, like, fifteen miles one way. Okay, hold onto the horn here"—I placed her hands—"and I'll boost you up." I heaved Casey onto the saddle, grabbing her shorts and stabilizing her when she almost pitched right back off the other side.

She grabbed the reins and stared at them like she expected them to tell her what to do from there. This was going to be a long day.

"Don't worry," I said. "Joker follows well, so you won't have to do much."

Lindsay, who was already working her horse in quick figure eights, said, "I'm fine with a long ride if you guys are." She clucked at Zeke softly.

A pain erupted deep in my throat at the thought of being away from the office—from Weston—for the whole day, but I couldn't shake the girls' conversation about how terrible the resort was. They couldn't know I was Craig's daughter—I looked nothing like him. But still, they talked about the place right in front of me without even a hint of embarrassment. Like it was such common knowledge that

Leisure Lodge was a dump that even the employees were in on the joke. I surged with a sick combination of pride and humiliation for Craig and decided it was my job to prove these two wrong. And if a thirty-mile horse ride on a hot day was what it would take, then that's what I'd do.

The ride to the lookout went relatively smoothly. Casey started complaining about halfway there about the saddle chaffing her bare legs, but she was determined to stick it out. Lindsay ended up being a huge help, guiding Casey when she struggled and coaxing Joker along once when he found a patch of clover particularly alluring and tried to take his rider off trail for a quick snack. When we got to the tower, she leapt from her saddle without even waiting for Zeke to come to a full stop, then trotted over to help her friend down as well.

After lowering myself from Epona, I led the three horses to a small creek for a drink of water. "How long have you been riding?" I asked Lindsay over my shoulder.

"Pretty much my whole life," she replied. Casey groaned and dropped to the ground, gingerly rubbing her inner thighs. Lindsay continued, "My parents were big into it, so of course I had to be, too. I rode English, jumping and all that? But when I went to college, it was hard to find a good arena, so I started riding Western." She crossed the clearing to me and helped guide the horses to the hitching post. With a gesture to the tower, she said, "We can check it out up there, right?"

"Of course," I said, and, with a little trouble coaxing Casey off the ground—the ride back would not be fun for her—we headed up the stairs and into the lookout.

I'd only been there once before. Craig took me the first summer I visited, when he was trying to show me all the cool things about the lake and the tiny town he called home. Over the past few years, I'd forgotten how breathtaking the views were. From one side, you could see miles and miles across the Swan Mountain Range; the opposite window looked down on the lake, which glistened in the sun as if millions of glittering sapphires and diamonds scattered across its surface. The Clearwater River cut through the trees, snaking its way through the valley. And the sky. The sky was everywhere, stretching out as far as I could see, and then some. It was like climbing those steps to the top of the tower took us out of the confines of the Larch trees and enclosed mountain valley and up into the infinity laid out before us. The view to the south was completely clear, crystalline blue; from the north, a mass of dark clouds tumbled over the mountain.

"What's that?" Casey's nasal voice cut through the silence, and I jumped. It was easy to be convinced I was alone in the tower, even with another person standing mere feet away. Lindsay and I followed Casey's outstretched finger with our eyes, until they settled on the gray-white haze nesting on the trees to the east of us.

"Fire," I replied.

"Seriously?" Her voice squeaked.

I nodded. "It's been a dry year. It's been burning for a while now, but it's contained. Nothing to worry about."

Casey stared, completely awestruck, and it hit me suddenly how young she looked, how frightened. "A couple years ago," I told her, "my friends and I thought it'd be a good idea to sit at the end of the dock during a bitch of a windstorm." I remembered the whitecaps that had covered the lake that day and the tree limbs that crashed to the ground behind us every few seconds.

Casey stared at me, her eyes prompting me to go on.

"Finally, we realized we were being idiots and decided to go back inside. Just as we were standing up, though, lightning struck."

"For real? What was it like?"

"Unbelievable. It was on the other side of the lake, but it seemed like it was right there." Never before had I felt so alive, and never since, despite my best efforts to recreate the sensation.

The horses whinnied below us seconds before a gust of wind rocked the tower. Casey shrieked, and Lindsay—almost imperceptibly—rolled her eyes.

"We better get back," I said.

No sooner had the words left my mouth than the first drop of rain hit the window, followed by a deluge of its brethren. It was as if the dark clouds from the north had planted themselves directly above our head and cut their own bellies open. In less than a minute, the windows were completely streaked with water and the view of the endless sky was distorted and blurry.

"I'm going to go move the horses to the post closer to the tower," Lindsay said, "so they can get under and away from the rain."

"I can—" I started, but she cut me off.

"Don't worry about it. I don't mind." She bounced down the winding staircase to the ground.

Guilt tugged at my stomach as I remembered my initial view of Lindsay and the harsh way I'd talked to her. Lightning flashed, and Casey sunk to the ground, leaning against the wall beneath the windows. Her face had gone white, and once again, I noticed how young she looked.

"How"—I moved across the room and sat next to her—"did you and Lindsay meet? In college?"

She laughed and beamed at me. "No! We're sisters. Do I really look like I could be in college?"

I nodded. "I thought you were friends or something. You look the same age." Except when you're scared or excited, I didn't add.

A shake of the head. "Nope. Lindsay is twenty-one, and

I just turned fifteen. I know." She laughed. "I'm the baby of the family. My parents wouldn't ever say it, but we all know I was an accident." She smiled.

Lindsay came back in, shaking the rain off her shirt, and I remembered the deftness with which she handled Zeke. "But you didn't ride like Lindsay?" I asked Casey.

Lowering herself to the ground on Casey's other side, Lindsay answered for her sister, "My horse kicked Case when she was five. It messed her up for a while—she had to be in the hospital and everything."

Casey blushed furiously. "I was always scared of them afterward. Lindz has been bugging me forever to give them a try again."

Another gust of wind shook the tower, and the color drained from Casey's face as quickly as it had appeared. I stood and dug my cell from my pocket. "I have a tiny bit of service," I said, looking out at the clouds and still-darkening sky. "I'll call and see if someone can bring a trailer out for us. I don't think this is going to let up anytime soon."

Lindsay looked like she might argue, but I cut a quick glance to her sister, who had started to shake slightly, and she nodded her agreement.

Craig's phone went straight to voicemail, as did Rory's. Karissa had taken her mom to Missoula for an appointment, so there was no point calling her. I called The Place, but the gruff voice that answered told me Derek wouldn't be on until night shift. Derek's cell rang about fourteen times before cutting me off. Finally, I dialed the office number. Two rings, then the distinctive click of the phone being picked up.

"Mountain Lake Lodge, this is Weston. May I help you?" Even over the crackling phone line, his voice melted me slightly.

"Hey, it's me."

"Laney?"

"Yeah, Laney. Sorry."

Thunder boomed above us, and the horses sounded an alarm below. "Where are you? I can barely hear you."

"Bad service. I'll talk fast."

I told him where we were and what he needed to do to rescue us then hung up and dropped back to the floor. "Okay," I said to Lindsay and Casey, "he's coming."

A few minutes passed in silence, then Casey said, "So, um, are you and that Weston guy, like, a thing?" Lindsay's eyes jerked to my face, her thirst for my answer apparent despite her attempt at indifference.

Were we? After what happened yesterday, I wasn't sure what we were. As we'd walked back to the resort, I could feel Weston pulling away from me. My hand was in his the whole time, the heat from his body crashing into me, we were so close. But still, it was like a gulf had opened up between us, threatening to swallow me whole. As soon as we reached the resort, he'd dropped my hand. With a quick excuse, he ducked into the office, and I walked the rest of the way to our cabins alone. The rest of the day, he was stubbornly business-like, spending most of his time on the phone with travel agencies, convincing them to give Mountain Lake Lodge favored recommendations. He only spoke to me when he needed to ask for something or share some work-related information. Our normal chattiness was completely dead for the day. Several times, I thought to call him out, to ask what the hell was going on, but his complete shift in mood had left my head spinning so fast I couldn't form a coherent question.

But still, what happened under the bridge *did* happen, there was no denying it. The thought of his mouth on mine, his hand tangled in my hair, his thigh pressed between my own...brought a rush of heat between my legs and a breathless twirl to my head. Those few moments with him on that rock were some of the most intense of my entire life. My heart fluttered, and I replayed the moment when his lips first met mine over and over in my mind.

The sound of rustling fabric brought my attention back to the room. Lindsay was removing her soaked outer shirt, showing off her toned, tan arms. I realized with a start that Casey was still watching me intently, waiting for my answer.

"Oh, West?" I said, trying to sound more flippant than I felt. "No. No, we're not dating."

"Do you want to be?" she pressed.

*Yes.* Out loud, I said, "Nah. He's a friend. That's all."

Lindsay leaned forward and put her elbows on her knees. She stared at me, scrutiny clear in her eyes. Her gaze bored through my skin and into my soul, and I was sure that, for a moment, she could read what I was really thinking. To her credit, she didn't challenge my answer, simply shrugging and sitting back up, shaking the rest of the water droplets out of her now straight hair.

As we settled back in to wait, she shot me another glance, and there was no question in her eyes: she knew how I felt.

Derek's old truck pulled in half an hour later, Craig's horse trailer bumping behind it. Weston hopped out of the cab and ran to the stairs at the base of the tower. He came into the room, shaking the rain from his hair in much the same way Lindsay had done earlier. "I think we are going to owe Derek for this one," he said. "I caught him as he was about to head out. It's a good thing he likes you."

Flames crawled into my cheeks. Lindsay was watching me again, cataloguing my reaction. I turned from her and started to the stairs. "Thanks for coming," I said to Weston. "I'll go load the horses so we can get out of here."

"Would you like help?"

"No," I said, too quickly. "Y'all hang up here. I'll be back."

Weston looked like he would come with me anyway, but finally shrugged and turned to the girls. Over his shoulder, I could see Lindsay cut me a knowing stare.

The cold rain was a welcome relief on my blazing skin, but the work of loading the horses failed to keep my mind from drifting to Casey's question. Why was it bothering me so much? We weren't dating. Of course we weren't. What happened between us didn't change that. I'd never dated anyone before. It was just easier that way. Dating caused all kinds of problems. Entanglements. Broken hearts and shattered feelings. What was the point, I'd always asked myself, of dating someone when it would end? It was so much easier, it made so much more sense, to hook up and have the fun without having to make any empty promises and ridiculous declarations.

So why was the lack of those promises such a problem this time?

Lindsay, Casey, and Weston came back down as I was shutting the horse trailer. Weston, if possible, was even more breathtaking with the rain rolling down the planes of his face. Casey stared up at him, unabashedly infatuated, and Lindsay followed behind, her eyes on my face, sly.

"It's going to be a tight fit," Weston said, opening the

passenger door for us, "but I think we'll be okay."

Lindsay giggled, a sound seeming out of place now that I'd gotten to know her. "We'll be fine," she said with a flirty lilt to her voice. "Tight spaces don't bother me." She climbed into the truck and motioned for Casey to follow her. I squeezed in last and pulled the door shut. The bare metal of the truck door was cold and hard against my side, and I glared out the window. Weston looked back at me, one eyebrow raised, before shrugging and circling the front of the truck to his own side. He pressed into the cab, forcing us all to practically sit in each other's laps, and struggled to shut the door. "All right," he said with a slight chuckle, "I think we're ready." He cranked the engine and slowly circled the tower to turn us back toward the road.

When we reached the highway, a mile from the resort, Lindsay broke through the pregnant silence in the truck. "So, Weston," she said, the false twang back in her voice, "tell me about yourself." Staring straight ahead, I couldn't help but notice out of the corner of my eye how close her left hand was to his thigh. Her fingers twitched slightly as if she longed to reach out and rest her hand on him.

"There's not much to tell." His voice was tense, and muscles bulged in his neck and arms. He held his back unnaturally straight.

"Oh, sure there is," she said, oblivious to his discomfort. "Everyone has a story. Let's start with that accent of yours."

Red blotches appeared on his neck, and his eyes squinted slightly. "I grew up in South Africa....College in England," he added, voice clipped.

The truck jerked slightly, and my stomach jumped. Casey fidgeted beside me, her face turning red. Lindsay's hand, freed from all self-control, now rested on Weston's thigh, her long, manicured fingers snaking dangerously close to his crotch. My chest tightened, and my shoulders hunched up.

"I think," she said, stretching her words out for eternity, "it's *very* sexy."

Weston's knuckles whitened around the wheel, and I worried he would crush it in his grip. Thankfully, just then he jerked it to the left and pulled the truck into the resort parking lot. The second the horse trailer was clear of the road, he slammed on the brakes and jumped from the cab, leaving the truck running. The horses whinnied in protest, their hooves slapping the trailer bottom as they fought for purchase against the sudden stop. Weston sped around the front of the truck and opened my door, helping me down before reaching a hand in for Casey.

"Thank you, ladies," he said, and his voice was devoid of the professional politeness it normally held when he talked to guests. "Laney and I will take care of the horses from here." He turned from the truck before Lindsay got out.

"Thanks!" Casey said to me. "It was a lot of fun."

I didn't believe she'd actually enjoyed her day, but her smile seemed genuine, so I returned it with a soft, "You're welcome."

Lindsay lowered herself from the truck and sauntered to the end of the trailer, where Weston stood. "Hey," she said loudly, "after I drop Casey off, I'm free for the night. What do ya say I come back and pick you up? We could go to dinner. Or...whatever."

"Um..." Weston shifted on his feet. Rubbed a hand over his neck, pushing his ponytail to the side. Stole a quick glance over his shoulder at me. "I can't." As an afterthought, he added, "I'm sorry." He didn't sound sorry.

To my surprise, Lindsay beamed at his rejection. She brushed past him and walked toward her car, where Casey was waiting by the passenger door. As she passed me, she squeezed my hand.

"He's all yours," she said with a wink.

# DAY FIFTY-ONE

"GOOD MORNING," I CALLED AS I strode into the office this morning. Weston was standing at his desk, phone to his ear. He held a finger up to his mouth, silencing me. I mouthed, *sorry*, and dropped into my chair.

"Yes, sir, I understand," he said and scribbled something an a notepad. His forehead wrinkled up, and he pushed his glasses against his face with the back of his hand. "Yes, sir. Craig and I will look over the contract this afternoon. I'll call you first thing in the morning to finalize things....okay. Thank you for your time....Yes....You too...have a great day."

He dropped the phone back on its cradle and sat with a groan. "Shite," he said under his breath.

"Everything okay?"

"Yeah." He rubbed his eyes behind his glasses. "It's fine."

"You wanna talk about it?"

"No."

I sat back in my chair, stunned. His voice was cold and harsh. Even when we'd fought, I'd never heard him sound like this. Whatever that call was about must've been really bad. Slowly, I rolled my chair across the room. He sat with his head resting on the back of the chair, eyes closed. His chest rose and fell steadily with deep, slow breaths, and the muscle in his jaw popped under the skin.

"Hey," I whispered, "what's going on?"

He shook his head, and I reached my hand out to him. I needed to touch him, to feel that connection between us, to make whatever was bothering him be okay. I squeezed his knee, and his whole body tensed up. "We have work to do. I need you to make sure all the books are up to date. The accountant will be here in two hours, and I need to know he won't find any problems."

"They're fine. Now what's going on?"

"Laney," he snapped, "please, just go make sure. We don't have time to mess around." He jerked his leg out from under my hand and turned to his computer, an obviously dismissal.

My skin prickled with a cruel mixture of anger, humiliation, and shame. His rejection washed over me, and

I sat stunned, waiting for him to say something else. To acknowledge me there, still by his side. He didn't. Instead, he typed away at his computer, laser-focused on the screen. If it weren't for his rigid posture and the way he sat turned slightly away from me, I would have thought he didn't even know I was still there.

Numb, I pushed myself back to my own desk and turned the computer on. The ancient beast took a full five minutes to boot up, and I spent the time checking through the files in my bottom drawer. Nothing in the accounts receivable or the accounts payable folders. Not that I expected anything to have turned up since last night. What was Weston's deal? He knew I updated the books every afternoon, if there was anything to input. His dismissal had nothing to do with the accountant coming—he just didn't want me.

Once the computer was running, I fired up Quickbooks and created an accountant's file and transferred it to a flash drive. That done, I spent the rest of the morning updating our database of guests, vendors, and other contacts. I was just finishing up when a small man with brown hair and an ill-fitting suit walked into the office.

"Hi," he said, and his voice was surprisingly strong, a drastic contrast to his mousy look. "I'm James Prescott, here to meet with Weston."

I forced a smile and introduced myself. "I made a copy of Quickbooks for you," I said, handing the flash drive to him.

"Mr. Prescott. Weston Beaumont." Weston offered his hand to the accountant then turned to me. "Laney, could you go check on the horses, please? And when you're done, Rory could use a hand with his chores today."

"What? Don't you want—"

He cut me with his look. "Mr. Prescott and I have some things to go over here. Please, just go."

Mr. Prescott shuffled his feet, purposely looking anywhere but at Weston and me. Fury built beneath my skin, racing through my veins and cementing to my bones. I wanted to scream at him, punch him, whatever I had to do to get him to snap out of this mood. But I couldn't. Not with Craig's accountant here. So instead, I clenched my hands into fists at my side, spun on my heel, and stormed out of the office, letting the door slam behind me.

# DAY FiFTY-THREE

"HEY, I GRABBED SOME BAGELS. You want one?" I called out as I entered the office this morning, a bag of bagels in one hand and my giant almond steamer balanced precariously on my other arm so I could open the door. I was sick of the awkwardness that had permeated the office since that morning under the bridge. Over whatever funk Weston had been in. After my anger dissolved yesterday, I figured maybe if I made an effort to bring things back to normal, Weston would follow suit, so I made a plan for this morning. Now, I looked up, and the door swung back into me as I stood in surprise. Hot milk sloshed from my cup and onto my shirt sleeve. "Oh, hey, Angie," I said.

"Good morning, Laney." A smile lit her face, smoothing her scars into her otherwise flawless features.

Bag held in front of me, as if it would somehow corroborate my story, I said, "You want a bagel? I got the ones with everything on them." Which were Weston's favorites.

"No, thanks." She lowered herself into Weston's desk chair, using her arms to slow her descent.

"So, what's up?"

Angie shuffled some papers on the desk then looked up at me. "Craig and Weston went to meet with the bankers this morning." A flash of worry crossed her face. How important was this meeting to our survival? "I'm filling in for Weston."

"I can handle the office," I said. Then added, so it wouldn't sound like I didn't want her there, "But you can hang out if you want."

"Actually, Rory is in Missoula picking up the new beach loungers. Craig asked Karissa to spend the morning getting the beach ready, and I'm sure she would love some help. And company." Again, Angie's face broke into a dazzling smile.

Leaving a bagel and tiny envelope of cream cheese on the desk in case she changed her mind, I headed off to spend my day on the beach.

Karissa was at the shoreline when I arrived, earbuds in, her iPod turned up so high I could hear the faint roar of music from ten yards away. She had a rake in her hand, and she alternated between using it to smooth the sand and collect the lake junk the lake had deposited on the shore overnight—Larch needles, seaweed, and tons of goose shit—and using it as an air guitar, jamming hardcore to whatever obscure band she was listening to. I sneaked up behind her, careful not to let my shadow cross into her line of vision. I reached out, let my hands hover over her shoulders, and—

She spun so fast her head was nothing but a pink blur in my vision. The rake's handle caught me below my breast bone, and all the air pressed from my lungs. I doubled over and gasped.

"Fucking hell, Laney! You scared the shit out of me." She ripped the earbuds out of her ears and glared at me.

When I could stand again, I motioned to her pocket. "Whatchya listening to?"

"It's a demo Rory gave me. It's actually pretty good."

She held the earbuds out toward me, and I tapped them into my own ears. The previous song was winding down, so I was given a brief period of silence before a guitar cut back in, feedback high, but somehow pleasing. It reverberated through my skull for a full five seconds before the bass drum started, giving a steady beat. Pretty soon, they were joined by a second guitar and an electric violin. Rory sped up the drums, crashing the cymbals, brushing across the snare. The bass drum pounded faster than I thought possible, and I realized that he'd finally conquered the double pedal he was struggling with so much last summer. The music pulsed its way into me, filling me head, body, and soul. It was like I was one with the song. It understood my hurts and my thoughts, and the wailing guitar and weeping violin played exclusively for me. I closed my eyes and faced the sun, letting its heat mix with the euphoria I was feeling.

The music faded back down until only the violin played on, longing and sorrowful in the background, a melody that tugged at my memory, but that I couldn't quite place. And then the words started, and my eyes popped back open. Rory was singing, rather than their lead, Cash or whatever his name was. Straining to hear his words, his voice richly melodic, but soft, I motioned for Karissa to turn it up.

*Soft skin shining in the silver moon;*
*Red line cutting across white marble;*
*Little girl, unable to see*
*Anything but the relief it brings*

*Where are you now, girl of fire?*
*Where did you go? Why did you leave?*
*Turn around, turn around, back to me.*
*There is no love at the razor's edge.*

I ripped the earbuds away from me and tossed them back to Karissa. I couldn't listen to any more, couldn't stand to hear Rory's pleading voice in my ears, singing the song I knew had to be about me. Did Karissa play me that one on purpose? She was watching me like she was afraid I might explode, but her face held no signs of guilt. Maybe she hadn't known.

"Hey, are you feeling okay?"

A hand to my forehead revealed I'd broken out in a sweat. If my churning stomach was any indication, my face was probably even more pale than normal. Not trusting my voice, I nodded to her, forcing a plastic-feeling smile on. I tucked my shaking hands against my sides.

Karissa returned my smile, skepticism clear on her face. "They've gotten really good this year, haven't they? I think they might have a shot once they get to Texas."

"Yeah." My voice was gruff.

She wrapped her earbuds around her iPod and dropped the bundle into her bag. Handing me her rake, she ran to the boathouse for a second one, and we set to work cleaning up the water's edge.

An hour later, we'd successfully cleaned the debris off the sand, leaving perfect rake lines in our wake. The guests' sand toys were piled neatly at the top of the beach, and their chairs had all been folded and leaned against the lone tree offering shade to the sand. Karissa took my rake from me and headed back to the boat house as Rory began backing his truck across the lawn toward us. His pickup bed was overflowing with large boxes, tie-down straps straining to keep everything inside. He was lucky he made it back from Missoula without losing anything.

"I think you might need a bigger truck," I called as he hopped out of the cab.

He looked over his packing job. "Yeah." He ran a hand through his hair, which was long enough now to fall into his eyes. "I was supposed to take Craig's, but it's acting weird, so he took it to the shop. I got everything in just fine." Challenging his point, the boxes shifted, emitting a low groan. Rory shrugged.

Karissa joined us, and we set to work liberating his cargo, alternating positions every few seconds so we could use our bodies to hold the boxes in the truck bed while Rory loosened the straps. It took about fifteen minutes—and easily three times as many curse words—but we got all the boxes on the ground with only one smashed finger to show for our work.

We all three dropped onto boxes, breathing hard. "So," I said to Rory, "the band sounds good."

His head jerked up. He recovered quickly, but not before I saw the surprise in his eyes. "Kris let me listen," I explained.

"Oh, yeah. Thanks."

"I didn't realize you sang?"

At my words, Rory's face turned a deep shade of scarlet and his shoulders hitched a tiny bit closer to his ears. He didn't answer me—he didn't need to; the look on his face was enough to tell me what I wanted to know. He wrote the song. It was about me. And, with the slightest glimmer of his eye, he showed me how proud of it he was.

I had no idea how long Rory had known about my wrist. Maybe Craig told him when my mother passed on the news. Maybe he'd barely seen the scar and the song was new. Maybe, maybe, maybe. But he knew, and for the first time, I realized how much he was affected by it. Looking into his face now, I was reminded of the pain laced through his words, lining his rich voice with a raw edge.

It never occurred to me that night five months ago how my friends would react. As I pulled the blade across my skin, my mother's face flashed into my mind. Angry, hurt, embarrassed. But never sad. The vision was quickly replaced by one of *him*, his face too close to my own, the pungent smell of stale alcohol crossing over me. The red across his cheeks and in his eyes, the sweat building on his forehead and temples. It all built up, and I pushed the blade harder.

Maybe I would have stopped had my mind been filled with a picture of Rory, smiling. Or Karissa, ranting about whatever cause she'd taken on. I guess she was right, I did forget about my friends this year.

"Okay," Karissa's voice cut through my thoughts, "what the hell is going on with you two?"

My facial muscles struggled to reform into an expression of indifference. "Nothing," I said, and I was pleasantly surprised at how calm my voice sounded. "Tired."

Rory jumped to his feet, acting much more normal than I felt. "Let's get going on these," he said and pulled his polo shirt over his head. Sweat glimmered on his chest, and I was reminded again how much he'd changed since I'd seen him last summer. "Aren't you two hot?" he asked. "It's like eighty degrees out here already, and you're dressed like freaking Eskimos."

Instinctively, I clasped the sleeves of my long-sleeved t-shirt between my palms, pulling the fabric tight over my wrists. Karissa crossed her arms tightly over her chest, and I realized for the first time that she, too, was wearing long sleeves. Karissa, who lived in tank tops, shorts, and flip flops. How the hell had I not noticed before?

"I'm fine," she said tersely. "Let's get this over with."

The first chair took us a full forty-five minutes to assemble. It came with an instruction pack, but everything was written in some other language—Dutch, maybe?—and the pictures weren't worth a shit, so we had to wing it. We only put four or five pieces on incorrectly before we started to figure out what went where. Once we got it together, though, we worked out a pretty quick system, and each of the other six only set us back about ten minutes. We finished up the last chair and started to pull the side tables—thankfully already assembled—out of their boxes.

"Hey, I hate to be a slacker, but I'm already, like, five minutes late for practice," Rory said.

"No problem." Karissa threw her car keys to him. They hit his outstretched hand and bounced into the grass, where he bent to pick them up. "Take my car so we can load these boxes into the back of your truck."

He nodded his thanks to Kris and ran for the parking lot. As soon as he was out of earshot, she turned to me. "All right, he's gone. Now what the hell was up between you two earlier?"

My thumb brushed across the opposite wrist involuntarily, feeling the raised edge of my scar. My brain told me to stay quiet, desperate to keep the rules I'd been so good about enforcing. But my mouth begged to finally say something. "Did you listen to the song Rory sings?" I heard myself say, as if from far away.

Her surprise almost knocked me over. "No shit? Rory sings one?"

"I thought you'd already heard."

"That was my first time through the album. Why? Is it

terrible? Oh, god, do we have to break it to him?"

"No," I said, surprised I felt no relief she'd not yet listened to the song. "It's actually pretty good. It's just—you should listen to it later."

She pulled her iPod from her pocket and started to unravel the earbuds. "Not now," I said. "Later, okay?"

"Um...okay? Whatever. Later is fine." She pocketed the iPod again, and we took turns heaving empty boxes into Rory's truck.

"You want lunch?" I asked when we finished. "I'm starving."

"Yeah. Let me move the truck off the grass." She jingled the keys in her hand. "Meet you at your cabin in a few minutes?"

I nodded. With a look over our work—the beach did look better with the loungers and tables lining the edge where it met the grass—I turned toward my cabin.

Nearly at my door, I saw Craig heading into the woods toward the stables. My gaze scanned the lot until it landed on Weston's car, and fire raged in the back of my mind, my sudden anger surprising me. Without thinking, I spun on my heel and marched back to the office. The door slammed against its hinges when I jerked it open, and I hoped Angie wasn't still there to witness my tantrum.

Thankfully, she was already gone, and the only person in the office was exactly who I was coming for. Weston sat in his chair, bent over some paper work, his black-framed glasses back on his face. He looked up at me calmly, the slamming of the door behind me having zero effect on him, and his cool ease enraged me even further.

He stared at me, not even saying hello, as if he knew I was here to yell. So I did.

"What the hell is your problem?"

"I'm sorry?"

"What. Is. Wrong. With. You." Each of my words was punctuated by more heat rising into my face.

"I'm not sure I know what you mean." He didn't look confused at all. He looked scared, and a little...sad?

"Bull shit. You know exactly what I mean. You took me to that bridge—"

"I'm sorry," he interrupted, and the fight fell out of me as fast as it had come. It was as if I were being physically deflated. His sorrow and apology was written all over his face.

"Sorry?" The word escaped my mouth on a sigh.

"Yes. I am so sorry about that. I never should have—"

"Wait. You're sorry about what now?" The returned edge to my voice pleased me.

"The bridge," he replied, almost a whisper. "We...shouldn't have..."

I dropped into my chair and tilted my head back so I could stare at the ceiling. "Fuck," I moaned. He was *sorry* about the bridge?

His chair wheels squeaked as he rolled closer to me, slowly. My head snapped back toward him. "That is not what you should be sorry about," I snapped. He stared at me, wide-eyed, so I continued, "I'm not sorry about what happened under that bridge, and neither should you be. But all this horse shit since then? Since when do you treat me like I'm some stranger—some business contact? What happened?"

Weston removed his glasses and rubbed a hand over his eyes. As he rubbed, I noticed a crease forming between his eyebrows and remembered why he was gone this morning. Had the meeting with the banker gone well? What if I was dumping all my feelings and neuroses on him immediately after he and Craig had been handed bad news?

"Laney," he whispered. My heart shattered at the pain in his voice. "I *am* sorry. You are so much more than a business contact to me. You have to know that." He held his hand up to stall my interjection. "But we—*I* shouldn't have...what happened between us shouldn't have."

"Why?"

"I'm twenty-three years old. A college graduate. And you're—"

"Seventeen," I finished for him.

He nodded, and the rage that had pulled me into the office in the first place roiled beneath the surface again.

"You didn't care about me being seventeen when you were making me come under the bridge," I spat at him.

His reaction to my crudeness was exactly what I'd hoped for, but his cringe and blush left me feeling empty, rather than justified. His hands raked through his hair, forearms straining and knuckles whitening when he grasped the ponytail at the end. "You're right," he said, "but I should have."

I stood and pushed my chair away from me; one long stride had me standing directly above him. Weston jumped to his feet before I had a chance to lower myself into his lap. "Come on, West," I said in my most seductive voice. "I'm practically eighteen. What's the big deal? It's not like my age mattered before."

He tilted his face to the ceiling, eyes closed, and pulled a long breath through his nose. With a groan, he said, "It's different...now." He looked back down at me, his eyes piercing.

"Different? Different than leading me along all fucking summer? Taking me out hiking, holding my hand? Different than what we did in the lake?"

"I'm sorry about that, too. I told you it couldn't happen again, Laney." He grasped his hair in a fist again, pulling chunks out of his ponytail.

I dropped into my chair. "Are you kidding me right now? You can't"—I fought the urge to scream—"you can't just tell me no more and then move on like it never happened. That's not how life works. We kissed in the lake. Under the bridge? That happened."

"You're right," he said, solemn. "You have to know..." His eyes squeezed shut, and his hands clenched into fists at his sides. "I didn't intend for any of this to happen. I shouldn't have let it. But you—I can't get you out of my head, Laney. I thought I could make it work just being your friend, but obviously I can't. I'm sorry."

"Oh my god, stop saying you're sorry about this like I'm a big fucking mistake!" My hands shook in my lap, and my eyes prickled with tears I refused to let surface.

Weston's face softened, and he reached toward me, hand stopping just short of my cheek. Instead he grabbed my hand, pulling me to my feet then stepping back, creating an uncomfortable space between us. "Look at me, Laney."

Reluctantly, I raised my face toward his. He stared directly into my eyes, face sincere. "You are *not* a mistake. Never could you be. But I need some time, okay?"

*Fuck this.* I looked up at him with my eyes wide, my lips slightly parted. The face I'd used more times than I could count to snag whatever guy I wanted. Raising myself to my toes, I snaked my arms around his neck and pressed my lips softly to his chin.

Weston tensed under my touch, and I pressed myself

closer to him. He groaned deep in his throat, pleasure mixed with pain. He turned his face toward me slightly, allowing our lips to caress each other. And then his hands clasped my own, pulling them back from around his neck and pressing them to my sides. His chin jerked away from me, and he stepped back, creating a gap between us again. Eyes closed, a pained expression on his face, he leaned down and pressed his lips to my forehead, lingering there until my skin burned with the kiss. Breath tickled the hairs at the base of my neck when he leaned down and whispered into my ear, "Three weeks, love," and walked out of the office.

I stared at the open door, following his trail with my eyes. My fingers slid across the place on my forehead where his mouth had been only moments before, and my heart jumped.

Three weeks.

In three weeks, I would turn eighteen.

# DAY FiFTY-SEVEN

MY EARS WERE RiNGING.

"So, what did you think?" Rory asked, shoving his drumsticks into his back pocket.

"It was definitely loud."

"Very funny." He nudged me with his shoulders, and I wrapped my arms around his waist.

"You know I'm kidding. You guys were amazing." His body shook with silent laughter. "Seriously! I was impressed. Really."

Rory had burst into the office first thing this morning, asking if I could come to band rehearsal after work. They'd booked a gig in Missoula for Saturday night, and they needed to test the new set out on me and Karissa. I'd come over as soon as Weston and I locked up the office, and watched as the band—currently called Into the Lion—set up in Rory's basement and got to work tuning. Once everything was ready, we milled around, waiting for Karissa.

She never showed up.

The set was manic, the energy amazing. Cash worked the imaginary crowd, using every inch of the cement-floor stage. Charisma spilled off him; it wasn't hard to imagine him performing at major venues, audiences of thousands screaming his name, throngs of groupies waiting in the wings.

The bass guitarist kept to his side of the room, in his own world, jamming to the beat. He was a big fan of slap-bass, which gave a fun, unique sound. Opposite him was a small Japanese guy who practically made love to his electric violin for the whole show.

And in the back of it all, keeping the other three together, leading the charge, was Rory. His curls tumbled over his forehead, sweat dripping off them by the end. His arms flew around his drum kit, blurring with the speed of his motion. Cash may have been the face of the band, but Rory was obviously the heart, pounding out the rhythm, giving life to the music. He was incredible.

But, despite the obvious love he had for his music and the energy with which he played, I could tell he wasn't connected to the band tonight. His eyes flicked between the basement door and the wall clock almost constantly, and his scowl deepened the later it got.

Now, the two of us waved to the other members of Into the Lion as they walked to their houses. "Thank you for coming," Rory said.

"Of course. Hey, I'm sorry—" I was going to say, *I'm sorry Kris didn't make it*, but the look on Rory's face stopped me cold. His head cocked to the side for a moment, and then he took off at a run, nearly knocking me off the porch as he rushed past. I scrambled to follow him.

He burst into Karissa's yard, shoving the rickety gate to the back open with a clank. I rounded the corner just in time to hear Karissa's dad.

"You're as bad as your whore sister," he screamed, his red face about two inches from Karissa's unnaturally pale one, spittle flying from his mouth onto her cheeks. "She was a little cunt, too."

Rory's hand connected with the side of Mr. Goodman's head with a sickening crack. The older man lost his footing, and Rory toppled over him onto the grass. Holding him to the ground with a knee on his chest, Rory pounded his fist into Karissa's dad's face over and over again, his whole body shaking.

"Rory!" Karissa's shrill voice rang out over the sound of bone hitting flesh. "Stop!"

His hand froze in the air, blood dripping from his

knuckles. Mr. Goodman's face was a painting of red, but he was still conscious, moaning and rolling his head back and forth in the grass. As if he were in a trance, Rory rose and turned to Karissa, who stood shaking violently. Staring at her father.

"Kris," Rory said carefully, "I'm sorry. I—"

Her eyes hardened, and she balled her hands into fists at her sides. "It's okay," she said then turned to me. "Can I stay with you for a while?"

"Of course," I stammered.

"Then let's go."

✳ ✳ ✳

Rory and I stood together in front of Craig and Angie's front door. Karissa was sleeping in my bed. After a refusal to call the police, she'd not said a word to us for the rest of the evening. She'd packed a bag and crawled into Rory's truck, where she sat staring out the window until we got back to the resort. She stalked into my cabin, unpacked her few belongings, and dropped onto the bed. She was asleep in minutes.

Now, Rory held his hand in front of the door, hesitating to knock. We were betraying our best friend, we knew, but there was no other choice. I nodded, and he pounded on the wood.

Angie opened the door. Her face was clean of makeup, and her hair was piled on top of her head in a messy bun. She wore a too-large t-shirt and yoga pants. It was obvious they were heading to bed, but she opened the door wider and invited us in.

We sat in the living room, Craig and Angie on one couch with me and Rory on the other, like some kind of surreal double date. "What's going on?" Craig asked.

Rory and I stared at each other. He rubbed the fingers of one hand over the cut knuckles of the other. Angie's gaze followed the movement, her eyes widening when she saw his injury.

"It's about Karissa," I began, and Rory and I took turns filling in the details of the evening.

Craig and Angie listened patiently, and when we were done, he asked, "Where is she now?"

"Sleeping in my cabin."

Angie rose from the couch and walked to the back of the apartment. The three of us sat in silence until she returned, a small box in her hands. Passing it to me, she said, "You think you can patch him up? This baby has made my stomach way too weak." She gave Rory's bleeding knuckles a glance and cringed.

I set to work cleaning up Rory's hand, wiping the blood away with the cold washcloth Angie draped over the edge of the box. His hand shook in mine, and he cringed as the clothe scraped across the broken skin. "Sorry," I whispered. As gently as I could, I spread Neosporin over his cuts then wrapped his hand in a long strip of gauze.

When I finished, I looked back up at Angie and Craig, Rory's hand still held between mine in my lap. "What do we do?"

Craig ran a hand over his face, and for a moment he looked much older than he was. "We have to report him," he said.

"Can we do that?" Rory asked. "I mean, we've never actually seen him do anything more than yell at her. And there's no way she'll admit to anything more."

"They might take him in on emotional abuse," Angie said. "You two will have to talk to the police, though. Reports have to be made by either the victim or a direct witness."

"She'll hate that," Rory said.

"She'll hate *us*. Can't we maybe—" I stopped talking when Angie shook her head.

"I'm sorry, you two, but I can't just let this go. We'll have to report."

Craig groaned beside her. "Ang is right. Kris is welcome to stay here as long as she wants. Hell, I hope she stays here until she goes to college. But we have to report Mr. Goodman for that to happen. I'm sorry, kiddo."

They were right. I knew it—I knew before we even got there. But still my mind revolted against the idea of going to the police. It felt like a betrayal to Karissa, no matter how right it was. For all my bravado and desire to be my own person, I was relieved to be able to turn to my dad for this. I don't know if I would have had the strength to go to the police without his and Angie's push.

"So," I said, "do we...?"

"Go to bed, sweetie," Angie said. "She's okay for the night. We'll take care of this in the morning."

We said our goodbyes, Angie hugging me extra tight, keeping me in her arms for an almost awkwardly long time. As Rory and I walked back down the stairs and into the night, I grabbed his hand and prayed we wouldn't lose our best friend for good.

# DAY SiXTY-ONE

THE DOOR TO MY CABIN SLAMMED into the wall and Karissa stormed into the room. I shot up in bed, pulling the comforter to my chin. "What—"

"No!" she screamed. "You don't get to ask questions. Just shut up."

I stared at her, wide-eyed. Her face was wet with tears and deep red, rage clear in her eyes. "When the fuck were you going to tell me you had my dad arrested?"

"I'm sorry." I had no other words.

She stomped through the room, grabbing her few things and throwing them into a backpack. Makeup clattered to the floor as she brushed all the items off the vanity and into her bag. She swore under her breath and bent down to pick it up.

I slid my phone off the bedside table and tapped out a quick text message to Rory. To Karissa, I said, "Pease don't go."

"Screw you."

"You can't go back to that, Kris."

Her whirlwind froze for a second, her hand hovering over her bag, and then she was back to it, searching the area for anything she'd forgotten. "It's fine," she said. "He's in a program now, learning to deal with his anger. I'm okay." But her eyes refused to touch mine when she said it.

Rory's truck sounded from outside, engine wailing followed by squealing brakes and crunching gravel. He was in the cabin faster than seemed possible. "What the hell is going on?"

Karissa turned to me, her face even deeper red, if possible. "You told *Rory*? You really can't keep shit to yourself, can you?"

"Please, Karissa," Rory said, crossing the room to her. "Please just stay here."

Her face crumpled, and she spun away from him to face the wall. I sat on my bed, silent and unmoving, afraid to set her off again. Her shoulders rose sharply, and a small sniffle escaped her. Rory stood behind her, frozen in space, apparently just as worried of movement as I was. Time hovered in limbo, the three of us in an uncomfortable stand-off. Karissa's small frame shook silently, and she dropped her bag.

Finally, she turned to face us, wiping tears from her face with the backs of her hands. She stared at Rory for a moment then shifted her focus to me, her gaze boring through me. "You two don't get a say in this. It's my life. *Mine.*" She picked her bag back up.

Rory closed the gap between them and took her upper arms in his hands. She flinched away, but he didn't let go. "Kris," he said with such pain in his voice it was like being cut with a hot knife, "please, *please* don't go. We're sorry. We should have told you about your dad. Don't go back to him."

For a moment, I thought he'd gotten through to her. She stared up at him, and her features softened. The grip on her bag loosened, but then tightened immediately back up. Her eyes turned to ice again, and she jerked out of his grasp. Without even sparing a glance back at us, she walked out of my cabin, slamming the door behind her.

"Hey," I said, and Rory turned to me, his eyes misty. "Thanks for coming."

He didn't answer, just stared at me, his head shaking slowly from side to side. At his side, his hands clenched into fists, then loosened, over and over again. The muscles in his jaw twitched, and his breath came in deep huffs. Finally, he said, "I need...I just have to get out of here."

I watched him leave, listening until I could no longer

hear the whine of his engine. Then I sent Weston a text message, letting him know I'd be late.

His response was almost immediate. *I heard. I'm so sorry. Take as long as you need.*

With my phone clutched in my hand, I buried myself back in my covers and tried to sleep the past half hour out of existence.

✳   ✳   ✳

There were only two vehicles in the parking lot of The Place when I pulled in. Derek had called ten minutes ago, asking me to come get Rory before he got into trouble. He'd been there all night, not answering his phone, not returning text messages.

I got out of the car and headed to the door, but stopped when I saw the figure sitting on the ground, leaned up against the side of the building. "Rory?" I stepped a little closer.

He was a mess. He wore the same wrinkled clothes he'd had on this morning—what he'd slept in last night, I was sure—and he reeked of stale booze. His eyes were swollen and bloodshot, and his face shone with a combination of sweat and tears. I reached down to him. "Let's get you home."

It took several minutes to coax him from the wall and into the car, but once he made it, he settled into the seat and closed his eyes. I started the engine back up and headed toward his house.

"She's gonna ruin her life," he said, and more tears streamed down his face. "I jus' wanna help." He belched then moaned. I prayed he wouldn't puke in my car.

"Me, too."

"Why'd she go back?"

I pulled the car to the curb and cut the engine. "I don't know why she left. We just have to deal with it and help her however we can."

He barked out a cruel laugh. "I don't want to deal with it."

"I know you don't." I got out of the car and circled around to open his door. "Let's get you inside."

It was some sort of miracle, but I managed to steer Rory into his room without waking up his parents or any of his younger siblings. After tucking him into bed, I made my way to the kitchen for a glass of water. By the time I returned, he was already asleep with his mouth hanging open, snoring unevenly. I put the glass on the milk crate by the head of his bed and adjusted his blanket. I bent over and kissed him softly on the corner of his mouth. "It'll be okay," I told him.

I hoped with my whole being for it to be true.

# DAY SIXTY-FOUR

"HEY!" RORY SNAPPED HIS fingers in front of my face. "Where are you?"

"Huh?"

"It's your turn."

Automatically, I pulled a cardboard tile from the stack in front of me. With barely a glance, I attached it to an existing road and plopped one of my small wooden men onto it. Rory scoffed. "You're totally not into this game, are you?"

"Sorry." He raked the tiles off the table and into a mesh bag. "We don't have to quit," I protested half-heartedly.

"It's fine, really. This game is hard to learn if you're not into it."

Rory had shown up at my cabin five minutes after the

work day ended, the bag of game pieces in his hand. It was some kind of strategy game where the players took turns building roads and castles then claiming them with wooden figures. He swore I would love it, so we set it up on the kitchen counter to play.

That was half an hour ago, and I hadn't figured out what I was doing yet. Rory finished picking up the pieces and went to the kitchen to get a drink.

"How's your hand?" I asked when he returned with a glass for each of us. There was a faint cut on one knuckle still, and the back of his hand was a yellowish bruise.

He set the glasses down and tightened his hand into a fist several times. "Doing great," he said with ice in his voice. "Better than the bastard's face."

We'd not seen each other since I picked him up at The Place, and neither of us dared bring up that night now. I didn't even know how much he remembered.

"Have you seen her?" he asked, his voice soft and sad.

I shook my head. "She told Craig she needed a few days off to help her mom."

His shoulders slumped. More silence.

"You miss her, don't you?"

"Don't you?" he shot back.

"Of course." But something told me it wasn't the same.

He downed the rest of his water and thunked the glass back onto the counter. "I—" He threw himself back in the chair with his hands behind his head. The skin on his temples pulled tight when he clutched his hair in fists. "I don't know how to help her."

"Me, either," I whispered.

He stared at me, his eyes burning. "Can I ask you something?"

I nodded, dread settling in the pit of my stomach.

"Why do you push people away? Why can't you let someone help you?"

He looked frantic, like he was moments away from cracking, and, not for the first time, but perhaps with the most clarity, I realized how profoundly I affected those around me. It was so easy to fold in on myself, to focus on my own pain and forget about the people who loved me. It had become such habit by now that not even the desperate look on Rory's face could coax me to unfold.

Instead of answering him, I said, "You told me a while back that you thought Kris was embarrassed of her dad. You're right. I'm sure she's humiliated."

"But she didn't do anything wrong."

"I know, but you know how she is. She's proud. And her stubborn streak could reach the moon."

He dropped his arms back to his lap. The fire left his eyes, replaced with a glassy sheen. "I don't know what to do," he moaned.

"Be her friend," I said.

"How?"

"I don't know," I admitted. Then, "Don't give up on her. When she finally comes around, please let her."

After I quit the team, I stopped eating lunch with the other runners—my closest friends at school. I spent lunch periods in Burt, picking at whatever I'd brought from home. For a while, they tried to get me to come back and eat with them again. I was asked every day at first, then a couple times a week. One day as I pulled apart a stick of string cheese, I realized I couldn't remember the last time I'd been invited to eat inside. I'd pushed my friends away, and they'd let me. I couldn't let the same happen to Karissa, no matter how hard she tried.

"Of course," Rory said softly. "I'll always be there for her."

And I knew he would.

# DAY SiXTY-SEVEN

I STOOD IN FRONT OF THE mirror, fighting my hair into place. Red curls cascaded over my right shoulder, standing in stark contrast to the poison green of my dress. I pinned a glimmering flower behind my ear and turned to admire the view from the back.

The dress clung to my body nicely, highlighting my subtle curves. The deep v-back showed off the smooth skin between my shoulder blades, and for a moment I was loathe to cover it. Maybe I shouldn't. I fastened my bracelet around my wrist and turned again, taking in the full effect.

The skin around my collar bones shimmered, and a slight blush rose on my chest as I imagined how Weston would react to this dress.

I didn't have to wait long. A light rap sounded on the

door, and my neighbor peeked his head inside. "Laney, they're about to start. Are you ready?"

"Coming!" With one final look, I turned on my heel and walked into the main room. Weston was standing just inside the door, studying a piece of paper he held in his hand. He wore khakis and a light-blue button-up. The top two buttons hung open, revealing a leather cord with a thick metal disk resting at the hollow of his throat. I fought to control my breathing. "Hi," I said.

His head rose to meet mine, and he uttered a soft, "Whoa." My cheeks flamed. "You— " He paused and took a deep breath, a soft blush rising in his cheeks. "You ready?"

Nodding, I crossed the room, and he held out his arm to me. Slowly, I placed my hand on his. His breath hitched, and he froze in his spot. Was this too much for him? I started to pull away, but Weston relaxed and pulled my hand through the crook of his elbow. With a deep breath, he led me out of the cabin.

We made our way across the lawn to the rec lodge, and I pulled the light cardigan I'd grabbed on the way out the door over my shoulders, securing the sleeve around my wrist, acutely aware of the soft fabric rubbing the skin of my back.

Angie had decorated the lodge with little twinkle lights, and a sheer white tent stood outside. Paper lanterns hung from the trees, casting a soft glow on the grounds.

Small white folding chairs with wide blue ribbons tied around the backs lined the sides of an aisle leading across the lawn to a carved altar.

"Wow," I whispered. "That's gorgeous."

We walked up to the altar, stopping just short of standing under it. "Her brother made it," Weston said. "It was delivered a few hours ago."

"Delivered? Isn't he here?"

He shook his head, and a dark expression covered his face. "No. He doesn't approve of the marriage. He only sent it because he believes in propriety."

I watched Angie and Craig approach from the far side of the lawn. She was radiant in her flowing lavender dress. "Doesn't approve? What's wrong?"

He lowered his voice. "Angie grew up on the reservation, did you know that?" I shook my head. "Yeah. Her family was pretty traditional, too. They were excited for her to go to college, but pretty unhappy that she decided to go so far away. When she took the job working back on the reservation, her brother was elated. Until then, he was scared she would leave them."

Glancing over my shoulder to make sure they were still too far away to hear us, I asked, "So what happened?"

"She left her job and is marrying a white man."

"Seriously?"

He nodded. "Joshua likes your dad just fine, but he feels

like Angie is leaving her roots—and the family—behind."

I opened my mouth to respond, but he jerked his head the slightest bit, and I snapped it back shut. Angie and Craig stepped up next to us. "You kids ready?" Angie asked.

"I don't see why we have to practice this," Craig grumbled. "I can walk in a straight line just fine. Let's just skip to the food."

It turned out that, while Craig could walk just fine, he did need practice with the rest of the ceremony. Weston and I had to walk down the aisle about four hundred times before it was decided we all knew what we were doing. Each time he held his arm out and I laced my own around his elbow, my body blazed with the contact. I would have been happy to walk the aisle all night. As it was, we didn't head inside for dinner until the sun had already lowered beneath the mountain ridge.

Dinner was a wonderful spread of finger foods from The Place, which stood in stark contrast to the formality of the rehearsal. I loaded my plate with chicken strips, fried clams, baby sandwiches, and an array of chips, veggies, fruits, and their various dips. All around me, people I barely recognized chatted with each other; across the room, I spotted Angie sitting alone at the bar.

"Hey," I said, sliding in next to her, "this is quite the party for a couple of people who wanted to elope."

She smiled—a little sadly, I thought. "Your dad knows everybody in this town, I swear. We should have gotten married tonight. Everyone was already here. I don't see why we have to go through this again tomorrow."

"We have to go through it all again because you have to dress up in a pretty dress and have everyone 'oh' and 'ah' over how beautiful you are. Plus, maybe tomorrow, Craig will take his baseball cap off."

She sighed. Strange how it didn't bother me at all—she sounded nothing like my mother. "I don't know, Laney. Sometimes I think maybe we should have eloped after all."

"Ang," I said, "what's going on?"

Her eyes filled with tears. "Your dad didn't even tell you about the baby."

"Hey, it's okay. It's not a big deal."

"Maybe, but I can't help but think..." She turned her focus back to her food. "I put on the dress last night to make sure it didn't need any adjustments....I feel so foolish wearing a white wedding dress eight months pregnant." A tear ran down her nose.

"Hey, it's okay. It's exciting, you know? You guys are starting a new life together. The baby is part of you now, and you look great."

"Thanks, but that's not it, exactly."

"What is it then?" I asked.

"Laney, why do you think your father didn't tell

anyone about this baby?"

I shrugged. "You know Craig. He's not exactly the touchy feely type. He probably figured people would find out along the way."

"Or, maybe he didn't tell anyone because he's ashamed."

"You're crazy! He loves you. He's *marrying* you. And I know he is excited about this baby. Why on Earth would he be ashamed?"

She stared past me out the window, and more tears spilled over. Her chin quivered. Slowly, she reached a hand up and ran her fingers across the scar on her cheek. The truth hit me like a Sherman Tank.

"Oh, god, I didn't realize." Heat rose in my cheeks. "When Weston told me what happened, I had no idea—" My dinner pushed up my throat. If I didn't get out of there, poor Rory was going to be cleaning my puke off the lodge floor. I clasped Angie's hand in my own. "I'm so sorry, I—" I threw a hand over my mouth and ran for the door.

Craig and Weston looked up from their table as I ran past. Someone called my name, but I was already out the door, the familiar whooshing filling my head. I ran past the white chairs with their blue ribbons, past the tent and all the twinkle lights. Trees blurred in my vision, and tears streamed down my face. Rory sat beside the tent, a bowl of chips in his lap. I ran past, ignoring his puzzled look.

By the time I hit the pavement of the highway, I found my stride. The night air blew the hair off my shoulder, and sweat dewed up on my face and neck. The thud-thud-thud of my ballet flats hitting the road mixed with the roar in my ears, completely shutting out the forest sounds. I willed the night to swallow me whole, to make me disappear completely. I was terrified to stop running, to let the pain catch me. Maybe if I never stopped running, I would never have to turn and face my past.

A mile and a half later, I found myself doubled over in front of The Place. My throat burned and my sides ached. My stomach spasmed again, trying to force its nonexistent contents to the ground to join my dinner. I wiped my mouth on the hem of my cardigan and straightened.

Derek stood leaning against a lamppost. Great. This was so not the image of me I wanted to give him. I turned and stumbled back toward the road.

"Hey," he called after me, "hold up."

"I need to go home." My head spun. My toe hit a rock, and I pitched forward. Gravel dug into my palms; I rolled onto my back and threw an arm over my eyes. A rock stabbed my back below my left shoulder blade, but I couldn't bring myself to roll off it.

"Come on, girl." Derek's arms wrapped around me. He lifted me off the ground and carried me toward the bar. I buried my head in his chest, letting blackness overtake me, leaving the night behind.

"Laney?" Someone was shaking me. "Laney, it's time to get up, love."

I pried my eyes open—the lids felt like sandpaper scratching over my corneas—and looked around. I lay in a bed, facing a window. It was still dark out. None of the decor of the room was familiar to me, but I knew where I was—the blanket I held tucked to my chin smelled like Derek. God, I hoped we didn't do anything stupid. I rolled over to face him.

Weston sat on the bed, looking down at me. I bolted upright. "What time is it?"

"About two."

"In the morning? Ugh."

Derek came into the room, my cardigan in his hand. "Here," he said and tossed it to me. "You got this pretty good. I washed it for you."

"Thanks," I mumbled. "Why's West here?"

"Ouch, thanks," Weston said with a faux look of hurt on his face.

Derek laughed. "I called him. You were in pretty bad shape, but I couldn't leave, so I called for someone to come get you."

"And you picked Weston?"

"Actually," Weston said, "he called Karissa, who was fast asleep, so Rory answered her phone."

"Okay," I said, only partially understanding that wherever Kris was sleeping, Rory was with her, "so then why isn't Rory here?"

"Because Rory met a new friend tonight in the form of Long Island Iced Tea. He's not in proper form to go anywhere right now."

"Anyway," Derek said, "you can stay here if you want, but I figured since your daddy's getting married tomorrow, you should probably get home."

Oh, the wedding. I couldn't believe the scene I'd caused at the rehearsal. Craig and Angie were probably so mad at me for ruining the evening. Angie's face as I pressed her about the baby came to my mind. How could I have been so damn stupid? She'd obviously been upset, but I wouldn't let it go.

"Laney," Weston said, "do you want to come back?"

"No," I replied, but I stood and headed to the door. He followed, thanking Derek on our way out.

We got into his car, but he didn't start the engine. We sat in silence. Weston coughed. I played with my bracelet. It was obvious he wanted to talk about what happened, but was unsure how to broach the subject. I decided to break the ice for him.

"Listen," I said, "thanks for coming to get me."

"Of course." He turned in his chair to face me. "What happened to you tonight?"

I sighed. "I was talking to Angie and she started worrying about tomorrow and I freaked out. It's whatever."

"I get it," he said. "Sometimes something makes me think of Uncle Luke and I lose it again."

"It's not like that, though. It would make sense if I'd lost someone like you have, but I didn't. I just snapped."

"Love, I think what happened tonight is exactly like that."

"How so?"

"Well, what were you and Ang talking about when it happened?"

I froze. How the hell did he know? "Nothing," I muttered. "We were talking about nothing."

"Laney."

"What?" I snapped.

"You can tell me what happened."

"Can I?" I felt the heat rise to my face, pushed into my cheeks by my anger. "I can just spill my guts to you, but you don't want to be with me? You can't have it both ways, Weston. You're not my boyfriend, and I don't have to tell you shit."

He flinched beside me, and I turned away before his wounded expression could crack through my rage. "Love," he said, his voice soft, "we might not be together, but that doesn't mean I don't still care for you."

"Whatever."

"I mean it." He placed his hand on mine, and my body recoiled. "We're still friends. Talk to me."

Fire burned through my veins, and my heart thudded in my ears. "You wanna talk? Fine let's talk. Why don't we talk about how you think it's okay to lead me on all summer and then drop me for no damn good reason? You want to talk about that?"

"Laney..."

"Fuck you, Weston. Just take me home."

And to his credit, he did.

# DAY SiXTY-EiGHT

THE WEDDING WAS BEAUTIFUL. We all made it down the aisle without any tripping or ankle twisting, and Craig said his vows with only a couple "ums" and "ahs" mixed in. All around, a good ceremony, despite the tension between me and Weston.

Now, Karissa, Rory, and I sat in folding chairs against the lodge wall, where they'd been moved to make way for dancing. Karissa had come to the wedding, acting as if nothing had happened. Rory wasn't sharing what happened between them the night before, but I was grateful he was able to bring her back to us. Craig and Angie twirled around the lawn under the tent, somewhat awkwardly. Craig would never be mistaken for Fred Astaire. Despite the occasional stumble and the constant checking of their feet, they looked fabulous. Angie's smile glowed—all traces of the sorrow and worry from last night gone.

Weston dropped into the chair next to me and nudged my foot with his. "Can we talk?"

I shrugged, fighting against the angry blush already rising into my neck.

"Hey, I'm really sorry." His voice cracked, and I looked up at him. His forehead wrinkled in concern, and his eyes sported tiny dark circles. Did he sleep at all last night?

With a deep breath, I said, "Me, too. I'm sorry."

"What are we all sorry for?" Karissa asked. Weston and I both stared at her. She flung her hands up out of her lap. "Geez. You two keep your secrets. I'll just be here listening in."

Rory excused himself and strode across the floor to the beverage table. Karissa watched him the whole way.

"So," Weston pressed, "are we okay?"

I nodded and smiled at him. "Yeah. We're good."

"Good to hear," Karissa said. She turned to Weston. "So, aren't you going to ask her one of your little questions now? Don't you want to know whether she prefers boxers or briefs?"

"Boxer briefs," I said without hesitation.

"Boxer briefs? What kind of cop-out answer is that?" Weston said.

"It makes total sense," Karissa chimed in. "They don't

have nearly the nerdy-little-boy factor of tighty whities, but they also don't bunch up and get all annoying-like around your hips when you wear more fitted jeans."

"So," he said, "boxer briefs. Good to know."

"Yep," I said, "the perfect compromise."

"I hate to interrupt this thrilling conversation," Rory said when he returned, handing a drink to Karissa, "but Craig and Angie told me to get the wedding party out on the dance floor."

Weston shrugged then bumped his shoulder against mine. "Let's dance then," he said, standing and offering me a hand. After a brief hesitation, I took it, and he pulled me out of my chair and led me to the dancing area. Some sappy love song, the kind that seems to be mandatory at wedding receptions, played over the speakers Craig and Rory had mounted to the trees earlier in the day. Weston tugged on my arm, twirling me into him.

He held me away from him, in proper dance form. Formal, not intimate at all. This close to him, my body ached for him to pull me in all the way, to line us up together on the dance floor, setting the night on fire. But the back of my mind screamed with the reminder of his rejection the last time I'd tried to be with him, so I continued to move along the with him, the music dictating our dance.

"Whoa," I said. "You've been holding out on me."

He spun me around. "I don't know what you're talking about."

"Right. Likely story."

Another spin, a dip, and a flourish. "I've hidden nothing from you. You haven't been looking in the right places."

"You mean, like in the third drawer on the left of your dresser, where you keep your ballet shoes?"

"Exactly."

Weston dipped me again, then pulled me back up, closer to him. He toned our pace down, ignoring the music completely in favor of slow swaying. The hand at my shoulder blade slid to my lower back, fingers spreading out and pulling me slightly closer to him still. He used his other hand to loop my arm around his neck. Then he softly pushed my hair away from my eye, pulling in a shaky breath. His hand trailed across my cheek, then followed the curve of my side down to my hip, where it finally rested. He leaned down, his cheek pressing softly against mine, and we danced.

Too soon, the song ended, and Weston dipped me deeply, then pulled me back to his chest. He held me tightly for a second before stepping back, conflicted desire clear on his face.

Just then, Craig walked over and clapped him on the shoulder. "Hey, kiddo," he said to me, "I think it's time for the traditional father–daughter dance. What do ya say?"

"I say the dance is usually about the bride and her father, not the groom and his daughter."

"Yeah, yeah. Technicality. Ang's father passed away a few years ago, so the only father-daughter here is us. Let's go." He held his hand out to me.

I took it. "Okay, but I'll have you know that if some cheesy, overdone, I-love-my-daughter-so-much song starts playing, I will walk away and leave you dancing with yourself."

"Fair enough," he said.

The opening riff of "Sweet Child O' Mine" played, and Craig beamed down at me. The first summer I'd come to stay with him, the year after we first met, I brought him a DVD I'd made. It was a slideshow of pictures set to music, all the memories he'd missed while I was growing up because my mother was too proud to tell him about me. The first song on the DVD had been this one. My eyes welled up when Axl Rose's voice blared out over us. When had I become so sentimental?

Craig's eyes misted over as well. "Thanks so much for standing up there with me today. It means so much to me. And Angie, too."

"Are you sure?" I asked. "I think I might have hurt her feelings last night."

"Hey, don't worry, kiddo. She's fine. You didn't do anything wrong."

The tension in my shoulders relaxed. "Okay. Good."

We danced to Axl's words for a couple minutes without talking. As the song was ending, Craig slowed our circling. "So," he said, "you wanna talk about what happened last night?"

"No," I said, too quickly. "I don't."

"Okay, but you know if you ever need to—" The song ended and I dropped his hand.

"Thanks," I said, already backing away. "Well, uh, I better not monopolize your dance time. You are the belle of the ball tonight."

"Shhhh," he said, "don't tell. People seem to think Angie's supposed to be the pretty one." His eyes crinkled up with a smile, making him look much younger than his forty years.

"Don't worry, padré. Your secret's safe with me."


We danced into the wee hours of the morning. Once the party had gotten started, the guests trickled out of their cabins, wondering what was going on. Before long, everyone at the resort was dancing under the stars. The kids clasped hands in a circle and spun around and around until their chain broke and they all fell to the ground. Little girls stood in line to dance on Rory's, Weston's, and Craig's feet.

Karissa spent the evening alternating between dancing

with Rory—she declined every time Weston asked her to dance—and hiding behind the boat house with a drink. I tried to join her once, but Old Man Hellings from cabin two insisted on one more dance. Three songs later, Karissa returned with an empty cup. That had been my night since the first time Weston had pulled me out to dance: song after song spinning on the floor, passed between Weston, Rory, Craig, and the old widower.

Now, I leaned my head back against the wall and watched Rory and Karissa. His arm was wrapped around her waist, holding her tighter than he had me during any of our dances. She beamed at him, the adoration clear on her face. How long would it be before they finally came out and told the rest of us they were together?

Craig cut across the lawn toward me. He'd always been one of those "early to bed, early to rise" kind of people, and the late hour showed on his face. "Hey, hey, married man," I called to him. "Quite the little shindig you threw here."

"I know. Who knew Old Man Hellings was such a party animal, eh?"

"Who knew *you* were such a party animal? I guess you didn't need Rory to rally the troops after all."

His face twisted in confusion. "What are you talking about?"

"You know," I said, "earlier, when you sent Rory over to get us all dancing?"

"Um, I don't know. I didn't do that."

"Oh, maybe it was Ang." Why would Rory make that up?

Craig squeezed my knee. "Kiddo, I'm headed up to bed. But, um..." He stared at me.

I giggled nervously. "You need the wedding night talk or something, Craig?"

He laughed, somewhat uncomfortably. "No, I think I'll be fine."

"All right then," I said. "I'm going to bed. Kris and I will clean up what's left in the morning so you don't have to worry about it, 'kay?" I stood to leave.

"Laney, wait," he said, and I froze. "Angie wants to talk to you before bed. She's waiting for you at your cabin."

I turned to him, forcing a smile to my face. "I better not make her wait anymore, then. I'll see you in the morning."

Angie was sitting on the porch swing when I got to my cabin. She'd traded her wedding dress for lounge pants, a tank top, and flip flops. She sat with one foot pulled up underneath her other leg. The flip flop on her free foot dangled from her toes, swaying with each flick of her ankle. Her hair was still pulled up from the wedding, with tendrils falling around her face and at the base of her neck. Dancing had loosened the up-do, giving it a carefree, messy look. Moonlight played against her scars, casting a soft luminescence.

There was no avoiding this. Part of me wanted to walk the other way, to ignore Angie altogether, but I couldn't do it. For one, I lived behind the door she was sitting by; if I never went in, she would either know I was avoiding her or assume something had happened to me. For two, she was my stepmother now, and I had a feeling that meant a lot more in my life than a new stepfather did. I squared my shoulders, fought to control the shaking in my arms, and walked up to the porch.

"Hey," I said, my quaking voice betraying my nerves immediately. "Congratulations. You looked great tonight."

"Thanks." She smiled at me sadly and patted the swing next to her. "Wanna sit?"

*No.* I crossed the porch and lowered myself onto the swing. My muscles tensed, ready to flee at any moment. Angie reached a hand toward my arm, thought better of it, and returned it to her own lap.

"Listen," she said, "I want to talk about last night."

"I'm so sorry I ruined the party. I don't know what came over me."

"It's not about the party—you didn't ruin anything. But I was wondering why you reacted so strongly. If there's anything you want to talk about?"

*Yes. Yes, oh god, yes,* part of me screamed. "No. Like I said, I don't know what happened. I flipped out, okay? No reason."

278

It was obvious my lie didn't take hold with Angie. I stood to go inside, but she grabbed my arm.

"Please, wait. I want to tell you what happened. Please sit."

The whooshing built up in my ears, intensifying with each beat of my pulse. My feet were glued to the deck. My breath grew shallow, and my vision blurred. As if I were wrapped deep in a layer of cotton balls, I vaguely felt Angie pull me back down onto the swing next to her. And then she told me her story.

"It was a Wednesday night, and it was cold outside. I remember because I can always run longer in the cold air, you know, and I'd been running for a while already. It's funny the things I do remember about that night. I mean, the fact that it was cold is etched into my memory, but I can't recall what the guy looked like to save my life. At first they sent me to a therapist and the whole nine yards to try to help me remember, but then I realized I didn't want to. They kept telling me how if I couldn't ID the guy he could do this to someone else, so I tried for so long to remember. But I would never get my life back if I didn't let it go, so that's what I did.

"Anyway, it was a Wednesday. I was in Philly for some continuing education workshops. It'd been a long day and I needed to burn off some energy, so I went running. After a while, I wasn't sure where I was anymore. I must have looked lost, because after a few minutes, a car pulled over next to me. A little old man leaned out the window and asked if I needed help. I told him where I was staying and he pointed me back toward the hotel. Then he drove off, and I was alone on the road again.

"The guy must have watched the whole thing, because as soon as the old man's car was around the corner, he came out of a run-down building behind me. I don't remember his face. All I can remember about him is the knife he was carrying.

"Everything happened so fast after. He dragged me back into the building and started ripping at my clothes. I took a self-defense course when I was in college, but it did no good. All I could do was stand there shaking and trying not to cry. He laughed a lot—sometimes I can still hear him laugh at night—and flashed his knife in front of my face over and over.

"I don't remember much else. The therapist I went to says my brain shut down to protect me. All I know is he raped me and cut me up. I don't know which he did first. The scars on my face aren't the only ones he left—I also have cuts on my thighs and on one side.

"When he was done, he left me there in the cold, empty building where nobody could find me. I thought I would die there, and I almost let myself. For a while I lay there bleeding, not even trying to move.

"Eventually, though, I knew I had to fight. It hurt too much to walk, so I dragged myself across the floor and out into the street. I was about ready to give up again when Weston came along."

"Wait," I interrupted, surprising even myself, "Weston found you?"

"Yeah. That's how we met. Lucky, too. He didn't usually take that street, but there was an accident on his normal route, so he went around. He called 911, but he didn't want to wait for an ambulance, so he lifted me into his car and drove me to the hospital himself. He stayed there with me all night and most of the next day, too. He's such a sweet kid."

Angie wiped a tear from her cheek, and I was embarrassed to find I'd been crying, too. She reached over and squeezed my knee. "Listen," she said, "I didn't tell you that so you would feel sorry for me. I wanted you to know the whole story. And I want you to know that if you ever want to talk about it—or anything else—we can, okay?"

"Yeah, sure," I mumbled.

"Well," she said as she stood up, "I better get back to your dad. He'll be wondering what's taking me so long." She smiled at me and headed across the lawn.

"Hey, Angie?" I called. She turned. "Um...why did you keep it?" I gestured toward her growing belly.

She placed a hand protectively over her stomach. "Oh,

sweetie, I had to."

"But isn't it hard? To be reminded every day, I mean."

She came back up the porch. "Yes," she said, "it's hard. But it's beautiful, too. After it all happened and I was trying so hard to remember, I was so, so unhappy. A couple times I thought about ending my misery." She reached out and grabbed my wrist. She held on tighter when I tried to pull out of her grasp. Her thumb traced my scar, under the edge my bracelet. "Then I found out I was pregnant, and everything changed. That's when I stopped trying to remember. I decided I would take the baby and turn it into a blessing."

"I don't get it."

"There's nothing to get, really. After it all happened, I was in such a dark place, Laney. I didn't think I would ever be okay again. Then I found out about the baby, and it was like I had a little ray of hope in my life. Now, whenever things get bad"—she rubbed my scar—"I sit still for a minute and wait to feel the baby move, and it gives me the hope I need again."

"Things got easier, then?"

"I don't know if it ever gets easier. I think maybe I got better at dealing with it. I quit focusing my energy on the bad and instead looked forward to the joy a baby will bring me. I still have hard days, but I've learned how to cope with them. I have something to help get me through."

I swallowed the lump that had grown in my throat. "Thank you, Angie."

She pulled me into a tight hug. "Anytime, sweetie. If you ever want to talk—about anything—I'll listen.

I watched her walk across the lawn toward the office, awe overwhelming me. Here was a woman who went through a horrible ordeal, worse than anything I could even imagine happening to me, and she handled it with such grace and optimism.

Why was I too weak to do the same?

# DAY SEVENTY-TWO

## FOUR.

Four days.
Only four days till my birthday.
I would be eighteen.
And Weston would be mine.

# DAY SEVENTY-SIX

AT FIRST I THOUGHT I'D BEEN sucked into a psychedelic dream. My vision swirled with colors—pink, blue, purple, green, and yellow bouncing off every surface, flowing through my hair and over my bare skin. I was floating in a sea of multi-hued balls, flying through a rainbow. My eyes slid shut, and I was in the black again.

I sat straight up in bed, my heart pounding. Not a dream. Blinking furiously, I forced my eyes to focus. Balloons covered every surface of my room. They bounced on the bed with each movement I made; not a square of the carpet could be made out beneath them. Even the kitchen counter was littered with them. They hung from brightly colored streamers, taped to the ceiling. More streamers created a curtain between this room and the bathroom.

Pulling my sheet securely around myself, I stepped from my bed and ventured into the rest of the room, kicking the colored balls aside as I walked. There must've been hundreds of them crammed in there with me. I peeked around my curtain and out the window. Dew still clung to the grass, the sun's rays barely shining through the trees.

My fan rotated noisily in the corner, blowing balloons haphazardly across the floor. Streamers swayed in the breeze. A flutter of paper beside my head caught my attention, and I pulled it from where it was taped to the inside of my front door.

The card was simple, a fold of off-white linen paper with a colored pencil sketch of a cupcake on the front. The paper was rough, but somehow still smooth between my fingers, and I rubbed my thumb across its surface, just below the drawing. My heart fluttered. I pressed the card open.

*Happy birthday, love,* it read in Weston's slanty handwriting. *I wanted to be the first to wish you so. Come outside once you're up.*

Something darted around in my stomach, like a hummingbird flitting back and forth, looking for the perfect flower. I read over his words, and it struck me: *I am eighteen years old.* Free. I could do what I pleased, be where I wanted.

Without a second thought, I burst from my cabin, Weston's card still clutched in my hand. The cool air assaulted me, raising bumps along the exposed skin of my legs. Stepping off the porch and into the still-wet grass, I inhaled deeply, wanting to drink in the freshness and promise the morning brought with it. My face tilted toward the sky, and the smile that broke across it traveled all the way to my toes.

A rustle behind me tugged me back to reality, and I spun around to find Weston sitting on his side of the porch, waiting like he had so many times before. A wry grin cut across his features, pressing dimples into his cheeks. His eyes, behind the black rims of his glasses, looked directly into mine. Intense, yet soft.

"Um, hi," I said and shrugged at the silliness of my earlier actions.

"Having a good morning?" he asked as he put a scrap of paper between the pages of his worn book and shut it. He reached down beside the chair and pulled up a small box wrapped in plain brown paper with a sparkly blue bow attached to the top.

I hopped up on my toes. "For me?"

Weston motioned for me to join him, sliding over on the swing barely far enough for me to fit. When I sat, one foot tucked up under my butt, we were touching from shoulder to knee, and my body crackled with the closeness.

He shifted beside me, breaking the contact, but before I could even feel the coolness left behind, he was back, his arm around my shoulders, me tucked up against his side. He pressed his lips to my head. "Happy birthday," he whispered.

The paper was scratchy in my hands, which were shaking. Squeezing the box tighter in an attempt to stop the tremble, I hoped he wouldn't notice. But how could he not? It wasn't only my hands. My whole body quaked slightly at his side, electrified by our connection. His fingers around my body flexed and extended, rubbing softly along my ribcage, and I leaned into him even closer.

The tape Weston used to wrap the box could have been used to piece together a space shuttle, should the need ever arise. After fighting with it for several seconds, I looked up at him with one eyebrow cocked.

"Sorry," he mumbled and raised his hips off the swing, plunging his hand into a pocket. I forced myself to stare at the shiny bow so I wouldn't be caught eyeing his crotch, which was expertly highlighted by his jeans. His hand returned from the pocket wrapped around a small knife. Holding it out to me, he explained, "The paper's quite stiff. That's all I could find to hold it down."

Our hands brushed when I reached to take the knife from him, and my whole arm ignited. He wrapped his fingers around mine, the knife still firmly between us, and pulled my hand to his mouth. His soft lips stood in stark contrast to the scratchy stubble left behind from a day unshaven. My eyes drifted closed, and I let the ecstasy of this moment, so simple and chaste, boil through my being, rippling across me, wonderful and dangerous at the same time.

The knife dropped to his lap, his hand making its way to the back of my neck, fingers tangling in my hair. A flash of light behind closed eyes—the sun breaking through the trees. Weston's scent overpowering me, as familiar as my own.

His lips brushed against mine lightly, so soft the kiss was almost non-existent. Adrenaline raced through me, making my insides dance, and I pushed even closer, opening my mouth to him. But instead of giving me what I hungered for, he pulled away slightly, talking with his mouth still against my own: "Open your gift, Laney." Even as softly as he said it, the excitement in his voice was palpable.

Armed now with Weston's pocket knife, I sliced through the super tape and released the package from its wrapping. The box was non-descript, dark blue and plain, giving no hints at all as to its contents. I clutched it tightly, drawing out the suspense, and looked back at Weston. He stared down at me, eager anticipation clear on his open face, which suddenly looked so childlike it was almost comical. With a deep breath, I pulled the lid off.

It took me a few seconds to realize what I was looking at. Staring at me from the bottom of the dark box was a simple leather cuff. Smooth and weathered-looking, it clasped together with two metal buttons. It looked much like the one he'd been wearing the day I first met Angie, but for one major detail.

Wrapped around the leather was a thinner strip of metal, taking up about half of the cuff's width, with leather showing on each side of it. My eyes followed the metal around the circle until it widened out into a short body, nearly as wide as the leather, and then four prongs. A fork! Three prongs were bent slightly at their ends, all turned into a tiny curl facing the outside of the cuff. The fourth, one of the middle prongs, was twisted all the way into itself, a curly-cue at the base of the fork body. Never had I seen something so strangely, wonderfully beautiful.

A soft gasp escaped my lips as I pulled it from the box, a smile pulling at my mouth. Weston released a breath beside me—I hadn't noticed how tense he'd gotten waiting for my appraisal. I turned to him, my face beaming.

"This is amazing!" I said. "You made this, right?" The image of him slipping the pizza parlor's fork into his breast pocket flashed across my mind. He nodded. "With that fork you stole from lunch with Angie?" I asked.

He laughed, and the sound made my heart soar, but he

was shaking his head. "I knew you saw," he said, "and wondered why you didn't say anything."

"Hey, who am I to make fun of the weirdo fork stealer?"

He continued, "This is actually a fork from The Place, the first night we all went out." I thought back to that night. Weston leaning so casually against a table, the diners gone, but the plates and silverware waiting to be removed, as we talked to Derek.

"So is this a thing with you? You steal forks and turn them into awesome jewelry?"

His smile widened, if possible. "And other things," he said. "I started after Luke died. After the service, we had to sit through this dreadful reception. A full formal dinner, not the buffet style you see after most funerals. I hated being there and was desperate for anything to pass the time. I had Luke's old multi-tool in my suit—I'd intended to drop it into the casket with him, but my father refused. Said it wasn't appropriate. Anyway, I had the tool, and the silverware was sitting there, all shiny and pretentious. Nothing Luke would have enjoyed. So I took those tiny pliers and started bending the metal—it molded much smoother than most restaurant silverware. It was real silver. My father probably had to pay to replace the pieces for my first creations," he added with a smirk.

Tears prickled the corners of my eyes, and I looked

back at the cuff, buying time for them to disappear. I ran my fingers across the aged leather. "It looks like yours."

"It is," he replied softly. "I shortened it a bit. I hope it fits."

He took my hand and pushed my thin shirtsleeve up above my wrist. Fumbling with only one available hand, he worked to unwrap my hemp bracelet. I sat frozen, knowing this would go faster if I helped, but unable to bring myself to do so, as he exposed my wrist to the world. A breeze caressed my scar when the bracelet fell to the ground. His thumb followed, touching so lightly I couldn't be sure he was actually making contact at all.

Weston slid my new cuff over my wrist, and I helped him connect the snaps. It hugged my arm perfectly, covering the worst part of my scar and making me feel clothed once again. I rotated my arm around, looking at it from all angles. My breath hitched in my throat. "Thank you," I whispered.

He didn't say anything, but pressed his lips to mine once more.

A few hours later, I lay on my bed, my arm held above me, examining my cuff, my lips still on fire from Weston's kisses, when Rory burst through my door.

"Happy birthday to yooooouuuu! Happy birth—what the hell!" he exclaimed when a balloon popped under his feet. He turned around quickly, taking in my new decorations. "Okay...well, obviously *someone* beat me to this."

I looked at the clock pointedly. "Of course someone beat you to it. It's almost noon already."

He shrugged, full-bodied and carefree. His shirt looked worn, a stark contrast to the brand new band shirts he usually sported. Against a dark gray background, a crowd of people was silhouetted in white. One figure, hot pink, stood out from the rest. *We the Me* it read, and I recognized the name as the one he'd told me when he first formed the band last summer. "I had a late night, and your pops didn't need me this morning. You know he totally spoils you by giving us all your birthday off." He launched himself across the field of balloons and onto my bed, nearly bouncing me into the wall in the process. "So," he said, a teasing note in his voice, "who are the balloons from?"

I gave a nonchalant shrug, but I could feel the heat rising to my face, giving me away. God, I would suck so hard at poker. I fought against the urge to touch my lips, to check if they were still swollen. Rory laid his head next to mine, neck cocked so his ear was against my shoulder. "I'm glad you're so happy," he said. And before I could respond: "Don't get all weird and deny it, Lane. You don't have to tell me details—in fact, please don't—but I'm happy for you." He squeezed my hand.

"Thanks," I choked out around my rapidly swelling throat. Who turned my emotions on full-blast this morning? My fingers laced around Rory's, and we lay there together, waiting for Karissa to come, bringing the rest of my birthday plans with her.

✳ ✳ ✳

My eyes snapped open at the sound of Rory's voice. "Wha?" I mumbled. When had I fallen asleep? Rory's body blocked the clock from view, and I pushed myself up on my elbows so I could see the digital read-out. 3:52. I shot the rest of the way up.

"I know." Rory laughed, groggily. He pushed his curls back from his eyes. One popped immediately back into his face, so I reached forward to push it away again. His eyes caught on my cuff, and he laughed. "Does *that* have anything to do with the look you had on your face when I got here?"

Again, I remained silent, letting my blush tell the story for me.

"It looks good on you," he said, followed by, "Where the hell is Kris? Wasn't she supposed to be here by one?"

I nodded and reached across him for my phone. I shot a quick text to our best friend. *Hey. You need a ride or something?* Her car wasn't the most reliable in the world, and she probably had too much stuff to walk to the resort. I checked for missed calls—maybe she'd tried to get us to pick her up already—but the list was empty.

Almost immediately, her reply chimed in. *Yeah. That'd be great. I'll wait outside for you.*

Rory and I piled into Burt, and he slid a CD into my player, his hand covering the top so I couldn't make out the artist. A few seconds silence, then the guitar and drums of The Beatle's "Birthday" blared through the speakers, filling the tiny cab. He yelled to be heard over the music. "We tried to record this for you last night, me and the guys, but Thom's equipment was being a bitch." He shrugged. "So I borrowed this from Weston."

We jammed to the song—on repeat—all the way to Karissa's house, where we finally turned it down. My ears rang slightly. As promised, Kris was sitting on her front steps, elbows on her knees, a pile of bags and boxes on the ground at her feet.

"Fuck," Rory said on a long exhale as he opened his door. At my confused expression, he nodded toward the driveway.

Karissa's Civic sat in the drive, behind the boat her parents never took out anymore. The hood bent up at a sharp angle, and the passenger's side door was caved in, the front quarter panel a mangled mess. The tire was completely flat, the wheel bent at the bottom. Through the broken passenger window, I could see the spider-webbed cracks across the windshield, meeting at a white point-of-impact to the right of the center console.

Rory ran toward Karissa, me following directly behind. "What the hell happened?" he shouted.

Karissa's eyes bulged, and she jumped up from the steps, waving her hand frantically, her head shaking. "Be quiet," she hissed.

"Was anyone hurt?" I asked, forcing my voice to be even and calm. I squeezed my eyes shut, but all I could see was the white spot on the windshield, cracks emanating from it. Like where a head hit. Why hadn't she called?

When I reopened my eyes, she was shaking her head. "No," she said, barely above a whisper. There was some stuff stacked in the front seat that hit the window."

When Rory spoke again, it was obvious he was having an even harder time keeping calm than I was. "What. Happened," he demanded.

Karissa shrugged and bent to pick up a bag. "It's not a big deal, you guys. Sorry I'm so late. I didn't want to bother you on your birthday for a ride."

I started to tell her it wasn't a bother at all, but Rory was already talking again. "Your father did this, didn't he? Was he drunk?"

"Stop, Rory. I said it's fine. Leave it alone."

But Rory wouldn't leave it alone. He grabbed her upper arm, forcing her to stand straight and drop the bag, which I now saw was filled with bags of tortilla chips. Karissa gasped, and tears sprang to her eyes as her face twisted. Her whole body tensed, her back totally rigid and her shoulders hunched up to her ears. Rory dropped her arm and stared at her like she'd shot him. "Kris," he said, all fight drained from his words. His face grew increasingly paler, a look of horror spreading across his features.

"Enough," she said, her voice hard and cold. "This conversation is over. It's Laney's birthday, and we are going to party." She smiled, and her face sparkled like always, but it didn't quite touch her eyes.

Conflict was obvious on Rory's face as he sorted through his emotions. We stood there, tense, as anger and sadness warred with his features. He closed his eyes and took several deep breaths, his nostrils flaring wildly with each. Finally, he tossed his head back and forth and shook the tension out of his shoulders. "Fine," he said, opening his eyes and staring at Karissa. "Let's go party. We'll talk later."

We loaded Karissa's boxes and bags into the back of Burt—she'd bought enough for a party much, much larger than the three of us watching horror movies—and she hopped into the small bed with them, claiming she wanted to feel the breeze on her face. We didn't argue with her, but Rory shot me a look over the top of the car. The words were clear in his eyes: *Nothing's changed.*

Kris insisted I wasn't to help with set-up for my own party, so I sat cross-legged on top of the pool table playing solitaire while she arranged the cups, drinks, and snacks. After having disappeared for several minutes, Rory skipped back into the lodge, Weston in tow. Together, they worked a giant, bulging tarp through the double doors, gently pushing and prodding at it to get it to past the threshold without too much pressure from the doorframe. Once safely inside, they shook it open, and a rainbow burst from inside. The balloons from my cabin spilled out over the floor, brightening the room. They folded the tarp up, and Rory headed back to the storage shed with it. Weston crossed the room to me, kicking balloons around on his way.

"It's the gift that keeps giving," I said with a smile.

"It was all Rory's idea," he said, leaning across the table to give me a quick peck before straightening and calling to Karissa, "Do you need any help setting up?"

"Nah," she replied, and the smile she gave him was wide and genuine. "I'm about done here. You go ahead and...entertain the birthday girl." She set back to work, humming to herself.

Weston leaned against the pool table, his elbows resting on the bumpers, back to me. Through his worn blue t-shirt, I could see the outline of his shoulder blades and the curves of his back and shoulder muscles. I scratched my nails across his upper back, and he groaned deep in his throat.

"I have to ask you something," he said, voice deeply serious, but, rather than the apprehension I'd once felt at these announcements, I was instantly elated. I'd missed this game. He didn't wait for my reply before continuing, "What's the best birthday present you've ever gotten?"

My hand snaked around his shoulder and across his chest, and his breath hitched. "You mean besides this bracelet?" I whispered. He nodded, barely moving, and took a deep, shuddering breath.

Memories of past birthdays flashed through my mind. Once my mother had become successful, birthdays always involved fancy dinners at exclusive restaurants and one big gift: a laptop last year, my iPod the year before. A plane ticket to Washington, DC, the year my class took a history trip there. A diamond tennis bracelet I almost never wore. But more than all these, one birthday stood out in my mind. "When I turned seven," I said, "my mother had just divorced her third husband, and we were poor. Like, ridiculously poor. Even that young, I knew I wouldn't be getting a fancy birthday party like my friends had. Mom wanted to make things special though, so we got dressed up in our fanciest outfits—I wore my dress from her last wedding, even though it was getting a little too small." I remembered the shimmering fabric of the soft, deep purple sundress. It was my favorite of all the bridesmaid dresses she'd put me in. "And then she took me to the board walk. All fancy with our hair and makeup completely done up, and we had lunch at a hot dog stand and dessert from the ice cream kiosk at the end of the pier. We walked the beach and played Frisbee in the sand. At the end of the day, she waded out into the water in her nice dress until she found me the perfect seashell." My voice hitched, and my heart ached for those days with my mother. "I could tell she wished she could give me more, but I thought it was the best present I'd ever gotten." A tear slipped down my cheek. "That's still one of my favorite days."

"Hey," Weston said softly, turning around and wiping my tear away with his thumb. "I'm sorry."

A small chuckle escaped my throat. "It's not like you could know I would get all sappy."

He kissed my forehead then bored his gaze into my eyes. "Let's try again," he whispered. "Do you prefer coffee or tea?"

"Tea, definitely."

A broad smile. "Good."

Karissa announced she was done, and we made our way into the next room. She'd set the table with food for a party of about twenty. A punch bowl sat to one side with an ice ring and frothy pink punch in it. In the middle of the table was the biggest bowl of tortilla chips I'd ever seen, surrounded by six different flavors of salsa. Finishing out the spread were rainbow-frosted cupcakes, arranged in a heart formation.

"Wow, you really outdid yourself this year," I said.

"Yeah, well, it's not every day my best friend turns eighteen."

"Thanks," I said. Maybe it was only for the night, but I was thrilled to have Karissa back and acting like her old self.

"How are we possibly going to eat all this?" Weston asked, grabbing a paper plate from the stack.

"Who cares," Rory said as he walked into the room. "The real question is, what are we gonna watch?" He dug through Karissa's bag on the ground by the table. He stood back up with four DVD cases in hand. "Really, Kris? You couldn't bring anything better than this?"

She grabbed the movies from his hand. "Whatever. It's Laney's night, and she likes horror. Suck it up. Besides, you're just gonna sleep through it anyway."

Karissa fanned the movies out in front of me. I studied the covers for a few minutes before settling on *House of Wax*. Campy enough for Rory's tastes, but hopefully scary enough to get my adrenaline pumping. We loaded up our plates, grabbed some punch, and made to settle in.

Craig had already removed some of the furniture from the lodge—something I was adamantly not letting ruin my birthday high—so we were left with one puffy chair and a loveseat. The four of us stood around awkwardly, staring at each other, none of us wanting to be the one to claim a seat and leave someone to sit on the floor. True to form, Karissa was the first to break, and she plopped down sideways in the chair, her flip-flop adorned feet hanging over one over-stuffed arm. Weston followed suit and lowered himself to the ground in front of one side of the loveseat.

"I can take the floor," Rory offered, but Weston waved him off.

"It's okay, mate," he said, "I don't mind."

So Rory and I settled onto the small couch, him leaning against one arm, and me settling in behind Weston. I curled my feet under my lap and wrapped a blanket around my legs despite the warm air in the room. The movie started, and we settled in.

The body count was at three when I heard Rory's first snore. Never had we held a movie night where he didn't fall asleep. I was impressed he lasted as long as he had, actually, especially since he was up so late the night before. Weston chuckled at him, and we returned to the movie. Less than a minute later, he nudged my knee with his shoulder. I followed his gaze across the room to Karissa.

She lounged in the chair, a jacket laid across her torso and clutched in her fists up to her chin. She was so into the movie that we could have held a dance party on the couch and she wouldn't have noticed, which was the only reason,

I was sure, she hadn't realized how far her skirt had slipped up her thigh. It was difficult to see clearly in the dark room, but the TV emitted enough light to show the ugly bruise spreading out from beneath the covering of her clothes. It took up the whole outer side of her upper thigh, mottled and patchy like it was older, trying to fade away, but too deep to do so gracefully. Weston reached over his shoulder and grabbed my hand, silently prompting me to come with him. We rose from our seats and slipped out of the room. Entrenched in the movie, Karissa's eyes didn't even flicker in our direction as we went.

As soon as we reached the covered porch, Weston dropped my hand and turned to face me. "You saw, yes?" he asked. I nodded. "I was wondering," he started then stopped and clutched his hands in the hair on both sides of his head, pulling much of it out of the elastic at the base of his neck. "Do you know what's going on with her?"

"What do you mean?" I asked, and even I could hear how fake my voice sounded. Of course I knew what he meant. We both knew it. But I couldn't be the first to say anything.

"When you were out with Rory one day, she came to the office and asked if we could order her some long-sleeved shirts to wear instead of the tank tops we gave her."

I stood silent.

"And," he continued, "I've not seen her wear anything

but long sleeves since. I thought she said it was just yelling."

"So," I said, hating the defensiveness in my voice. I wanted to tell him it didn't mean anything, but I knew it did, better than most. Who wore long sleeves in ninety-five degree heat, day after day? Only people who had things to hide. I'd thought the same thing Weston was thinking, but wanted so badly to be wrong I convinced myself I was. "She doesn't want our help, West."

"Hey," he said and pulled me to him. "It's okay." I was surprised to find myself crying. "Shite, I'm sorry. I'm ruining your birthday again."

I hiccupped and shrugged. "It's okay."

Weston shook his head. "No it isn't." A deep breath. "Okay, let's go finish that awful movie you picked." A slight quirk pulled the corners of his mouth upward.

"But what about—"

"Nothing's going to happen to her tonight, love. We'll figure something out. Promise." He laced his fingers with mine and tugged me back toward the door. I resisted.

"She says it's getting better, that her dad goes to some group or something now. But I think it's getting worse, West. She's getting more distant, and when we went to pick her up today, her car was smashed up in the driveway. Rory touched her, and she almost screamed. She won't talk about it. If we even suggest the subject, she gets nasty and shuts down."

He pulled me back to him once again and pressed a kiss to my jaw. A hand ran over the back of my head, smoothing my hair down.

"I...I don't want to push her away."

"Sometimes," he said, pulling back and looking me intently in the eyes, "that's what we have to do. I'm sorry, love, but she needs help, even if it is hard to do."

I nodded.

With a quick, intense kiss on the mouth, he turned back to the door again. "Let's go celebrate your birthday. We'll figure it out later."

We crept back into the room. On the screen, a girl was running around a campsite in an open bathrobe, showing off her bra and underwear, her long hair trailing behind her, tears all over her face. Karissa made no indication she saw us returning, but her skirt was pulled back over her thigh, expertly covering her bruise. While we were gone, Rory had stretched his long legs out over my side of the loveseat, and now lay on his back, one arm covering his eyes, the other trailing off the couch to the floor. Weston dropped back to the ground and pulled me down with him, his arms wrapped around me. I laid my head against his chest, his heartbeat keeping rhythm with my own, and continued celebrating the rest of the second-best birthday ever.

# DAY EIGHTY

ANGIE WAS IN THE OFFICE again when I came through the door this morning. Weston and Craig had spent all of yesterday taking meetings in Missoula, and hadn't gotten back until late. My body buzzed with the anticipation of seeing him again, and I wondered briefly how long it would be before the feeling wore off. Right now, it felt like it would never go away, and I hoped that would be the case.

"Oh, hey," I said to Angie, hoping I didn't sound as disappointed as I felt at seeing her in Weston's chair.

"Hello, Laney! Happy birthday. I'm so sorry I had to miss it." Her beautiful smile lit up her face, and a hand rested at the top of her growing belly. I'd always thought people were full of shit when they talked about the pregnancy glow, but with Angie I could finally see what they meant. She beamed at me, and it was like she was creating light from within herself. "I have a gift for you," she said.

"Thank you," I replied, "but you didn't have to."

She laughed, deep and throaty. "I did. The way Weston begged me, I couldn't say no. So I guess it is a gift for him as well."

My facial muscles contorted, and I could see my own expression in my mind: brows furrowed and mouth crooked, the same confused face my mother would get while trying to balance our budget back in the poor days. Angie stood and pulled me into a big hug, her belly forcing us to angle our upper bodies sharply toward each other. When we parted, she said, "I'm watching the office so you can have another day off today. Go enjoy yourself."

"Oh...wow," I sputtered. "Thank you."

She nodded her welcome, and repeated, "Happy birthday. Weston should be back soon to get you."

I turned to leave, but before I got the door open, she said. "Hey, Laney?"

"Yeah." My shoe squeaked on the wood floor when I spun back to face her.

"I know we don't know each other very well yet, but..." She bit her lip, and if possible, this concerned expression made her even more beautiful. "...Weston is

307

special."

My head bobbed in agreement, and she continued, "In the time we've known each other, I've never known him to take to someone like he has you. He's always been all work, totally focused on making something of himself. Proving to his father that he can, you know?" She didn't wait for an answer. Instead, she took a deep breath and said, "And when he does something—well, he puts everything into it."

"Okay," I said, drawing the word out.

She smiled again, this time reserved. "He won't love you partway, Laney. I just—I thought you should know before...in case...well, before things go too far."

Flames licked at my neck and face. "Does Craig know?"

Another laugh. "You know how your father is. He's totally oblivious, though I don't know how that's possible. The two of you practically blind the room every time the other is brought into conversation."

Oh, god, if I could slip through the floor right now.

"Don't worry," Angie said, "I won't say a word to Craig until you are ready. Now go have some fun."

I left the office in a daze as Weston pulled into the lot, driving Rory's truck. Two white boards, like overly large surf boards, were strapped in the bed. He hopped out of the cab, already dressed in a pair of board shorts and a fitted tank top. His hair was pushed back with a thin black headband, making him look intensely British. The hummingbird returned to my stomach, more violent now, larger. Perhaps a goldfinch. Heat tingled between my legs, and I said, a little breathy, "Nice truck."

He shrugged, and a grin lit his face. "I tried to use Craig's, but the transmission is acting up again."

"So, what, you and Rory are buddies now?" I hadn't intended to sound defensive—I wanted them to get along—but my voice was laced with it anyway.

"Something like that. He's a good guy." He held his hand out for me. I grabbed his fingers, and he pulled me toward him. Excitement crackled through him, reminding me of a little kid racing for the ice cream truck. Using his free hand, he dropped the tailgate then swept his arm in front of his bounty with a great flourish.

"What?—"

"Welcome," he said, "to our first official date."

He sent me to change into my swimsuit while he pulled the boards down to the beach. Once inside my cabin, I jumped around, pumping my fists in the air like a complete idiot. Weston and I were together all the time, and would likely be even more so now that he wasn't hung up on my age, but something about the way he said the word *date* planted a ticking bomb in my ribcage. With each second that clicked, my chest grew tighter, my heart filling the cavity to full capacity. My hands jittered, causing me to drop the strings of my bikini three times as I tried to tie it. A full troop of fairies danced in the pit of my stomach. I squeezed my thighs together tightly in a wasted effort to squash the heat away.

Finally, my suit was securely tied. I unsnapped my new cuff and set it on the table, replacing it with my double-wrapped hemp cord. The cuff pulled at my heart, and I hated to part with it so soon, but I knew I would hate myself more if I ruined the leather in the lake. Standing over my bed, I stared at the tissue-thin, long-sleeved t-shirt I normally wore to the beach. Picked it up. Dropped it back to the bed again.

A tank top in place over my bikini, I ran out the door to meet Weston.

He was standing by the water, a board on each side of him and a long paddle in each hand. I stood at the edge of the reeds, hidden from view, and studied the way the sunlight played off his features, setting some in bright highlight, others in muted shadows. He scratched the side of his face with the end of a paddle and turned to face the direction of our cabin. With a deep breath and a shake of my hands at my sides, I stepped out from around the tall reeds.

His chest rose sharply then held statue-still. I walked closer, a small smile playing on my lips. His breath flew from his mouth. "Whoa," he whispered; I was barely close enough to hear it.

"Hi," I said, and I sounded like I'd run a marathon. Breathless and raspy. Goosebumps prickled on my skin, despite the rising heat of the sun.

Weston stared.

Then the paddles fell to the ground with a clatter, and he took the remaining two steps between us, his eyes alight with passion. One hand clasped around my own, and the other snaked around my lower back, pulling me against him roughly. His lips crushed mine, and a surprised groan sounded deep in my throat. His tongue played across my own. For the briefest of moments, we two were the only people in the universe.

Breaking our connection, he stepped back and chuckled softly. "Sorry, love," he said, not sounding sorry at all. "I thought I might go crazy if I had to go through the whole date wondering if I would get a kiss at the end." He rubbed a hand down my arm and added, "I like your shirt."

Suddenly self-conscious, I toyed with my bracelet, making sure it was positioned properly. Weston picked the paddles back up from where they lay and handed one to me. "Ever been paddle boarding?" he asked.

✳   ✳   ✳

We reached the end of the lake and ran our boards up on a deserted beach. Weston took my paddle from me, his fingers lingering on my hand way longer than necessary, and leaned it against a tree with his own. As he crossed the sand back to me, he pulled his shirt over his head. Tanned skin across his toned chest captured my breath, and I followed the lines of his body downward. The dark curves of his tattoo peeked up over his shorts, accenting his hipbone. My fingers urged to trace those lines.

Following my gaze, Weston ran one of his own fingers across the thickest line. "It's for Luke," he said. I crossed the sand to him and reached out, tentatively, unsure of myself. My eyes closed. Then I felt his hand around my own. So gentle—soft despite fine callouses. "It's okay," he said, more breath than word.

Together, we traced the lines, thin and winding at the top, thickening as they lowered into a single cord under his shorts, which we slid lower as we moved. "What does it mean?" I wasn't sure the words had even left my mouth.

His breath hitched, and tiny bumps erupted over his skin. A tiny laugh. "I don't even know."

I looked up at him, having to lean back a little to meet his gaze. His hand held my own firmly against the skin covering his hipbone. My palm burned. I raised my eyebrows in question.

"Luke was always the tattoo guy, not me. He had a ton of them. It drove my father insane. A few months before he died, he took a trip to New Zealand. He found this weird little stone carving there and asked me if I could draw a tattoo in the same shape for him. I don't know what happened to the carving, but my sketch was in the glove box when he died. He never got his last tattoo."

"So you did," I finished for him.

Weston nodded, eyes closed, and then he was kissing me again. Tenderly this time, none of the rush of his previous kiss. His lips were soft against mine, moving together, connecting us as one. He released my hand, but I left it against his hip, relishing the feel of his smooth skin beneath my palm. Fingers tickled at my side, sliding under the hem of my tank top. Hesitating, waiting for permission. My arms lifted above my head, the soft fabric of my shirt following, our lips only parting to let it through.

Skin to skin, we pressed our bodies together. Tongues danced, and fingers clutched in hair, on hips, balled behind each other's backs. I couldn't get close enough. I wanted to drink him in, make every part of him mine.

And then I was plunged into icy water. Weston's hand found my bracelet, and he fumbled with the fastening loop. My muscles seized, and I stood stone still. Our mouths broke apart, and he lowered his forehead to mine. I squeezed my eyes shut, unwilling to look at him.

"Please," he whispered, and the sound of his voice sent a fissure across my heart. "Laney, I want to see all of you. Please, love."

My body responded before my mind did. As my brain

screamed at me—no, no, *no!*—my other hand crossed between us to my bracelet. I helped him slide it off my arm, and it dropped to the sand at our feet. My eyes opened.

Weston's face was so open, kindness and love written across it with a bold-tipped marker. His eyes traveled across my face, along the curve of my neck, and down my arm to my hand, still held in his own. They returned to my own, and he smiled, the skin around his gray irises crinkling. "Let's go," he said, and led me back to my paddle board.

We pushed our boards out into the water and lay on our backs, side by side, our intertwined hands stopping us from drifting apart. Every so often, Weston's thumb would graze my scar, softly and lovingly. After the first few times, I stopped flinching and started enjoying the feel of his touch on the piece of myself I'd kept so hidden away.

"Favorite episode of *FRIENDS*?" I asked.

He laughed. "What if I said I'd never seen it before?" I didn't respond, waiting. "Okay," he said, "it's probably the one where they remember their worst Thanksgivings and Monica cuts Chandler's toe off. Favorite book you had to read in school?"

No hesitation. "*Jane Eyre.*"

"Well, aren't you cliché?"

"That's me, a walking cliché. Least favorite game to play?"

"God, that's easy," he said, his voice turning the tiniest

bit cooler. "Monopoly. Father was obsessed with my business strategy. All I cared about was being the racecar." A long pause, then, "Why—" He stopped.

He lay silent so long I thought he had fallen asleep. I propped myself up on one elbow and looked at him. He wasn't sleeping, but staring at me intently, heartbreak clear in his eyes. My heart thrummed against my ribs. "Why...?" I prompted.

His chest heaved with a great breath. His eyes locked with mine, and I couldn't look away if I'd wanted to.

"Why," he repeated with a soft voice, "did you try to kill yourself?"

My heart stopped, then started back up with a frantic gallop, bucking and kicking in my chest. Sweat prickled on my forehead and the small of my back. My skin broke out in a thousand itches, like a swarm of mosquitos had landed on me and launched an attack all at once. The dull rushing sound rose in my ears again, overpowering even the noise of my jagged breaths. I was drowning.

And then Weston's voice cut through it all, reaching out to me, pushing the pain away. "It's okay, love." He squeezed my hand, rubbed a thumb across my fingers. "You don't have to answer me. Not until you're ready. But I had to ask."

It took a few minutes, but eventually the ice in my muscles began to thaw, letting me relax out of my rigid posture. Weston's eyes held my own the whole time, never pushing, only caring. Simply being in the moment with me. The sun warmed my skin again, sending the itching, crawling sensation back away. My hearing came back last of all, and when it did, I realized Weston had been humming softly to me the whole time, some kind of classic lullaby.

Another squeeze to the hand. "Thank you," I croaked out.

He nodded. "Anytime, love. Anytime." Then he pulled our hands to his face, our fingers still tangled together. He turned my palm to face him.

And then he pressed his mouth to my scar, kissing it better.

# DAY EIGHTY-TWO

"THIS ONE HAS A CRACK RUNNING up behind the bed that'll probably need work," Melinda said, leading Weston and me through the front room of the cabin toward the bedroom. It was a Saturday, when most of the guests change over, so we were touring the cabins, making a list of repairs to focus on during the winter. I made a note about the crack on my notepad and followed Melinda to see how bad it was. It couldn't possibly be worse than the smashed bullnose in the last cabin, which looked like someone had hit it with a brick.

Just before we entered the room, Weston pushed me through the open bathroom door, which stood at a ninety-degree angle to the bedroom. My ass pressed against the small porcelain sink, and I somehow made a mental note that this cabin needed a taller vanity. Weston's hands were everywhere: tangling in my hair, tickling the side of my ribs, cupping around my hip bones. His lips played with mine, gentle, but captivating. Day-old stubble rubbed my chin and lips, and I moaned, part pleasure, part pain.

I broke away from him. "We can't. Melinda's waiting."

Weston pushed himself even closer, his desire clear against my belly. He pressed his lips against my throat; my pulse fluttered beneath the kiss. "You didn't seem to mind when you had me flat on my back in the last cabin," he whispered in my ear. His hot breath set my skin on fire.

A loud bang sounded, and we jumped apart. Shooting Weston an I-told-you-so smirk, I joined Melinda in the bedroom, where she was remaking the bed. The bang must've been the log headboard hitting the wall as she shifted it around. A large crack scaled the wall behind it, forking as it hit the ceiling.

"Oh," Weston breathed out as he entered the room. He held his hands awkwardly in front of his crotch and rocked back on his heels. "That is bad. There's another guest coming this afternoon?"

I nodded my affirmation.

"Any empty cabins?"

I thought back to the schedule on the computer, trying to recall if any of the cabins showed a red bar for the week. Melinda beat me to the answer. "Cabin three," she said.

"Angie says they cancelled, so it's last to clean."

"She's right," I said, remembering the sob story the woman gave me over the phone, trying to get her deposit refunded.

"Great," Weston said, rubbing a hand over his face and sighing. "Melinda, can I get you to clean that one first? We'll move this family over there for the week. This wall needs fixed now."

Melinda raised an eyebrow at him. "The view isn't as good from that cabin," she said.

With both hands raised behind his head now, Weston arched his back, stretching and making his shirt raise up to show a slice of stomach. My hands twitched, begging to reach out and touch his smooth skin. He emitted a groan of frustration.

"Okay," he said. "I'll pick up a bottle of wine for the cabin, and we'll comp them a weekend stay sometime in the winter."

Melinda gaped at him, but didn't argue. I watched as she picked up her cleaning bucket and headed out the door to cabin three. Weston turned around and flopped onto his back on the half-made bed, fists clutched in his hair. "What a nightmare," he murmured.

"I don't know," I said, sidling up to the bed. "It looks like you got rid of any interruptions and scored us a bed to ourselves." My fingers crawled up his thigh.

"Laney," he groaned, "we have to fix this wall. And go buy some wine before the guests arrive for cabin three. We don't have time."

Leaning closer, I pushed his knees apart with my thighs and stood between them. "If you're in such a hurry," I teased, "why are you still on the bed?"

He glared at me, a mischievous grin on his face. "Fine," he said, his voice full of faux chagrin. "Five minutes." Quick as a flash, he grabbed my arm and yanked me onto the bed on top of him.

Some time later—it could have been five minutes or five days for all I knew—we split apart, gasping for air with our legs tangled together. I shifted myself so his leg pressed against the ache between my thighs, and moaned. Weston rubbed a hand over his face and laughed lightly. "Wow." His voice quavered.

"Yeah." My hips tilted, pressing me tighter to his thigh, and he laughed in earnest.

"Don't think I don't know what you're doing."

"I don't know what you're talking about."

He spun over me, pinning my arms above my head and pressing his hardness against me, his thigh still snug between my own. My heart jumped into my throat, and I bit back a scream. A familiar panic clawed its way up my body, biting at my limbs and freezing me on the twisted bed sheet. I fought for breath, pulling tiny gasps of air into my lungs.

And then his lips were on mine, so soft in contrast to position he held me in. My muscles loosened. The roar that had been seeping into my ears dissipated before it could reach the deafening pitch I was used to. Weston released my hands and lowered his full weight onto me, as if he couldn't get close enough. I wrapped one hand in his hair and slid the other down his side. My fingers teased along the skin at the top of his pants, the contrast of its smooth warmness and the rough ridge of denim making them tingle.

I hooked two fingers into the front of his pants. Weston moaned deep in his throat and thrust against me. My mouth opened as I gasped, and he pulled my bottom lip between his teeth, nipping lightly. My back arched.

A blur of motion crossed my vision, followed immediately by, "Hey, are you in—Oh, my god!" Angie spun away from us as Weston and I struggled to untangle ourselves from the sheets and each other. "I am so, so sorry," Angie squeaked.

"Not at all," Weston mumbled as he straightened his shirt out and hastily pulled his hair back. "Not at all."

If I could've disappeared, it would've been great.

Angie turned back to us, her face as flushed as mine felt, her scars shining brightly against the deep blush. "Melinda said we are moving the Abermans into cabin three?" A broad grin spread across her face. "Is this why?"

"Oh my god," I groaned, covering my flaming face with my hands. "I—"

"The crack behind the bed can't be ignored any longer," Weston interrupted, having somehow regained total composure already. "We'll fix it this week so it's ready for the next guests."

I dared to lower my hands to peek at Angie. She looked directly back at me, but the expression of disappointment and anger—maybe even embarrassment—I expected to see was nowhere to be found. Instead, her eyes glinted with happiness, and her wide smile was knowing. My pulse slowed as my heart worked its way back to a normal pace.

"Mel also mentioned something about wine and free nights?"

Weston fidgeted beside me, close enough for me to notice without looking, but carefully too far for us to touch. "Yes. Uh...since cabin three is not as, um, desirable as this, I thought—"

"You did well, West," Angie said.

He nodded his thanks, and we all stood in a loose triangle, staring anywhere but at each other. Certainly the awkwardness would suffocate us all. I curled my toes in the edge of the sheet we'd dragged to the floor in our hasty exit from the bed.

322

"Okay," Angie said, finally breaking the silence. "I'll run to town for some wine if you two want to arrange a voucher for the free nights. And if you could find Rory and fill him in on what needs to be done here, that'd be helpful."

"Thanks," Weston and I mumbled in unison.

Angie flashed another dazzling smile and headed out of the bedroom. The front door creaked, and then she called back, "Oh, Laney?"

My feet carried me into the living room, though I couldn't feel them connect with the floor. Weston followed on my heels. When I stopped, he placed his hand discreetly, and so lightly, on my lower back. I leaned into his touch. "Yeah?" My voice was barely a whisper.

"My promise is still there"—a relieved sigh escaped my lips—"but you'll want to tell your dad soon. It could have been him who came looking for you."

I nodded, and she walked out the door, leaving us alone again. The second the door latched, Weston burst into laughter, wrapping his arm around my waist and pulling tight. With him pressed against my back, I could feel his want coming back to life. "Come on, pretty girl," he whispered, and his hot breath tickled against the skin below my ear. Electricity shot through my body. "Let's go finish what we started." My stomach flopped, and I pressed back into him. He took a step back, pulling me with him, but I broke loose long enough to lock the front door before joining him back in the bedroom.

# DAY EiGHTY-FOUR

WHEN I RETURNED FROM MY run this morning, I saw the familiar figure on the porch swing. My already pounding heart increased its tempo and leaped around my chest. "Hey," I called out as I jogged across the lot.

The voice that greeted me caused my step to stutter. Craig, not Weston, rose from the seat. "Good morning, sweetheart." I scanned his face—features relaxed and carefree. He wasn't angry or disappointed, thankfully, but what was he doing here so early?

"'Morning," I replied. "What's up?"

"Um, maybe...let's go inside," he said. I led him into my cabin, thankful I hadn't left any bras or underwear out to be seen. Crossing through the kitchen, I grabbed a glass of water and offered one to him. He declined. Instead he said, noticeably uncomfortable now, "Sit down, kiddo."

Shit. Throw an auburn A-line on his head, replace *kiddo* with *honey*, and you'd have my mother. I'd heard the "Sit down, honey" opener more times than I cared to remember, always followed by, "Martin/Dwayne/Steve/Larry and I have separated. We're getting a divorce." Except the last time she'd said it. Then it was followed with, "Mike told me what happened...." But thinking about that forced acid into my throat.

I clutched the back of a chair. "Uh, it's okay. I'll stand. What's going on?" Angie's pretty face flashed through my mind. I braced myself for the bad news.

"Have you heard from Karissa?"

"I don't—" My voice cracked, and I swallowed the lump that was growing in my throat. "I don't really know. She won't talk to me about it. If I even try to bring it up, she completely shuts down."

Craig's throat bobbed with a thick swallow, and he averted his eyes.

"You know something?"

"I talked to Rory," he said. "Karissa has been staying at his house for a few nights now. I know it's hard, kiddo, but she's safe"

"Thanks." A weight lifted from my shoulders, a strange mixture of emotions washing over me: relief that she was out of her house and jealousy that she'd talk to Rory, but not me. It wasn't much, I knew, but the fact that she was out of her house was a huge step.

"Laney," Craig said, making me jump, "how long have you and Weston been dating?"

My body froze, and my mind scrambled to keep up with the sudden change of topic. "How...we're not—"

With a flick of his arm, he waved off my concern. "Laney, you'd have to be blind to not see what's happening with you two. I said something to Angie last night." Reading my mind, he continued, "She didn't tell me anything, but her silence said a lot."

My face burned, and we stood staring at each other until I realized he was waiting for an answer. "Oh, just since my birthday. Really," I said sheepishly, my gaze falling below his left ear.

He laughed. "If that's your story. Hey, it's okay. I don't mind if you want to date Weston. He's a great young man. But..."

The way he said "but," the heavy silence as his sentence trailed off, pressed on my chest. "But?" I prompted.

"I talked to your mother yesterday."

"My mother?" I nearly shrieked.

Now it was his turn to avoid my gaze. "She called me last night. Apparently you missed a scheduled call? She was freaking out, so I made something up to cover for you."

"Oh, god," I moaned. "What did you tell her?"

"I, uh...I said you'd gone out with Weston for the night and that you must have forgotten your phone back here." He shuffled on his feet. "It was the fastest story I could give her. I didn't know she would react so..."

"Shrilly?"

"Yeah."

Yesterday was Sunday. How could I have forgotten? We'd gone to the Farmers' Market in the morning, where we gorged ourselves on fresh cherries and lemonade. The rest of the day was spent on the beach with Rory. Or back in my cabin, tangled in the bed sheets with Weston, coming closer and closer to fully giving in to our passion. I thought it would happen yesterday evening. We were so close, wrapped around each other, hands grasping at bare skin. He'd pressed his weight into me urgently, his need hard against my pelvis, his mouth covering my own. And I wanted him. Oh, god, I wanted him so, so bad.

But I couldn't bring myself to do it, couldn't grab hold and lead us to that next moment. Weston never asked, never pushed, and I knew he never would. He would wait for me; it would always be my choice—a choice I wanted so desperately I felt the urge start to bubble deep within me thinking about it now. So why hadn't I done it?

My phone trilled on the counter, and I nearly jumped out of the kitchen, blushing as though Craig could see what I was thinking. "Shit."

He chuckled. "Speak of the devil?"

I glanced at the phone screen and nodded grimly. "Sorry," he said and backed out of the cabin, leaving me to face her alone.

"Hello?" Thank god, my voice was even.

My mother's was not as she said, "Good morning, Laney. So nice to hear your voice."

Silently, I waited for her to start lecturing, reminding myself I'd done nothing wrong.

She didn't disappoint. "We had a deal, Laney." My mind flashed to my first morning here, when she'd said those same words in the same voice. It seemed like a year had passed between, not two months. She continued, her voice rising, "You were supposed to call yesterday."

"I forgot."

"You forgot? Listen, if you can't—"

"Mother," I almost yelled before she could go any further, "I am eighteen now. Your threats won't work anymore."

Dead silence. Nothing was said for so long I pulled the phone away from my ear to check that the connection hadn't been lost. As soon as I replaced it, she started again, her voice laced with more venom than I'd ever heard. "If that is what you want, then fine. But your father told me about your little boyfriend. I can't say I'm surprised, Laney. It's not the first time you've jumped right into some boy's bed. But if you want to be a big, powerful adult, fine. Don't come crying to me when you get knocked up and left alone."

The phone clicked in my ear. I stood there in the kitchen, statue-still, as her words washed over me. My own mother thought I was a slut. It wasn't a shock—she'd said as much before, on the darkest day, but it still cut me to the core. Tears sprang to my eyes, and I clutched a hand to the counter to steady myself.

But then the sadness was pushed away by something else. Something hard and cruel. Anger climbed my body, starting at my toes and clawing its way up to my heart, scratching all the while, opening my wounds to bleed again. It felt as though I'd been rubbed raw. Black danced at the edges of my vision, and I heard a noise tearing its way out of my throat.

My scream was raw and guttural. Light played off the window where it vibrated in its screen. Still I shrieked. And when my breath ran out and the sound finally choked in my throat, I pushed the rest of the pent-up energy down my arm to my hand. It lashed out fiercely, and my phone sailed across the room, shattering against the off-white wall. In the back of my mind, I registered there was another divot to be fixed. Tears, hot and angry, ran down my face and neck and splashed on the tile floor at my feet.

I didn't hear the door open, didn't see him coming

toward me. But then I was wrapped in Weston's arms, the two of us lowering to the floor. He held me there with our backs against the lower cabinets as I screamed and sobbed into his chest. My voice grew coarse, and my eyes dried up. The skin on my face pulled tight, stiff with the salt of so many tears. I hiccupped.

He held me tighter. Pressed a kiss to the top of my head, smoothed a hand over my hair. When I had sat silently for a few minutes, and my breathing had grown steady again, he stood, helping me to my feet. No questions were asked—he brushed his lips across my forehead and said, "I'll take care of the office until you're ready. Take your time." And with a squeeze of my hand, he left me there, love and peace filling the void left behind by my rage.

After work, Karissa lay in my bed, playing with her necklace as I told her—again—about my mother's call. My anger flared on and off, but the memory of Weston's embrace kept it at bay. I finished my story with a *humph* and flopped back onto the bed beside her.

Still studying the necklace, she said, "Well, what did you expect? You told her you would call on Sundays, and you didn't. Of course she was upset."

I pulled my wet hair around the front of my neck, sighing at the relief the cool tendrils gave my heated skin.

The cold shower had helped, but the heat was rising again already. "I didn't so much tell her I would call every Sunday as she told me I would either call or go back home."

Kris sighed. She sounded so much like my mother I almost couldn't stay in the room with her. We'd been talking in circles for almost ten minutes now. All I wanted was to vent my frustration to my friend. Why did she keep defending my mother? "And the things she said! Who says that to her daughter?"

"I'm sure she was overreacting. She worries about you. All moms do. It has to be hard to have you so far away and not be able to keep up with what you're doing." In the back of my mind, I could hear her voice saying, *It's not like she was wrong about you.* She would never say it out loud, but I couldn't help but wonder if she thought it. If all her jokes and jabs about me being a slut came from a place of truth rather than teasing.

"It's not even so much that she got mad," I said. "It's that she called Craig instead of me."

"She was worried." Boredom crept into Karissa's voice, and anger bubbled under the surface of my skin, different from the rage that had overcome me this morning. Where was my best friend? The one who knew to let me rant about my mother and who nodded in all the right places, showing her solidarity. Was it so much to ask for Karissa to be on my side? Heat slipped into my voice as I said,

"Whatever. She didn't have to call Craig. I have a phone."

"Right," Karissa said, finally dropping her necklace and turning to face me, "because the last time she confronted you about something, it turned out so well for everyone." She cast a pointed stare toward my wrist, wrapped in Weston's fork cuff.

I recoiled. She couldn't have hurt me more had she punched me in the gut. The ache centered above my navel and spread like wildfire into my limbs, which were now shaking. Acid bit at my throat, the taste in the back of my mouth so familiar by this point that I welcomed it. "Wow." It was all I could say.

The room closed in around me. There was not enough air! Numb to the world, I rose from the bed and crossed the room to my dresser. My sports bra snagged on my hair as I pulled it over my head; shorts slid up over my hips, and I slipped into a thin, long-sleeved t-shirt I'd dug out from the bottom of my drawer. I secured the cuff back around the shirt, holding the sleeve safely to my wrist. The walls pressed against my chest and shoulders as I laced up my running shoes.

As I crossed the threshold, Karissa's voice reached my ears, soft, hitching when she said my name. But by then the door was already closing, and the buzzing in my ears was too loud for me to be sure I'd heard her at all.

# DAY EiGHTY-FiVE

WESTON'S CABIN WAS DECORATED so sparsely one might think it was unoccupied. No wonder we spent our time at my place. It had the nearly clinical neatness of a new apartment waiting for a tenant, as if it were still sitting untouched after the renovation. Only the collection of mismatched silverware and the sketchpad on the bedside table gave any indication that someone might live here.

I lay on the bed and waited. Weston should be home from his morning canoe ride any minute now, and the office wouldn't be opening for another hour. We had plenty of time.

My phone buzzed near my head. I didn't bother checking the Caller ID, but silenced it automatically. I knew who it was. Karissa had called twelve times during my run last night, and twice more this morning.

After I left my cabin, I ran for a solid hour in a futile attempt to leave her comments behind. She had cut me deeper than any blade could have, and I couldn't figure out how she had become so cruel over the past year. The old Karissa never would have said something so hurtful. I'd ignored her first calls, so angry I couldn't even fathom speaking to her. She could seethe in her guilt for all I'd cared.

Now, though, I wasn't sure anger was motivating me anymore. As I'd turned my run around to come back to the lodges, I realized Karissa's comment was exactly the sort of thing she would have said in the past. She's always been nothing if not brutally honest. The one who'd changed in the past year was not Kris, but me.

I ran on, thinking over the past few months, realizing the person I'd become. Last-summer me wouldn't even recognize the girl wearing my skin. Then, as my feet hit the dirt lot of the lodges, it dawned on me: last-summer me was *happy*.

Glimpses of the old me had broken through my mask this summer, more and more as I spent time with Weston. My heart ached for the girl I used to be—I missed her. And so I decided: I could be last-summer Laney again. I *would* be. No more trying to be the good girl, playing it chaste. What had that gotten me? Nothing but pain and heartache and reminders of what I'd lost.

The doorknob jostled, and I sat up on the bed. Weston pushed the door open with his back and shuffled into the room, juggling bags in his hands and his phone pressed between his shoulder and ear. "Yes, I know," he said, "but I don't think it's going to work." He paused, letting the other person speak while he shoved all the bags onto the kitchen counter. I recognized the supplies we'd loaded into the back of his car after a trip to the hardware store yesterday. "All right, why don't I call a contractor to come look at it, and then"—the phone slipped on his shoulder, nearly falling to the floor when he finally saw me—"listen, I'm—I'll have to ring you back."

Weston turned and stared at me full-on. I won't lie: I'm not unaware of the effect my body has on men, and as I sat there now, propped up on his bed in nothing but a bra and panties, I was clearly having the same effect on Weston. All summer I'd kept myself hidden under long sleeves, only showing more a few brief times. Now I watched as Weston took in the whole of what was before him. His eyes raked up my legs, long and lean from years of running, and across my pelvis to my stomach. They hesitated there, taking in the gentle curve of my hipbones and navel before moving upward. I wore my favorite bra, one I hadn't put on since *before*. I knew how it accentuated my breasts, and I didn't want that kind of attention anymore. But I craved it now, and Weston was happy to oblige. He raised his eyebrows in appreciation and stared at the line where the lace met my flesh. Finally, his eyes reached my face. I'd let my hair out of the confines of my usual ponytail, and a shock of red fell across the corner of one eye.

"Hi," he said, breathlessly.

"Great opener," I teased. "You pick up a lot of girls that way?"

"No." He took a step toward the bed. "But I'm hoping it works now."

I stood and closed the gap between us. With my arms wrapped around his neck and my hands entangled in his hair, I whispered, "I think it just might," and pressed my mouth to his.

Having seen the way he looked at me and feeling the very sexual charge to the air, I expected him to return my kiss full force. Never did I expect him to back away from me and gather my hands in his own, holding them between our bodies. But that's exactly what he did.

"Whoa, love, have you been drinking?"

"It's seven in the morning."

He cocked an eyebrow at me.

"Really," I said. Then, "Okay, maybe I had a few late last night, but it's been hours. I don't even have a buzz anymore. It's nothing."

"You're sure?" He took another step back, so I stepped

closer to keep the charge between us.

"Of course."

"I don't know...."

Pulling my hand from his, I reached up and pushed his hair behind his ear. "Please tell me you aren't going to give me the whole 'I can't take advantage of you' speech right now."

"Well..."

"Well, nothing," I said. "If anyone's taking advantage here, it isn't you."

He laughed. "You've got me there." He placed a hand on my hip and pulled me a little closer. Warmth spread through me from the point of contact, setting my nerves alight. "You're sure about this?"

"Absolutely. Aren't you?"

"Yes, but I wonder where this all came from. You've been so cautious, and now I find you in my cabin like *this*." He stood so close now I could feel the heat from his chest.

I tilted my face up toward his. "I just realized I don't know what the hell I'm waiting for anymore."

He groaned. "I love that answer."

And he finally gave me what I was waiting for. His kiss was urgent, but not rushed. His lips molded against my own, and his tongue searched my mouth. I pressed myself against his body, desperate to maximize our contact.

He backed me across the floor to the bed. In one swift

movement, his shirt was lifted across his body and over his head, our lips only breaking contact for a brief second. Skin to skin, we dropped to the bed, exploring each other's mouths with our tongues and bodies with our hands.

Weston's hands had grown rough and calloused from the extra work he'd been putting in around the resort, but they were as gentle as silk on my skin. I buzzed with excitement along a heat trail his fingers left wherever they went. I couldn't get enough. My body ached for his touch, and he was happy to give me my fix. He traced the lines of my legs and arms, across my abs and over my shoulders to my neck. Fingers wandered across my lacy purple bra often, until that, too, was removed and they found my bare chest.

He teased my nipples with a tender touch, setting my whole body on fire again. I pressed my mouth even harder into his, a moan passing from my throat, and my fingers clutched at his back. My spine arched. His hand left my breast, replaced by his mouth.

"Oh, god," I groaned, and a spasm started to build deep within me.

His knuckles grazed along my ribcage, leaving a trail of goose bumps in their wake, until he clutched my hipbone in his palm. His tongue flicked across my nipple, and I cried out again. I could feel his satisfied smile. Fingers played across the waistband of my panties, and my hips lifted toward him. He slipped them under the elastic, pressing farther, and then—

Oh, my god, I was going to be sick. The memories came crashing back to me: *his* body pressed against me; rough, calloused fingers pushing their way into my underwear. Touching me exactly where Weston's hand lay now. The familiar acid taste rushed to my throat, and I pushed him off me, hand clamped over my mouth.

"Laney?" Weston wore an expression of total shock.

"I'm sorry," I croaked through my fingers. "I—I gotta go." I jumped off the bed and ran for the door, bending to grab my shirt on the way out. My favorite bra still lay on the floor by Weston's bed.

My skin shone with sweat, a combination of excited dew brought to the surface by Weston's touch and the clammy wetness that comes with vomiting in the bushes. When I was finally able to stand again, I pulled my shirt back over my head—taking care to pin the sleeve down with my bracelet—and pulled my hair back into its usual ponytail before heading back to my cabin.

Karissa jumped off a kitchen stool as soon as the door opened. "Laney," she shouted, "I'm so sor—shit, are you okay?" She rushed to my side, but I shrugged her away.

"Fine," I managed to say. "I think I'm getting sick."

"Can I do anything?"

340

"I need to sleep." I fell onto my bed. "Just don't—don't let anyone in, okay?"

"Of course," Karissa said, and then my best friend watched over me as I slid out of consciousness.

# DAY NiNETY

"SHE DOESN'T WANT TO SEE ANYONE, especially you."

"But I—"

"But nothing. I don't know what happened, but last time she was over at your place, she came back looking like a mess, and she hasn't gotten out of bed since."

"I know. That's why—"

"I said no. If she wants to see you, she'll come over."

I rolled over and peeked out from beneath my comforter. Weston stood outside the door, leaning forward and pressing into the room. His hair was loose from its normal ponytail and wild around his face. Even from my position on the bed, the worry etched on his face was obvious.

It'd been five days since the morning in his cabin, and I

had successfully avoiding seeing him. It was actually pretty easy, since I hadn't left my cabin. I slept most of the time, leaving the bed only to pee and eat, which I only did while Kris was out working.

She tried talking to me the first two days, practically begging me to tell her what had happened. At one point, she'd crumpled and cried, apologizing for the things she said to me the last time we'd talked. On the third day, she stopped trying to get me to talk. She hopped off the couch that morning—she'd started sleeping in my cabin—and went about her usual morning routine as if nothing at all were different, talking over the top of her book as she ate cereal. She jabbered on about some guy who had been at the beach the day before.

On day four, she told me the adventures she and Rory had at The Place the night before. Derek had made a new drink while his boss was out—terribly disgusting, but effective. The night ended with the two of them in the lake, naked. Nothing happened between them, she assured me, but she did catch a glimpse of Rory as he jumped off the dock. I could practically hear the blush rise in her cheeks.

Now, I watched as Karissa pressed herself against the door, pushing Weston to leave. He stood his ground.

"Karissa, please," he said. "I need to make sure she's okay." The desperate edge of his voice tore at my heart.

My best friend's voice softened. "I know, Weston. I want that, too. But we can't make her talk. Give her some time, okay?"

The door clicked closed, and Kris crossed the kitchen to the breakfast she'd left sitting on the counter. She ate in silence, and I found myself missing the random chatter of the past two mornings. Part of me yearned to hear about yesterday's happenings while she ate; instead, I got nothing but silence punctuated by the occasional crunch of cereal.

Karissa finished the rest of her morning routine and headed for work. She paused at the doorway and said, so softly I almost didn't hear it, "Weston's a good guy, Laney. You don't have to tell me what happened, but please tell somebody."

# DAY NINETY-FOUR

THE FEVER STARTED THAT NIGHT. In English classes, my old friends and I used to make fun of the heroines in Victorian novels, the way they always fell ill when they became distraught. *Poor sensitive souls*, we'd tease, *can't handle a bit of heartbreak without falling into a fit of fancy.*

I lay there, feverish and shaking, sent to my bed by an emotional blow. I was such a hypocrite.

"Do you need some water or something?" Karissa asked. I shook my head. "Your dad and Angie got back last night. I could go get them?" Another head shake. It was so long before she spoke again that I thought she must have left. But eventually she tried once more: "How about Weston?"

"No," I groaned, "let me sleep."

That was three days ago. Now, I could hear Karissa and Rory on the front porch, arguing.

"—don't think it's a good idea," Rory said.

"What else are we supposed to do?"

"I don't know, but I don't think this is going to help."

A new voice cut into the conversation: "We have to give it a shot," Craig said. "Veronica was there last time things got bad. Maybe she can help now."

I shot up in bed. My *mother*? Why the hell were my two best friends and my dad out on the porch discussing me and my mother? I focused on the conversation outside, straining to catch more details, but, as if they could read my mind, they fell silent, remaining so for an agonizing length of time.

Then I heard a voice that made my heart stop. "She's in there?" my mother asked, all business. She didn't wait for a reply—or maybe one was given silently—before she pushed the door open.

"What's going on?" I asked immediately, clutching the puffy comforter under my chin.

She gave an annoyed sigh. "What's going on is that I'm here to take you home, Laney." She folded her arms across her chest and stared at me. The crease in her forehead was deeper than I'd ever seen it.

"Home?"

"Yes, home. You've missed two weeks of calls now,

and your behavior is completely unacceptable. Now get up and pack your things."

I wanted to tell her I was an adult now, that she couldn't make me leave. She had no control over me anymore. Instead, I mumbled, "I'm sick."

"You're not sick, Laney, you're *dramatic*. Your little boyfriend told us what happened before you started throwing this tantrum of yours. Now get up and pack before Mike gets here."

"Mike's coming?" My voice, though it was barely a whisper, was packed with dread. The room began to swim in my vision, and the buzz picked up in my ears.

"Of course he's coming. Someone has to drive your car back home."

"But—"

"But nothing, Laney. You and I have a plane to catch. End of discussion."

Mike. Here. In my cabin, my safe place. My *home*. The thought made me gag. I rose off the bed, but I didn't start packing. Instead, I crossed the room, sidestepping my mother, and left. Grabbing my shoes on the way out, I laced them up just before I hit the road.

The sun beat down on the road, drawing heat lines up from the pavement, distorting the trees and cabins around me. My shirt trapped the heat against my body. My skin begged for a breeze to pass across it, but I wouldn't give into the desire. I held my sleeve in the palm of my hand, trying to pull it tighter, to hide my scar from the world.

Sweat dripped down my brow and into my eyes, but I made no effort to wipe it away. I embraced the salty burn. Pain was real—pain told me I was still alive when it would be easier if I weren't.

How long had I been running for? I'd lost track. I looked around me, trying to gauge my distance by the cabins I passed, but none were familiar. How long ago had I crossed the bridge? The muffled rushing had still filled my ears at that point; it wasn't until later that I outran the buzz and nausea.

I looked up at the sky. The sun was directly overhead, maybe a little to the west. It was barely after noon. Had I really been running long enough to put the whole morning behind me?

Without warning, my energy gave out. Maybe it was the realization of how long I'd been running, but one moment I was pushing forward, leaving my hurt and shame on the road, and the next I found myself dragging my feet, unable to go any farther. I stumbled off the side of the road and dropped onto my back in the grass.

A squirrel played in the tree above my head. It jumped from branch to branch, flicking its tail and rubbing its front paws together. Never did it stay long on one branch; its body stayed in constant motion. Every so often, it made like it would hold still—lowering down and curling its tail around its body—but, inevitably, it would jerk back up and hop to the next limb.

I lay there for what felt like hours, contemplating the particular sadness of the squirrel. Would he ever be content to simply *be*? Did he find joy in the movement, or could he simply not find joy in standing still?

My stomach dropped, leaving a heavy emptiness. Realization washed over me: I related more to a restless squirrel than I did to other human beings. More than I related to my old self.

Before, I ran for pleasure, heading toward something—a new personal best, a race win, a college scholarship. Now, I knew, I ran away. Never for exercise or for the love of running. I was trying to forget, to outpace the emotions building inside me. Like the squirrel, I couldn't settle down and let myself *be*.

Already, the familiar tingle was growing in my legs again. As my thoughts bordered on the dangerous and uncomfortable, the desire—the need—to run away overcame me.

NO.

I couldn't keep running. Eventually I wouldn't be able to go fast enough, and the past would catch up with me. I steeled myself and turned to face my emotions.

Once I opened to them, they came at me like a herd of

elk, one after another, trampling across my heart. I remembered that day—*him*—the confusion, fear, and anguish replayed in my mind as if it were only yesterday. My mother's face flashed before my eyes, so angry when I'd begged for her compassion, and my heart broke anew. With difficulty, I forced myself to face the desperation that led me to the bathtub that night, razor in hand. It tore at my gut, leaving jagged edges around the hole in my being.

I wrapped my arms around my midsection and squeezed. Maybe if I kept myself wrapped tight enough, I could stop the pain from overwhelming me. The hole couldn't be fixed. It would always be there to remind me of this time in my life. The hurt would never go away, but I finally knew I didn't need to let it control me anymore. I was stronger than the pain.

I was in charge.

My body protested getting up, but I forced myself back to my feet. Slowly, I unsnapped my fork cuff and peeled my sleeve away from my sweaty skin. Sunlight danced across the ridges of my scar, highlighting it on my otherwise smooth skin. With my sleeve pushed over my elbow, I was naked, even though I was still completely clothed. For so long, the scar had been one of shame, the scar of a victim, but I realized now it was something to be proud of. The scar marked me as a survivor.

With that thought circling my mind, I headed back to

Mountain Lake Lodge.

✳  ✳  ✳

The surprise was clear on Weston's face when he opened the door to me, standing in my running clothes, still sweaty and dusty. Without a word, he stepped aside and allowed me to pass by him into the cabin.

We sat together on his bed, neither of us saying anything. Energy crackled around us, and I could feel his curiosity. I'd made my decision—the time was now.

"I used to be a slut," I said.

"Laney—"

"No. It's okay. I just had to say that. I used to sleep with a lot of guys. It's part of who I am."

"Part of who you were," he said. I stared at him. "You said 'used to.'"

"Yeah," I agreed, "used to..."

He grabbed my hand and pulled it to his lap. His thumb found my scar, uncovered at last, and traced the line on my wrist. "Are you okay, love?"

"No," I admitted, "but I think I will be."

"What can I do to help?"

"You can listen."

Weston nodded, and I finally told my story. "It was..." I cleared my throat, trying to bolster my weak voice, then started over. "It was the night of our regional semi-final cross-country meet." The evening came rushing back to me, and the impact of the memories was nearly physical. I could feel the burn of my legs as I pushed over the course, the thrumming excitement at crossing the line in first place. Even the flavor of our celebratory dinner—my favorite shrimp scampi—filled my mouth, the memories were so vivid.

"I stayed up way too late. I was so tired." My vision blurred as tears sprang to my eyes. Weston gave my hand a reassuring squeeze, and I pressed on. "When the bed shifted, I—I thought it was the dog. She'd sleep with me sometimes." The tears spilled over my cheeks, and my whole body jerked with a sob. I forced a deep breath into my lungs and spat the next part out on the exhale: "But it was Mike—my mother's boyfriend. I laughed at him at first, thought he was drunk and lost. But—he wasn't. He wasn't drunk at all."

The pain that tore through me was like a knife tearing my flesh away from my ribs. My chest dropped to my knees, and I hugged my free arm around my legs. Darkness pushed in on me, and I gulped for air, trying in vain to force the pressure from my lungs. Screams tore through the room, and it took me a moment to realize they were coming from me.

In the background of it all, barely more than a whisper, Weston's voice soothed me. "It's okay. He's not here.

You're safe." Over and over he chanted those words with his arms wrapped around me, until I believed them.

Eventually, with my breathing under control once more, I sat upright, shrugging Weston's arm from around me. He pulled my hand gently back into his lap and squeezed it gently. As I forced my mind back to that night once more, something in me flipped. Rather than the all-consuming fear and pain I'd just felt, anger washed over me. It ran through my veins and laced itself into my words. When I opened my mouth again, my voice was steely and cold. "It was like being stuck in a nightmare. He shoved his hand in my underwear—into *me*. He pressed his body onto mine, forced his tongue in my mouth. The whole time I lay there, my mind screamed at me to do something. And when he...when it started, I tried. I kicked and thrashed, and I clawed at his back. I tried to scream—I really did—but only a squeak came out.

"It was over pretty quickly, I guess, but it felt like years. When he was done, he rolled off me then leaned forward and kissed my cheek like I'd done him a fucking favor. I fought with all I had to not puke. I wouldn't give him that, too."

I lay there for hours, crying and failing to process what had happened. Then, when the first morning sun peeked through my bedroom window, I did the only thing I knew how. I went into my bathroom and stripped out of my tank top. My panties were already pulled down, but I took them the rest of the way off. Looking at them made me lose control, and I finally vomited. They stared at me from the ground, and my stomach clenched again. I threw them, along with my tank top, into the sink. Digging through my vanity drawers, I finally found a book of matches; I dropped one onto my clothes and watched them burn.

Then I showered like I would any other morning. Only this time, instead of singing softly to myself and shampooing my hair, I turned the water on as hot as it would go and sat at the bottom of the bathtub as the stream scalded my skin, burning his touch away. I stayed there until the shower ran cold, and then I got out and toweled off.

Dressed in my biggest pair of flannel pajamas, I crawled back into bed. My muscles and joints were so sore I could barely move.

And I lay there on my bed, trying—failing—to forget what had happened.

Finally, I turned to look at Weston. Tears streaked his face, and he grabbed me and pulled me close to his chest. We cried together until my chest hurt and our eyes were puffy. "I'm so sorry," he said over and over again.

Finally, I pulled back. "There's more," I said.

"Okay...."

"I want to answer your question."

He stared at me, confused, and I turned my wrist to show him. "Oh," was all he said, carried to my ears on a huff of breath.

With a gulp of air, I squared my shoulders. "My mother came to see me when she got home from work that evening," I said. "I was still in bed. I figured she must be coming to check on me since I'd stayed home from school, but when she came in, she was livid."

"What'd she say when you told her what happened?"

"I didn't. I never told her." Weston's eyes widened in shock, and I continued, "Mike had already talked to her, she told me. He explained to her how I'd seduced him, come on to him when he was drunk and not thinking clearly. He'd apologized, and she forgave him." My stomach heaved. "She hadn't forgiven me, though."

"What did you say?"

"I wanted to tell her the truth—I did—but the way she looked at me and the things she said...I couldn't. She called me a lying, manipulative slut. Told me she was ashamed of me and that she couldn't figure out what she'd done so wrong to get a daughter like me."

"That's harsh," he whispered, a hard edge to his voice.

I nodded. "Yeah. After she left, things got so dark. I hurt so badly. It was like my heart had been torn from my chest. Her words hurt way more than what Mike had done, and at the time I didn't think I would ever recover. I didn't want to be alive anymore. I didn't want to *feel*. So—so I went to the bathroom and filled the tub with hot water, and I..."

I'd thought we were all cried out, but both of us spilled new tears. Then Weston leaned over and kissed me softly, tentatively. "Thank you for sharing, Laney."

"I need your help," I said.

"Anything."

"My mother and Mike got here today," I explained. "They want to take me back to Southport. I can't go with them, but I don't know what to do. They won't listen to me."

"You don't have to go, love. You're an adult now."

"I know, but you don't know my mother. I wouldn't put it past her to try to force me." I showed him my wrist once again. "She could claim I'm not stable, get the police involved."

"She wouldn't, would she?"

I stared at him, making it clear with my expression that she would. My mother couldn't stand to lose her control. Deep down, I knew she cared for me and was worried, that she truly thought bringing me back to North Carolina was the best way to help me heal. She was my mother, and, despite all our differences, she wanted what was best for me. She wanted to help, but she didn't know how to do it, and I was unable to tell her.

"I don't know what to do," I said, and tears threatened to assault my eyes again.

"I do," he said. The quickness of his response surprised me. He stood up, grabbed my hand, and pulled me toward the door.

"Where are we going?" I asked with a quaver in my voice.

"There's someone else you need to tell your story to."

# DAY NiNETY-SEVEN

I STOOD AT THE EDGE OF THE lawn with a steaming cup of hot cocoa in my hands, despite the already hot morning. Construction workers milled about, talking on cell phones and to each other, a few bent over a folding table, looking at plans and calculations. The equipment parked to the side of the rec lodge reflected the sun as it rose above the trees.

Demolition began today.

"How are you doing?" Weston asked as he walked up to me, holding his own cup. A familiar electric buzz shot through my veins at the sight of him, hair loose and wild, glasses on, flannel pajama pants loose on his hips. Beneath the jolt was something more subtle, but no less powerful. The connection we had now was something I'd never felt before, but one I wasn't ever going to let go of. He leaned against me softly, his arm pressing against my shoulder, and bent down to kiss to top of my head. "You sure you want to watch this?"

I nodded.

"It'll be better, love, I promise. Sometimes we have to go through the mess, and sometimes things need to be cut away to make everything stronger in the end."

"Wow, when did you become so wise?" I asked, trying to lighten the mood. He was right though—I'd learned that all too well over the last couple days.

One of the construction workers squinted toward us and yelled, "You guys stay back. No closer than that, okay?" We nodded our agreement, and he signaled to a man in an excavator. The machine fired up and crawled toward the building.

The noise of the excavator claw digging into the roof and front wall of the rec lodge was nearly deafening, but nothing compared to the chaos of the first wall hitting the ground. Dust and debris scattered everywhere, and a burst of air blew my hair around my face. Beside me, Weston jumped and dug his phone out of the waistband of his pajama pants.

He leaned into me and called over the clamor of the deconstruction, "We've got to go." I looked up at him, confused, and he beamed at me. "Angie's in labor."

✳  ✳  ✳

Angie had held my hand while I told my mother what Mike did to me. She was there, gripping my fingers through all of the denials. She never once let go as I explained to my mother that I would not be coming home, that I was planning to defer university enrollment for a year while I figured out what was next.

No charges were pressed—all the evidence had been long ago burned or washed away, and I just wanted to forget. But I wouldn't go back to Southport as long as Mike was still in my mother's house. "Call once he's gone," I'd told her, "and we can try to fix things between us."

The next day, Angie had held me again as I cried for hours upon hearing my mother was staying with Mike.

So when the call came in, I knew it was my turn to hold someone's hand. I sat at Angie's bedside while we waited for Craig to get to the hospital. She squeezed my hand fiercely with each contraction, but she showed no signs of fear. She'd been through so much worse. She was ready for this.

The door burst open, and Craig came running through. He rushed directly to Angie's side and kissed her forehead. "Sorry I'm late, baby. My truck wouldn't start, and I had to beg Rory to drive me back from Missoula."

Angie laughed, the sound light and musical. "I keep telling you to retire the old beast."

I dropped Angie's hand and backed toward the door,

making it almost to the threshold before Craig said, "Don't leave, kiddo. This is your new brother or sister. You should be here." Angie smiled her encouragement.

"That's okay, Dad. I'm going to wait in the hallway."

"You don't have to—"

"No, it's fine. You had to miss this the first time around. I want you to have the experience of a nervous first-time daddy. You can't do that with your daughter in the room." I winked at him.

"Thank you," he said. "I love you."

"I love you, too, Dad."

I found Weston in the lobby, leaned back in one of the outdated orange plastic chairs, reading *TIME* Magazine. He gave me a quick kiss when I got to him, and we waited together in silence, my head on his shoulder.

Two hours later, Craig rushed into the lobby, his face shining. "She's here," he said.

"She?" Excitement laced my voice.

"Yes," he practically shouted. "Another girl for me. I couldn't have asked for anything better."

"Congratulations, mate," Weston said.

"You two want to come see her? She's beautiful."

Angie's hair was sweaty and her face flushed, making her scars stand out even more prominently, but she'd never looked more beautiful. A tiny bundle of pink lay cradled in her arms.

She beamed when Weston and I entered the room. "Come on over, you guys." She turned the bundle slightly so we could get a better look. "She has your eyes, Laney," Angie said with a wink. The baby looked nothing like me—she was all thick, dark hair, brown skin, and almost-black eyes. She looked exactly like her mother.

We leaned over the baby, admiring her tiny features. Then Weston asked, "Have you named her yet?"

Angie looked at me, tears glistening in her eyes. She reached forward and squeezed my hand.

"Yes," she said, "this is my little Hope."

# DAY NINETY-NINE

I FOUGHT THE TEARS THAT BIT at the backs of my eyes. We'd promised we wouldn't cry. But as I watched Weston put the last of his bags in the backseat, my resolve began to slip. He turned to face me, and his expression tore at my heart. The heat of my first tear seared my skin.

"Hey," he said and stepped to me. His thumb caressed my cheek, pushing the tear away. "No crying, love. This isn't goodbye. It's just a—"

"A postponed hello," I finished with a sob.

He folded me in his arms and held me firmly against his chest. His heart thumped beneath my ear. I used the steady rhythm to stabilize my breathing, fighting to get under control. Weston ran a hand over my back, soothing me.

"I'm—" A hiccup cut my words short, and I took a deep

breath. "I'm going to miss you so much."

"I know." He pushed me back slightly and waited for me to look up at him. When our eyes finally connected, the love in his stole my breath away. "I'll miss you, too." He pulled me to himself again.

I'd known the day would come when Weston would have to go back to school. He still had a year left. No matter how badly I wanted him to, I knew he couldn't stay with me. But even knowing we would be together again in a few months couldn't hold down the pain rising in my chest.

"It won't be so bad," he said, his voice artificially cheerful. "I'm sure Angie will be calling on you to help babysit all the time. You'll be too busy to miss me." His voice cracked, betraying his cool act.

"I'm glad you got to meet her," I said into his chest.

Running his hand through my tangled hair, he said, "Me, too."

In that moment, the whole of the summer overcame me. I remembered our first meeting in the stables, that night in the lake. Countless questions, conversations. The bright smile Weston would give me when I said something he thought was funny. Our fights. His hands on me, lighting me on fire and calming me down at the same time. His lips brushing mine, my fists clenching his hair. My mind flashed back to that day on the paddle boards—our first real date. The kindness and adoration in his eyes when he asked why I tried to kill myself. The love there when I finally told him.

Weston squeezed me tighter. "What are you thinking about?"

I leaned back and looked up at him, letting myself be sucked into his gaze. "Everything."

When our lips met, the intensity of the summer passed between us, and my body electrified. My fingers tangled in his hair, pulling it loose from its ponytail as I clutched him even closer to me. He cupped my neck with one hand; the other splayed across my lower back, pressing me against him.

Sadness mingled with desire, and I opened my mouth to him. Weston moaned my name, the desire in his voice matching the hardness pressed against my belly. He turned us and lifted me to the hood of the car. I wrapped my legs around his hips, pulling him tight against me.

His tongue played across my teeth, and he pulled my lower lip into his mouth, nibbling gently. Salt of our tears mixed with the sweet taste Weston left in my mouth, and I never wanted to leave this moment.

Gasping for breath, Weston finally broke away. He smiled at me through his tears and pressed his lips to my forehead. "I love you, Laney," he whispered against my skin.

"I love you, too."

Later, Craig, Angie, and I stood together and watched as Weston drove out of the parking lot, making the long trek back to Philadelphia. Karissa and Rory had come for the farewell lunch, but left early, hand-in-hand. Now, it was just the three of us watching my heart drive down the highway, the soft static of the baby monitor keeping us company.

When Weston's tail lights fell out of view, Craig looped an arm around my shoulders. "How about a movie with me and Ang?" he asked.

Three months ago, I would have turned his attempt to comfort me down flat, but today, it was exactly what I needed. I couldn't think of a better way to ease the pain of losing Weston than an afternoon spent surrounded by love. I nodded.

We turned and went to their loft, Craig dropping his arm so we could walk freely. Hope's muffled cry chirped through the monitor, and Angie rushed up the stairs to tend to her. I reached the stairs just as my dad grabbed my hand, stopping me. I turned.

"Sweetheart," he said, not looking at me.

"Yeah?"

He wrung his fingers. "I was thinking...." He huffed a deep breath. "Ang has been seeing a woman in town ever since...it's helping her a lot, and I wondered..." His face burned scarlet under his tan.

I thought back to all those days my friends reached out to me, all the people who tried to help me who I'd refused. All the pain of the past year. It was time.

"Of course," I said. "I'd love to meet her."

With a smile, I climbed the stairs to go spend an evening with my family.

# 263 DAYS LATER...

THE BREEZE BLEW PAST LANEY, swirling hair around her face and creating waves in the grass, which was still overly long from the spring. She watched a boat on the water, an early season water-skier towing behind it. The back of her mind called for her to check the time, but she resisted. She would know when he got there. Laney let her eyes close and tilted her face toward the sky.

She felt him before she heard the soft footsteps behind her, like the cord to her heart, which had been pulled so tight these past months, had loosened. He laced his fingers with hers as he stepped up next to her. Pressing a soft kiss to her temple, Weston asked, "What are you thinking about, love?"

"Everything," she said, remembering the day he'd left.

Electricity shot down her spine, and an urgent heat built in her stomach, but she resisted, enjoying her last moments of anticipation.

"It's really something, isn't it?" he said, looking out toward the lake.

Gazing out over the expanse of lawn, the grass still swaying in the breeze, Laney could barely see the lines in the ground from where the old building had sat. He'd been right. It looked great this way. Better. The choice she'd hated, the one she fought against so hard, was the best one in the end.

"It's beautiful," she agreed, remembering the drawing she'd found in Weston's drawer so long ago. "Exactly how I'd imagined it would be." She turned, facing him for the first time in months.

Laney's breath caught in her throat. He was as breathtaking as always, with his wavy hair tied behind his neck and his black-rimmed glasses perched on his nose. The blond strands falling around his face stood in less contrast than they had the summer before, his tan having faded over the long winter in Pennsylvania. His gray eyes stared into hers, soft and loving. "I've missed you," he whispered.

And then he kissed her. It was a kiss that held all the excitement of a first kiss, but the connection and love of two people who had shown each other their souls.

It was a kiss Laney never wanted to end, and she joyed in the idea that it didn't have to.

This was her forever.

# GIANT THANKS

WHEN I SET OUT TO WRITE THIS BOOK, it was drastically different from what it is now. I couldn't have made it through without the love and support of many people. I owe enormous thanks and all the stars in the sky to:

Kelvin, my loving and supportive husband, without whose patience this book wouldn't exist. Thank you for all the time you spent alone while I hunched over my keyboard, for all the days you took Boy Sprout to the farm with you so I could have time to work, for all the meals you prepared when I forgot. I know I haven't made the journey easy on you, so thanks for sticking it out!

Connor Weston, my character may have had the name before you, but you're still my favorite. You were a trooper all those days I was working and you had to play by yourself. You're pretty much the best toddler ever, and I'm thrilled I get to be your mama.

Giant thanks to my mom for showing me what it means to really love books—you made me a reader. And to Gramma Ida and Aunt Amy: without you two there to listen to my tales to the point of exhaustion, I probably would not be a writer today. I'm forever grateful for days spent eating sugar-free candy and making up stories. Dad, you taught me how to practice, and the importance of doing so even when I'm naturally good at something. Without that lesson, I wouldn't have had the strength now to keep practicing my writing, making myself better each day. Thank you.

Ashley Maker, critique partner extraordinaire, this book wouldn't be nearly as good without your input. Your comments were invaluable, and your love for my characters and their story kept me going when I wanted to stop. Rory sends you a thousand kisses for your work. To Jessica Leighty, who was there the very first day in March 2010, who's had to listen to my excitement and angst through all the versions of this book... I'm pretty sure I would've lost my sanity long ago without you to bounce ideas off. Kristen Jex, Rory's band would have been totally nameless without you. Thank you for your brilliant mind.

My fellow Indie Ignites, you've shown me that I *can* self-publish and have supported me in this journey. Huge sparkly thanks. Extra sparkles and a fluffy unicorn to

Nazarea Andrews and JC Emery for putting up with my neuroses.

Kelly and Shanyn at Inkslinger PR, you two are Godsends. Not only are you both truly delightful women, but without your hard work and great ideas, Laney and her friends would be stuck out in the world with no one to read them. Thank you for the dedication y'all give your authors. Rock. Stars.

My friends and family at Seeley Lake: this one's for you. I can't wait to get back to the beach and see you all again next summer. I stole many of our memories for this book—huge thanks for being there to make them with me in the first place. Brian and Kerry, I can't express how grateful I am for your resort. You took the real-life Leisure Lodge and turned it into a place the Beaumonts would be proud of. The Lodges is my home away from home one week each summer, and I've gotten more inspiration there than anywhere else. Keep up the hard work.

Finally—and most of all—thank you to anyone who picked up this book and read it. I am truly grateful, and I hope you love my characters as much as I do. Each of you who showed me how excited you were to get your copy: you are the reason I was able to finish. It wasn't an easy story to tell, but with your encouragement, I did. I hope I did it justice.

Awkward hugs to all of you.

# ABOUT THE AUTHOR

RACHEL BATEMAN is a writer and editor who spends too much time thinking she can out-bake the Cake Boss. (Spoiler: she can't.) She lives in the middle of Montana, but dreams of the ocean. When not writing, editing, or reading books, she can be found playing with her husband, young son, and small zoo of animals.

*99 Days of Laney MacGuire* is her first novel.